## THEY ARE BEST FRIENDS AS MUCH AS MOTHER AND DAUGHTER. EACH HAS A SECRET THAT COULD DESTROY THAT BOND.

Small-town dress shop owner Anna's daughter Katya leaves home for art school in September 1965. After that, nothing in their loving and devoted relationship is ever quite the same.

Anna and her long-time lover Dave, who is married, first enjoy the freedom of Katya's absence until some threatening exposures move Anna to initiate a break-up. Her biggest fear is that Katya will learn of the affair. Instead of offering the peace of mind Anna hoped the split would bring, the separation brings frightening and dangerous results.

Away at art school, Katya is both thrilled and distressed by her attraction to fellow art student Paulette. Nothing in her protected small-town childhood has prepared her for being attracted to another girl. When they get to know each other in irresistible and frightening ways, Katya's biggest fear is that her mother will find out.

Inevitably, the worst happens and mother and daughter learn each other's secrets. Both react with hurt and anger and a desire never to see each other again. Can they regain their former devotion to one another or are they doomed to live out their lives bitter and unforgiving?

"This confection of a tale is spun with the technicolor dreams and nightmares of a teenaged girl named Katya on her way toward self-realization...The plot turns on many tantalizing events, expertly woven together and shot through with bright descriptive writing. Vivid characters quicken the plot and unwind the wraps on the mother/daughter secrets. *I Never T . . . . .* is a lovely story of Katya and *vard, author of Whiteout and 7*

"*I Never Told You* is a thought-provoking debut about betrayal, secrets, forgiveness, and forbidden identities. Set in the mid-1960s, and moving seamlessly between small-town culture and the flamboyance of Hollywood, it's the story of a mother and a daughter struggling—despite themselves—to find acceptance and love."—*Barbara Claypole White, bestselling author of The Perfect Son and The Promise Between Us*

"Bernie Brown knows how to spin a tale. Set in the 1960s, her debut novel offers readers a fresh and lively love story and mother/daughter drama woven through with a terrible tragedy from the past. At the same time, Brown bravely tackles prejudices and human dilemmas that continue to entangle us today. A captivating book from beginning to end." —*Elaine Neil Orr, bestselling author of Swimming Between Worlds*

*Katya took her by the shoulders. "Mom, talk to me."*

*Anna erupted. "What about? About your friend?" she said with scorn. "About how I shamed you in front of all your friends? About how I said things I should never have said. Saw things I wish I had never seen." She stopped shouting. In a small voice she said, "I saw you and that woman. I saw you. I don't know what this means, Katya. Tell me what this means." Hot tears flooded her cheeks.*

# I NEVER TOLD YOU

## Bernie Brown

Moonshine Cove Publishing, LLC
Abbeville, South Carolina U.S.A.
First Moonshine Cove edition October 2019

ISBN: 978-1-945181-696
Library of Congress PCN: 2019913613
Copyright 2019 by Bernie Brown

Cover painting provided by the author, back cover and interior design by Moonshine Cove staff.

## About the Author

Bernie is an Iowa farm girl transplanted to Raleigh, North Carolina. When she isn't writing, reading, or watching a British series like *Father Brown* and *Monroe*, she sews. Recent creations include silly stuffed monkeys and sparkly mermaid costumes for her incomparably cute and clever granddaughters. She plays the harmonica without much success. Bernie is a retired administrative assistant from

Digital Audio Corporation. Her Iowa childhood, travels in the States and Europe, and her contemporary life in Raleigh, NC influence her writing. She has published nearly forty stories and essays in print journals, ezines, and anthologies such as *Still Crazy, Modern Creative Life,* and the *Raleigh News and Observer.* Bernie has Bachelor of Arts and Master of Arts degrees in English from the University of Nebraska at Omaha. In addition to several short story awards won a decade or more ago, a recent story was nominated for a Pushcart Prize, and another one will appear in an anthology of contest winners by Grateful Steps Publishing. She is a writer-in-residence at the Weymouth Center for the Arts and Humanities and a member of the Women's Fiction Writers Association. Future writing projects include publishing a collection of ghost stories, completing a humorous novel about travel adventures and misadventures, and creating a novella about a character she deleted from *I Never Told You.* The history of her home state of Iowa always beckons her, and she hopes to write other novels with that in mind.

### <u>berniebrownwriter.com</u>

## Dedication

With much love to Mom and Dad in heaven. You always
believed in me.

# Acknowledgments

Writing a book is a long process, both wonderful and terrible. When that email comes from an editor telling you he wants to publish your book, you cry with happiness, thank the stars, and tell every single person within earshot and on cyberspace. The person who gave me that wonderful moment is Gene Robinson of Moonshine Cove Publishing. I will be forever grateful to him for making my dream come true.

Countless others helped me along the journey. The members of my critique group went through the entire book with me, chapter by chapter, Sunday after Sunday. Their advice and comments made me grow as a writer and helped my book fulfill its potential. A huge group hug to Sharon Kurtzman, Maureen Sherbondy, and Nancy Young. I trust your advice and know you always have my best interests at heart. Sharon gets an extra squeeze for sharing her "behind the scenes" look at work in a dress shop.

The writing community of the Triangle area of Raleigh, Durham, and Chapel Hill is vibrant and supportive. I have received nothing but encouragement and good feeling from Diane Chamberlain (also a beta reader), Therese Fowler, Sheryl Cornett, Barbara Claypole White, Kathleen Laughlin, Elaine Orr, Michelle Taylor, Robin Miura, and Janna McMahon. The late Anne Barnhill, treasured friend and also a Moonshine Cove author, encouraged me to submit to my now publisher. You ladies are the best friends I could ever hope for.

My siblings and their spouses have praised me, expressed their pride in me and my work, and supplied information about Iowa and the Midwest that I had forgotten or never knew. Thank you, all, Bev and Bill Gunderson (Bev was a beta reader, too), Rich and Sheryl Bro, and Barb and Bill Colbert. My two brilliant sisters-in-law, also writers, have cheered me on. Thank you, Mary Howard, (also a beta reader) and Cathy Tkacz.

The first friend I made in Raleigh, nurse anesthetist Brenda Haynes, answered my questions about surgery and recovery times for shoulder gunshot wounds. Registered nurse Vicki Sellner, also a beta reader, explained the dangers of staph infections. Vicki and husband Tim have been my believers and cheerleaders ever since our daughter married their son. They generously offered their Emerald Isle beach condo, The Sellner Strandhaus, for writing retreats several years running.

I am lucky enough to be a writer-in-residence at the gorgeous Weymouth Center in the Jim Boyd Mansion in Southern Pines, North Carolina. Thank you to Katrina Denza for the gift of many residencies when *I Never Told You* took shape, and to Alex Klalo who carted all my bags and writing gear up and down those winding steps countless times. Both Katrina and Alex came to my rescue the fateful morning I broke my wrist while on a residency.

The international writers group Women Fiction Writers Association, of which I am a member, has a Facebook Page, a spin off Facebook group called the Ink Tank, and a local chapter who meet regularly. Each of these venues supported me with feedback, encouragement, online education, and in-person meetings.

I salute Joe Rasmussen, lawyer in my Iowa home town, who explained small town storefront real estate. Also Laurie Lietz, executive director of the Surf Ballroom in Clear Lake, Iowa. She kindly answered my questions about running a ballroom.

Artist *non-pareil* and friend from grad school Bud Cassiday designed the gorgeous cover and clued me in on some Omaha facts circa 1965.

I am pleased and grateful our son Zach takes pride in me and my writing. Our daughter Jessie Sellner (also a beta reader) and her husband Daniel have been cheerleaders, plot brainstormers, and morale boosters of the highest order. Their bright and beautiful daughters Helen and Hope fill me with joy no matter what else is happening in the world or my life.

My dear and much-loved husband Ken has believed in me ever since I uttered those brave words "I want to publish a novel." Thank you for being my sounding board about plot, character, word choice, and all other writerly concerns. And for being the best in-house IT guy any writer could ask for.

# I NEVER TOLD YOU

# CHAPTER ONE
## Anna

Anna refused to cry. She squeezed her eyes tight to stop the tears, opened them, and concentrated on the scene out the taxi's grimy window. Chicago's skyscrapers whizzed by, horns squawked like geese, and cars darted in and out of traffic like Dodge'ems at the State Fair. In an artificially bright voice, Anna asked her daughter, "What do you think of Chicago?" She stopped herself from patting Katya's knee and calling her "Sweetie."

Katya's eyes danced as she gazed at the city streets, so different from Weaver, Iowa's sleepy Main Street. "It's the most beautiful place I've ever seen."

*It looks big and dirty to me.* Anna liked coming here on buying trips for her dress shop, but she didn't like this place today. Not one bit.

This day, September 10, 1965, her darling daughter Katya was leaving home for The Walker College of Commercial Art to pursue her dreams of becoming a fashion illustrator.

The house back in Weaver would be a tomb without her rushing up and down the stairs and the Dave Clark Five blaring from the radio. Fabric scraps and threads from Katya's latest creation would no longer litter the sewing room. And no more heart-to-heart talks, no more bowls of popcorn and late-night movies and costume critiques. Anna couldn't bear her daughter's leaving, but she would have to.

*I won't cry. I won't cry.*

She leaned back, closed her eyes, and wished they'd never find the school dorm.

But of course, they did. The taxi arrived at the front door a few minutes later. In the lobby, excited chatter bounced off the walls, and luggage tumbled from push carts. The eyes of fresh young women gleamed with excitement while apprehension marked their parents' faces. One mother, her forehead damp with worry or exertion, bumped Anna with the oversize carton she carried. "Oh, sorry," she said from behind her burden.

"That's okay," Anna said to the box as she tried to figure out where the line to board the elevator ended. She had lain awake countless nights thinking about things that might happen in a big city. What if Katya got lost? Or mugged? Or run over by one of those wild drivers? She might fail at art school.

Anna gave her head a shake to rid it of these crazy thoughts. Katya's destiny lay away from small town life. She had brains and talent. She would make friends, develop her gift, and maybe even find a boyfriend or two. Weaver didn't have the right boy to appreciate her daughter, this exotic six-foot-tall creature with hair like sable.

The elevator descended. Its bell rang, and the doors rumbled open. They squeezed their belongings and themselves in, shifting and rearranging, and the doors shut with finality. No one spoke. Anna wondered if the other parents jammed in this small space shared her desire to stop time and hang onto their daughters for dear life.

The bell rang at the second floor, and the doors opened. Two families got off with their belongings, leaving Anna and Katya alone and looking at each other. Katya's eyes shone with excitement. Anna smiled back, feigning confidence.

Before she had time to prepare herself, the elevator stopped at the third floor, Katya's floor. As the doors slid open, Anna hid behind the box she carried, afraid her face would show just how much she wished this day had never come.

CHAPTER TWO
Katya

Katya stepped off the creaky elevator. It didn't matter that the place looked more 1945 than 1965, her skin tingled. This was her dream. Her future. Her ticket away from small town Iowa. A musty, unused smell hung in the hall, but to Katya it smelled better than cinnamon rolls from the Main Street Café. The excited chatter coming down the hall made her impatient to join it.

Caught up in the moment, she almost forgot about her mom behind her, carting a big box held together with string. "Mom, you doing okay?"

"I hope this thing doesn't fall apart before we find your room."

Katya lugged the biggest suitcase they could buy filled with clothes for a Chicago winter. In her adrenaline-fueled state, it weighed nothing.

The door to Room 310 stood wide open. Inside, a short, round dark-haired girl argued with an older woman who might have been her twin, except for the age difference. "You always put your underwear in your top drawer at home," the older woman said.

"My panties won't know the difference if they are in the second drawer here, will they?" The girl noticed Katya and her mom. "Oh, hi. My name's Dottie. This is my mom. Ignore us. We fight all the time." Dottie's smile showed sparkling white teeth.

"I'm Katya." Right off she liked Dottie. Dimpled cheeks matched her dimpled knees peeking out from her short A-line skirt.

Was the favorite blue shirtwaist Katya had on hopelessly square?

As if Dottie read her mind, she said, "Like your dress. Blue looks great with your hair."

Yup, Katya liked her.

"I'm Anna," Katya's mom held out her hand. Dottie's mom. her hands full of underwear, extended a chubby elbow. "Fanny. No jokes about size, please." And they all laughed.

Katya's mom said, "Where are you from?"

Dottie said, "Jersey. Where else?" She shrugged her shoulders and laughed.

Katya had never been to Jersey. *Did Dottie mean New Jersey?* "We're from Iowa. We took the train."

Dottie's face registered uncertainty, too. "Nice. Well, I hope your bed's okay. Mine is lumpy. We each have drawers and a closet. Good luck getting everything in."

Katya's mom nodded to her. "We better get you unpacked."

Katya heaved her suitcase on the bed and snapped open the clasps. The lid popped open like it had been holding its breath.

In the cramped dorm room, the mothers and daughters wove paths in and around one another. Her mom put her hanging stuff in the world's smallest closet. Katya stowed underwear and socks in a jumble in the top drawer. In the second drawer, she arranged her sweaters, her favorite navy one with the collar on top. At last, clothes filled the closets and drawers. Empty luggage and boxes were put away. The sun no longer shone directly through the window. Now it gave off a gentler, late-afternoon light.

"I guess we're done," said Fanny. She turned to her daughter. "Aunt Louise is picking me up in fifteen minutes." The two from Jersey sniffled. "Now be good and lose some weight. See how thin Katya is."

"Ma, she's twice as tall as me." Dottie blew her nose with a honk, using her mom's lace-trimmed hankie.

Fanny said to Katya and her mom, "I always tell her to lose weight, but she's cute the way she is, isn't she?"

Dottie rolled her eyes.

"Don't go out with fast boys," Fanny said.

"Like they'd have me." Dottie wiped her eyes.

"Punkin', it's time. See you at Thanksgiving." The two hugged and cried. Dottie's mom gave her a sloppy kiss which left bright red lipstick marks on Dottie's cheek. When her mom tried to wipe them off with the crumpled hankie, they smeared.

Katya and her mom's lives revolved around each other, but Midwesterners didn't talk about things like that. They both looked away, uncomfortable watching Dottie and her mom's open display of emotion.

Fanny turned around twice more for hugs. When the Jersey woman finally left, Dottie heaved a sigh and plopped down on her bed. "Sorry. She's always like that." As if Dottie had been the picture of restraint.

Katya's mom looked at her and her dimpled roommate. "Why don't we three go out to dinner before I catch the train?"

She had barely finished asking when a soft knock on the open door pulled their attention to the most perfect creature Katya had ever seen. She had blonde hair as shiny and pale as Sandra Dee's and eyes as blue as Grace Kelly's.

The girl said, "Hi, I'm Paulette. A bunch of us are going across the street for pizza in about fifteen minutes. You want to come?" She looked at Katya's mom and said, "You, too."

Katya looked at the girl, then at her mom, and back to the girl, the motion tugging her heart between her old and new lives. Paulette's movie star presence drew Katya to her. It would be a thrill to be this girl's friend.

Her mom made it easy. "You girls go ahead. I'll get something at the station and read my book. I'm tired, anyway."

Katya smiled thank you at her and said to Paulette, "Thanks. I'm Katya. This is Dottie."

"I better be on my way," her mom said.

"I'll walk you down." They reversed the trip of a few hours ago, silent while the elevator carried them closer to saying goodbye. The doors opened to reveal carpet stains and spots she hadn't noticed before. Around them, other moms and dads gave their girls parting hugs, their presence unimportant to Katya.

This moment, this parting-from-her mom moment, this leaving-home moment loomed so large that no words could measure up. "Thanks for everything, Mom. I loved the train ride. I'll write right away."

Her mom nodded and avoided her eyes. Katya knew she was holding back tears.

Katya's arms encircled her mom in an unaccustomed hug, awkward and full of elbows. A kiss intended for her cheek landed on her ear. "I'll miss you." Now *she* held back tears.

Her mom looked up then and blubbered. She didn't quite pull off the laugh with which she tried to hide it. "I've got to get going, honey. Be careful. Chicago's a big city. Don't go out alone."

"Yes, Mom."

"Write to me."

"Yes, Mom."

"Bye, now."

"Bye." Katya watched her mom climb into a beat-up taxi, and her stomach clenched. Shrugging off a moment of panic, she pressed the elevator button hard, as if it could give her courage.

CHAPTER THREE
Katya

When the elevator again delivered Katya to her floor, Dottie, Paulette, and three other girls waited in the hall.

"You hungry?" Dottie asked.

"Always," said Katya. "Just let me get my purse."

\*\*\*

A pang of homesickness made Katya gulp when she saw the same green plastic-covered booths in Mandelli's Pizza as the booths in Weaver's Main Street Café. As if they had read her mind, the girls started talking about their hangouts back home. Dottie named several pizza places. "I've spent half my life eating pizza, as you can probably tell." She looked down at her stomach in case she hadn't made her point.

Katya didn't admit that the only pizza she'd ever eaten came from a Chef Boy-Ar-Dee mix. Mandelli's tasted as different from Chef Boy-Ar-Dee as Coke did from Kool Aid.

The sauce had no hint of bitterness and the crust made her think of fresh bread from Johnson's Bakery. Pepperoni slices like silver dollars surprised her with their spicy sweetness.

"I was named Girl Most Likely to Run a Restaurant by my graduating class," and the other girls laughed.

Paulette asked, "Did you ever think about doing that?"

Dottie said with certainty, "No, I don't know anything about cooking. Only eating." She laughed, and so did the others. Then she turned serious. "I want to make cartoons. I'll take Tweetie Pie, or even Mr. Magoo, over Steve McQueen any day." A chorus of "Not me" came from the three girls at the end of the table whose names Katya didn't catch.

Dottie added, "Well, not for a date, but, you know."

Paulette and a girl named Mona sat across from Dottie and Katya.

Mona looked out of place. She had a pretty face, but her hair style looked more fifties than sixties, like she used bobby pins instead of brush rollers. Her flowered shirt said church lady not flower power.

Mona didn't laugh at Dottie's stories, but said in a superior voice, "My *fiancé's* name is Steve. He's in Engineering at Northwestern." She said *fiancé* like it was her favorite word. On her left hand sat a ring with a tiny diamond. All Katya could think was, "Poor Steve."

Katya couldn't take her eyes off Paulette's face. She had never known anyone named Paulette, sort of like actress Paula Prentiss, who was beautiful and funny and almost as tall as Katya. Paulette said to Mona. "Your ring is pretty. Where is your fiancé from?"

Katya figured Paulette would be nice to anybody.

## CHAPTER FOUR
Anna

Dave kissed Anna's neck softly as a feather caressing it. She shuddered. The familiar scents of Old Spice and coffee clung to his skin, making her smile. Then she stiffened. "Where did you park?"

He kissed the other side of her neck, and she relaxed again, moaning softly. He said, "In the alley," the words muffled against her skin.

More kisses replaced words, and Anna got lost in making love.

\*\*\*

They lay sprawled amid rumpled sheets, smiling at the ceiling.

"This is nice, coming to your house. After years of meeting in back roads, we are in a real bed."

"We've been together in real beds before, in Omaha."

"Yeah, but you know what I mean. Here in Weaver, our own town."

A pang of guilt struck Anna right in her chest. "But we still have to hide. You're still married."

When guilt made her miserable, Anna told herself she wasn't the affair type. If she and Dave had not been connected by something that happened a long time ago, things would be different. They would both be faithful spouses. Instead, his wife drank, and her husband had run away.

Dave trailed his finger up and down her arm which rested on his chest. "What do you hear from Katya?"

"Not enough."

"It's only been a week."

"I feel like I'll never see her again." Her chest emptied out when she said it, hollow as an old tree trunk. "No music coming from her room. No clothes to wash. Do you think she's okay?"

Dave stroked her arm. "I'm sure Katya's fine. I bet she's having the time of her life."

Anna rolled over and fit herself into the curve of his arm, warm and familiar and safe, like a favorite bathrobe.

## CHAPTER FIVE
Dave

In the half dark of early morning, Dave let himself out Anna's side door, whistling softly. The sun shone pink gold as it broke the horizon. The smell of leaves and apples and soil surrounded him. Spending the night alone with Anna in her house had been better than in any hotel, and certainly better than in a parked car in a back lane. At times like these he let himself imagine that one day they'd be married.

But he knew it wasn't possible.

He'd long ago stopped feeling guilty for loving Anna. The Fran he had married, the Fran he had once adored, had died inside the day their son died. She blamed herself for Randy's death, and her only comfort came from alcohol. He didn't have the heart to leave her alone, which was why he was leaving the house of the woman he loved and going to the house he shared with the woman he married.

\*\*\*

Dave opened their back door and it creaked. "Fran?" No answer. She wasn't up yet. When he found her passed out on the floor of her bedroom, he tried not to feel disgust. Moving her to the bed made her moan, but she didn't waken. He tucked a blanket around her, and a pang of regret about their ruined marriage, the loss of their beloved child, and the hopelessness of their situation made him close his eyes and sigh.

Like a ghost in his own house, he showered, dressed for work, and left as quietly as he had come in.

\*\*\*

"Morning, boss. Coffee's hot." Moe's greeting cheered Dave. The gray-haired janitor and handyman kept the Majestic Ballroom looking as majestic as a thirty-year-old dance hall could. The place had seen plenty of good times, and it showed. Scratched wooden seats lined the walls. Jitterbugging, twisting, and waltzing feet had taken the shine off the parquet floor.

"What's happening today?" Dave poured a cup from the coffee pot Moe kept on the grill's back burner. The dented and discolored pot probably came with the Majestic.

"Couple of floor squares are chipped pretty bad. Somebody could catch their foot. I think there's still a few replacements in the store room." He paused and pointed to a broken seat on the second level. "Looks like a wrestling match broke the heck out of that."

Dave walked closer for a better look. "Damn, I don't know if that can even be saved. I'll have a look. You go ahead with the floor."

\*\*\*

By seven thirty opening time, the floor had been repaired and the chair taken away to the storeroom. Next time he was in Omaha, he'd look for a used one at a place he knew.

On stage, guitars were being plugged in, speakers positioned, and microphones tested by a new Beach Boys cover band. God knows what these Midwestern kids, who had never seen the ocean. loved about the surfing songs; but any song with a good beat and catchy vocals brought them out.

Two pretty girls came in first. "Hi, girls," he said.

They giggled and the blonde one said, "This band is going to be great. You should have them every Saturday."

He jollied them along, "I'll think about it."

\*\*\*

The band opened with "Surfin' Safari" and the kids moved out on to the floor, smiles on their faces, their feet and bodies in motion, synched to the fast-paced hit. Satisfaction put a smile on Dave's face. The right band, the happy kids, the music filling the night air were what his job was all about. Forget maintenance and cranky air conditioners and overdue bills. They took a back seat to a ballroom floor crowded with dancers.

The song lineup of "In My Room," "409," and "Little Deuce Coupe" had Dave's foot tapping. His foot stopped tapping when he saw the group of four regulars who came to cause trouble, not to dance.

Dave watched the signs. When the band took five, he moved closer to the late comers, alert for whatever might set them off. He could smell beer and cigarettes, and the tall one said, "Nice ass," as a couple passed them on the way to concessions. The girl in the couple was the blonde who had arrived early. Her partner turned, ready to land a punch when Dave stepped between them.

The tall one, the one who had made the crack, was Anna's stock boy. Anna liked him and said he kept the stockroom as orderly as a filing cabinet. But Dave knew this other side of him, the side that needed to make trouble.

*** 

With the band on a break, the kids flocked to the concession stand. These were the times when Moe shined his brightest. He had a way with the kids, remembering names, complimenting the girls, teasing the guys, who teased him back. Dave usually just lent a hand when the crowd was especially big. Tonight, he could see, Moe wasn't himself. His face was pale, he was sweating and without his usual smile lighting up his face. Dave went to lend a hand.

"You feeling okay, Moe?"

"Little tired tonight, boss." Then while handing a kid a bag of chips, he lurched slightly, dropped the chips and grabbed the counter.

Not wanting to embarrass him, Dave said quietly, "You go sit down. I'll take over here."

The band came back on stage, the dancers all dribbled away from the concessions, and Dave turned to check on Moe.

He sat on a chair, sipping a Coke, and looking brighter. "Sorry, boss. Don't know what came over me."

"Why don't you head on home. I'll close up. See you in the morning." He clapped him on the shoulder, and Moe gathered his things and left.

***

After closing and cleanup, Dave checked around the front parking lot before turning off the flood lights. One couple still made out in their car, steaming up the windows. Dave gave the hood a couple of knocks to send them home. *Go find a back lane like most teenagers.*

*And some adults.* Dave remembered with chagrin where he and Anna met before Katya went off to school.

CHAPTER SIX
Katya

The first few weeks of classes Katya struggled to get her schedule and supplies straight. She continually needed one more pencil, a 2B or an 8B or some other B. Before now, she had thought a pencil was just a pencil.

Once she accidentally stumbled into a room with cages holding turtles, baby chicks, and rabbits. She thought she had walked into a zoo, but it was Beginning Animation. The students were drawing animals from life. She saw Dottie, her head bent in concentration, and Katya backed out of the room hoping no one had noticed her.

Her favorite class was Textile Rendering. Her mom had taught her to love fabric. Rough tweed, creamy silk, fine lace, and sturdy gabardine. Now she was learning how to really see fabric. How dense it was, how shiny, the way it flowed or didn't flow.

There was so much to learn, to know. Katya worried she'd never learn it all, but it didn't matter. Her mind danced with the new knowledge. It filled her dreams at night. That and one other thing.

*\*\**

One night during the second week of classes, Katya was washing her face in the dorm's bathroom like she did every night. Paulette stood at the next sink, holding her glossy blonde hair away from her face. The way her hair lay against her bare shoulder made Katya's stomach go all funny and she dropped her hair clip. "Oops," Katya said.

When Paulette picked it up and handed it back, her Grace Kelly eyes locked on Katya's, like she had a secret she wanted Katya to know.

Those eyes made her warm all over, and she liked it.

The next afternoon, Dottie bounded into their room waving a letter. "Look, I heard from Carolyn Spade. We were in the same class." A letter-from-home happiness filled her voice. Katya knew the feeling. Two letters from her mom and one from her best girlfriend Charlie had cheered her up the same way. She had written back to them, telling them everything.

Dottie tore open the envelope, laughing aloud as she read. "Carolyn was the only girl in our group fatter than me."

"Was she your best friend?"

"Not best buds, but yeah, we had fun together. I think she might be a lesbian."

"A what?"

"A lesbian. You know, a girl that likes other girls. Don't they have lesbians in Iowa?"

"I don't know."

Katya stayed quiet a moment, and then said, "How do you know stuff like that?"

Dottie shrugged. "I don't really. Just stuff the boys whispered about her at school. She sounded kinda fake when she talked about cute guys." Dottie shrugged. "I'm just guessing."

Dottie's talk unsettled Katya, like she might throw up or cry. In the back of her mind a thought started. Would that explain why she thought Paulette was more perfect than even her favorite singer Dusty Springfield? That thought scared her, and she pushed it away as if it smelled bad.

Back in high school, she had gone out with John Cousins a few times, but he was a lousy kisser. Not that she had any other kisses to compare them to. At least, his kisses didn't make her want more. She had figured some other boy would kiss her some other time, and she'd like it. That hadn't happened yet, but she always believed it might.

For the briefest moment she let herself think about kissing Paulette, but the thought confused her, and she shut it away.

Now she didn't know. She didn't know boy from girl, a good kiss from a bad kiss. All of it seemed stupid.

# CHAPTER SEVEN
## Anna

The Baptist minister's wife inched around Anna's shop, touching everything with her pudgy fingers, screwing up her fat little face and shaking her head. Nothing ever pleased that woman. Prices? Too high. Styles? Too flashy. What would she complain about today? Anna called her Squirrel Face behind her back, but like a good shop owner, was polite to her face.

"Can I help you find something today?" she said in her best saleslady voice.

Squirrel Face sighed. "I guess I'll try this one on." She handed a blouse to Anna. A navy background covered in rich oranges and bright golds, flaming reds and deep purples created a stunning design on the silky Egyptian cotton.

The blouse was too pretty for her least favorite customer, but good business dictated Anna be polite. She showed Squirrel Face to the dressing room, hung the blouse on the hook, and pulled the curtain shut. Then she stuck out her tongue at the closed curtain before she returned to the shop's front.

A few minutes later, the sour woman came out of the dressing room and put the blouse on the counter by the register. "I guess I'll take it."

"It's a lovely blouse. I think you'll get a lot of use from it," Anna said.

"I'd better at this price."

As Anna bagged the blouse, Squirrel Face said, "I heard your daughter is at school in Chicago."

"Yes. She wants to be a fashion illustrator."

"A fashion illustrator?" Squirrel Face sneered. "How odd. And all the temptations and dangers in a big city. Aren't you worried about her? I don't know many parents that would have allowed their child to go that far away. I know I certainly wouldn't."

Anna ground her teeth to keep from spitting at her. *You don't have children, you old cow. And I'd feel sorry for them if you did.* Anna didn't even fake a smile when she handed the purchase to the loathsome woman.

But Squirrel Face wasn't done. "Of course, sin is everywhere, even right here in Weaver." Her untidy eyebrows arched in emphasis, and she headed for the door.

Anna wanted to slap her face. What did she mean by that? Was it a threat? A warning? Did Squirrel Face know about her and Dave? As she watched the woman leave, Anna's face burned with worry and anger.

***

Anna rarely phoned Dave, but today she would make an exception. She needed to sound off about that idiot woman. She needed to hear Dave's calm and reassuring voice.

***

"Is Mr. Frank there?" Anna said to Moe when he answered the phone. Dave had told her he thought Moe knew about them, but he was too loyal to tell anyone. The few times she had called Dave at the Majestic, she had pretended it was a business call.

Dave said, "Yes?"

"It's Anna Simms."

"Hey, Moe. I'll take this in my office."

Anna waited to hear Dave pick up. When he did, she said. "That evil woman, the Baptist minister's wife . . ."

"Squirrel Face?" Dave asked with a chuckle.

"Yes, Squirrel Face. She was in the shop today and insinuated that a good parent wouldn't let their child go to a big city. Too much sin there. She just infuriates me." Anna tried to keep her voice low in case someone came in the shop.

"Don't pay attention to her. She's a nutcase. You're ten times smarter than she is."

Anna sighed. "I hope you're right. Then she went on to say that sin was everywhere, even here in Weaver. I got the feeling that she was referring to us. Do you think she knows?"

Dave laughed. "Don't let a petty little woman like that get under your skin. She's pathetic."

"She frightens me a little."

"That's why she does it. She's jealous."

"Jealous of me? Why would she be jealous of me?"

"Because you're smart and beautiful and everyone loves you. Whereas she is dumpy and disliked."

That made Anna laugh. They said goodbye and Anna hung up, more confident that she had felt before the call.

## CHAPTER EIGHT
Katya

At the end of the first week of October, Katya stayed after her last class to organize her portfolio. Leaving the classroom later than usual, she ran into Paulette in the hall. Her end-of-week tiredness vanished.

"Hi. You headed back?" Paulette asked, and Katya nodded.

They talked all the way to the dorm. "What's your favorite class?"

"Do you like your teachers?"

When they reached the front door, Paulette asked, "Do you want to go see the new Jack Lemmon movie tomorrow?"

Sparks shot through Katya's veins, and she rushed to accept before she lost her nerve. Was it just two girlfriends going to the movies together, or was it more than that? Katya wondered how much she should tell her mom about Paulette.

\*\*\*

On Saturdays, many of the girls deserted the dorm to go to football games with guys from Chicago colleges. The few who stayed behind either had plans for big nights on the town or boyfriends back home. The quiet made Katya, with Paulette at her side, happy to step out into crisp fall air, sparkling sunshine, and a sky as blue as her friend's eyes.

"What do you want to do after graduation?" Paulette asked.

"Movies. I want to work in movies," Katya stole a peek at Paulette to judge her reaction. This was the first time she had admitted her dream to anyone but her mom. She feared people would laugh at her. A small-town girl wanting a Hollywood career. Ridiculous! With Paulette, Katya didn't have that fear.

31

She went on. "I want to draw sexy gowns for musicals. And chaps for cowboys and hats with feathers for saloon women. And big floppy feet for clowns." She stopped to draw breath, and then said, "I want to do it all." Then she feared she had said too much and put Paulette off.

Paulette chimed in. "Yeah, do it all!" she shouted to the sky, and it was Katya's turn to laugh and say, "Do it all!"

The people around them barely noticed. That's what Katya liked about the big city. In Weaver, shouting on the street would have made people stare, and word would have reached her mom by dinner time. In the city, you could be just about any way you wanted to be and people didn't care.

"What about you?" Katya asked Paulette.

"Comic books. *Archie* is my favorite. Jughead and Betty and all the gang. I want to create someplace like Riverdale. Or maybe a girls' club. I don't know."

Katya had read comic books, but never thought about how they got put together. "You mean you want to draw them?"

"And make up the stories."

"I always liked *Casper.* He's cute."

"He is cute. But *Archie* is my favorite." They had reached the theater. A line of about twenty people waited for matinee tickets. In Weaver, a line of five people would be a mob.

Standing in line beside Paulette made Katya want the wait to last forever, just so she could stand beside this glowing creature. They chose seats half-way back. Sitting next to Paulette thrilled Katya even more than standing by her. When Paulette nudged her shoulder a little closer to Katya's, she couldn't concentrate on the movie.

During the scene where Virna Lisi wore a simple white dress with draping at the neck, showing off her cleavage, Katya whispered to Paulette, "Wow, that dress. It's gorgeous. I would love to create something like that."

Paulette reached into Katya's lap and took her hand, holding it under her coat so no one could see. Katya's hand answered Paulette's with a squeeze.

*Did Paulette take her hand because she had shared the excitement about the white dress, or was there another reason?*

CHAPTER NINE
Katya

The week following the movie, Katya itched to tell Dottie about her confusion regarding Paulette, to get reassurance from someone she trusted. Several times she nearly did, but then held back. She finally risked it one night as they both sat on their beds drawing in their sketch pads. Katya didn't look up when she said, "I think I really like Paulette."

Dottie continued sketching. "She really is nice. You'd think somebody so gorgeous would be stuck up or something, but she's not at all."

Katya looked up from her work. "No, I mean I *really* like Paulette."

This time Dottie looked up, too. She put her pencil down. "I noticed you watching her." She asked the all-important question. "Is it like with Carolyn Spade?"

Katya knew what Dottie meant, though neither of them said the L-word. They exchanged a long steady look. A tightness clenched Katya's throat all the way down to her stomach. Thoughts whirled around inside her head like pinwheels. She said, "I don't know. How can I tell?" Her voice grew louder. She started to cry. "Am I a pervert? I don't want to be a pervert. I just want to be me. Back home the guys would always make jokes about a couple of old ladies that lived together. Dykes, they called them. I thought that was their last name and they were sisters. Is that what they meant? Am I a dyke? This is so new and so weird."

The usually brash Dottie came to sit by Katya and patted her shoulder. "I wish I knew what to say."

"It's okay. It is just a huge relief to tell somebody, to say things out loud, and not have them get all disgusted." Katya sniffed, and

Dottie passed the box of Kleenex. With closed eyes, Katya breathed long and deep, trying to rid herself of the knots inside her. She hiccupped and said, "Don't tell anybody, please, please don't tell anybody."

Dottie's voice softened. "I won't. I promise."

Katya blew her nose. "I'm scared to death."

Katya thought the conversation was over, but Dottie continued. "Since we're telling secrets, I've got one of my own."

Katya couldn't imagine. "Yeah, what?"

"You know Mr. Hayward, the Intro teacher?"

"Yeah."

"He keeps flirting with me." Dottie dipped her head, and her voice lowered. "He even hinted that we go out sometime."

Katya did a double take. She hadn't thought of Dottie in that way. But why shouldn't she attract guys? Except Mr. Hayward was old. He was probably thirty. "Well, maybe you should tell somebody, like your advisor. He could get in trouble."

Dottie jerked her head up and shook it. "*He* is my advisor. And no, I don't want to get him in trouble. I like it. I like him."

Katya could not think of one thing to say except, "Oh."

"He kissed me."

Katya stared, and another "Oh" came out of her mouth.

They gawked at each other and fell over backwards on the bed, exploding in laughter. The tension sputtered away.

"I gotta have a candy bar," Dottie said when she caught her breath. "Ya want one?"

"Sure."

Dottie rooted around in her top drawer and came out with two Milky Ways. She tossed one to Katya. They unwrapped their candy and the only sound was the chewing of caramel.

# CHAPTER TEN
## Anna

Fall's good corn crop loosened the usually-tight purse strings of Weaver's farm families. Anna's sales rose, and by the week before Thanksgiving, she sold out of Villager cardigan sweaters in pumpkin, a color she'd taken a risk on. She hoped the restock rush order arrived before Christmas.

Her bank account grew, she paid all her bills, and she almost succeeded in getting her mind off Katya. Anna had never spent a holiday without her.

"Do you have Thanksgiving plans?" one of her favorite customers asked.

"No. My daughter isn't coming home till Christmas. When we planned to spend Thanksgiving apart, we thought we would be okay, but now I don't know."

"It's hard when they leave home."

"I did get an invitation from my cousin in Cedar Rapids. I think she feels sorry for me." Anna laughed. "I'm not sure I'll accept. My throat is a little sore." She passed the woman's purchase to her. "What about you?"

The woman sighed. "My turn this year. The whole family." She dragged out the word "whole" so long, it might have included the entire town. In a stage whisper, she said, "Don't tell, but I would rather be you."

Anna smiled sympathetically. "Well, try to enjoy it."

The woman smiled back. "I probably will." She turned and left.

The bell on the door tinkled, and Anna was alone. She had hated lying to the nice lady. She did have an invitation, but she had invented the sore throat. Staying home, maybe having a few stolen hours with Dave, would be better than spending the whole day with a bunch of relatives she barely knew.

*\*\**

Midafternoon on Thanksgiving Day, Anna heard a knock at the side door. She smiled to herself. Her day was made. Dave had come. She hurried to pull the door open.

"Happy Turkey Day!" Dave held up a paper bag, shook it, and it crinkled.

"Where'd you get turkey?" Anna's eyes narrowed in doubt, but her lips curved in a smile.

Dave pulled out two sandwiches wrapped in wax paper. "Sympathetic neighbor. Not exactly turkey dinner, but they *are* turkey!" His eyes gleamed in a way that told Anna something besides turkey made them shine.

Anna gave him a big, sloppy kiss. "Sounds good to me." She took the bag from him and grabbed two plates from the cabinet. Unwrapping and putting a sandwich on each one, she arranged them carefully, as if they were the whole feast. She turned to Dave, who was setting the coffee pot to brew. "Let's eat on the couch," she said.

He'd learned his way around Anna's kitchen this fall. "Got any chips?"

"Over the sink." Anna studied his face while he wasn't watching. Yes, he definitely had something on his mind. Something good. She wanted to ask him about it, but decided to wait until he was ready to talk.

*\*\**

Within a few minutes, only bread crumbs sprinkled their plates. A football game played softly on television while Anna and Dave sprawled on the couch. She had her legs tucked under her, her loafers on the floor. He had loosened his tie and rolled up his sleeves.

Anna admired his well-shaped forearms. She wondered if men knew how attractive that part of their body was, curved, slimming to the wrist, hair curling neatly. She ran her fingers down it and took Dave's hand. "I'm glad you came."

"I wouldn't have missed it, even if it was just turkey sandwiches." He raised their clasped hands and kissed the back of Anna's. He put their hands back down on the couch and laid his head back. "I've been thinking."

*Here it comes.* She wouldn't have to ask him.

"What about?"

"Fran."

Anna pulled her hand free. Her stomach clenched. "Fran? What about her?"

Dave took her hand again, and she let him.

"I'm thinking of giving her an ultimatum. That I will leave by spring whether she is sober or not." Dave's words came out slowly, like he had to think about each one before he said it.

Anna's heart pounded, and her head told her to take it slow. "Do you think that will work? Are you sure?"

He shrugged. "Maybe."

Anna could tell he wasn't sure at all, and her heart stilled.

"I know you feel all twisted with guilt about Randy's death and Fran's drinking."

Dave stared at his thighs. "I'm listening."

"Honey, you know what happened to Randy wasn't your fault. I think that you feel guilty because as his father it was your job to protect him, and you think you failed."

Tears glistened in his eyes. "Wouldn't you, if something happened to Katya?"

Dave's question hit home. She did worry that something might happen to Katya. And if it did, it would be Anna's fault because she had let her go to the big city, just like that idiot Squirrel Face said, a city of full of dangers and temptations. But that was all wild imagination. Katya was safe and Dave's son was dead.

"You were a wonderful father. I saw you with him lots of times. The love you and Fran had for that little boy showed in everything you did. You can't fix what is wrong with Fran. You can't fix what happened to Randy. You couldn't have stopped it. Don't you think it's time you stopped letting those things control you?"

Dave put his arm around Anna and pulled her close. They just sat that way, heads together, each lost in their own thoughts. The football game was at halftime, and a marching band played "When the Saints Come Marching In" softly from the television.

"Honey, it's going to be a busy night at work. Holiday crowd. I better get on up there and give Moe a hand."

Anna kissed his cheek, his breath smelled of turkey, a homey smell. "I'm glad you came, not just because of the sandwiches, but because. . .we brought things out in the open."

Dave pulled her close, and talked into her hair. "Agreed. Just give me some time. I know it's been forever already, but today I knew something has got to change. This was the first time I even thought I could make that happen." He let her go while he put on his overcoat. "Did you write to Katya?"

"I did." She pointed to the sealed letter on the coffee table. "I really miss her."

"Why don't you call her tonight? You never call her."

"It's too expensive."

"Come on. Didn't you say you were having a good November at the shop? Treat yourself a little."

"Maybe."

"And December will be even better, and then she'll be home for Christmas in no time."

Anna nodded, still not sure she should call, but tempted. She usually just called on Sundays when the rates were lower. Katya probably wouldn't even be there, probably hadn't given her mom a thought all day.

# CHAPTER ELEVEN
Katya

"It's me." Katya gave Paulette's door a knock, and Paulette opened it wide.

"Happy Thanksgiving!" Paulette handed her a cup of coffee. Katya didn't really like coffee; but all the other girls did, so she pretended she did, too.

The cup warmed her hands as she sat down on the second bed in Paulette's room. "Thanks."

With a flourish, Paulette passed Katya a Twinkie on a Kleenex.

"Yum. I love these." She dunked it in her coffee the way she had watched farmers at the Main Street Café dunk their cookies.

Paulette watched, cocking her pretty head. "Is that good?"

"Try it."

Paulette gingerly dipped the corner of the spongy yellow cake in the coffee and took a bite. Her eyes lit up. "Hey, that is good. What other exotic Iowa habits do you have?"

Embarrassed, Katya laughed. "I think that's the only one." Katya wasn't about to tell her how she and Charlie had emptied bags of salted peanuts into their Coca Cola.

Paulette settled on her bed, legs crossed, Twinkie crumbs sprinkling the front of her robe. She wiped her chin, and declared, "I want to know everything about you."

***

The two talked and drank coffee most of the morning with The Supremes and Petula Clark providing background music. Somewhere around eleven thirty, when they had just emptied the second pot of coffee, Paulette suggested, "Let's go out for a nice Thanksgiving dinner. My parents sent me some money. It'll be my treat."

Katya hadn't expected that. Her impulse was to go, but her insecurity kicked in. "No, that's too expensive."

"You don't have to pay me back. You'll be doing me a favor, keeping me company when my family is far away."

Katya yearned to say yes. She pictured herself sitting with Paulette in a big city restaurant. She shut her eyes, mustering her resistance; but it refused to appear. "Well, if you put it that way. Yes! I would love to go."

"Great. My mom suggested Berghoff's. That's their favorite when they come to Chicago."

"We better get dressed, then."

In a fog of caffeine and happy anticipation, Katya went back to her room. She didn't want Paulette to be embarrassed by how she looked. What could she possibly wear?

## CHAPTER TWELVE
Katya

Ladies wearing hats, men in suits, kids dressed in their Sunday best all sat in Berghoff's dark-paneled dining room. Katya took in the laughing, chattering voices, the clink of china and cutlery, the bustle of waiters, as she followed Paulette, and Paulette followed the host to a corner table of dark wood with black chairs. The room had high windows along the ceiling, but the main source of light was the multi-tiered light fixture, a veritable hanging pyramid of shaded light bulbs.

Katya's purple A-line dress with a black panel down the front fit right in. Realizing that, she straightened to her full six feet and held her head high. Paulette, of course, looked like a pop star. A mass of tousled blonde curls tied with a black satin ribbon sat atop her head like a crown. Her pale blue Chanel-like boucle suit had three overlarge buttons down the front. When she walked by the other diners, they looked up, drawn irresistibly by her shining appearance. Katya hoped they might be admiring her purple dress, too.

"What do you think?" asked Paulette, as she sat down.

"It reminds me of Hilltop House in Omaha. My mom took me there one time. I had Chicken Kiev."

"Is that good?"

"It's perfect. Thank you."

Paulette shrugged. "It wouldn't have been any fun alone."

\*\*\*

The turkey dinner probably tasted good, but Paulette's presence and the restaurant held Katya spellbound. Not the food.

"This is nice, but not as good as my mom used to fix. She made the best Thanksgiving dinner. Is your mom a good cook?" Paulette asked.

"Yes, when she isn't too tired. Her shop keeps her busy all day, so we usually had something simple like tomato soup and grilled cheese during the week. On Sundays, we went to the cafe. I always had a cheeseburger and my mom had the special."

"I would love a grilled cheese and tomato soup. Maybe we should have gone to a diner today." Paulette laughed. After a pause where she appeared to be thinking, she said, "Did you date in high school?"

Paulette's question, so unexpected, made Katya's heart flutter. "A little. Some guy took me to prom."

"Did you like him?"

"He was nice enough. Kind of dull. I didn't like when he kissed me." Katya regretted adding the part about the kiss. That might be opening up a territory she wasn't sure she wanted to enter. "How about you? Did you date much?"

"I went to some formals with a friend's brother. He needed a date, and I was curious."

"Curious about what?"

"About guys. I went to an all-girls school."

Katya's chest and shoulders grew tense. Apprehensive, she held her breath. This conversation flirted with subjects that made her nervous, threatening to ruin this perfect day. She just knew Paulette was going to ask her something personal.

"When did you know you liked girls?"

A painful flush consumed Katya's body. *Please don't ask me. I don't know. I'm confused.*

"I've made you uncomfortable. I'm sorry." Paulette smiled her starlight smile, the one that made her eyes shine and her face glow. "You don't have to answer."

With sudden and unexpected certainty, Katya decided she wanted to talk. "I never knew until I saw you, and then I didn't know what was happening to me. I had never heard of such a thing. You must think I'm a complete idiot. Dottie told me what she knows, which isn't much." Katya laughed a nervous laugh, and then Paulette laughed, and they both laughed and the tension floated away to the high ceiling.

Paulette said, "I don't know much, either. There was this tennis coach one summer. She was always asking me to stay after practice to help put away the equipment. Once in the store room she kissed me and we messed around a little. It smelled funny in there. I felt really guilty, but I also liked it. That's about all I know. After that I looked at all the girls at school, wondering if they knew I had kissed Miss Harding, wondering if they ever felt like that. I never found out, and the tennis coach moved away. I never played tennis again."

The waiter appeared, removed their empty plates and gave them dessert menus.

"It's Thanksgiving, so I should have pumpkin pie; but this place is German, and they make great strudel. That's what I'm going to order," said Paulette.

"Me, too." Katya took a deep and satisfying breath. She knew later, the self-doubting would return; but for now, happiness seeped down to her very toes. They finished off their desserts in contented silence.

*\*\*\**

The crisp air and brilliant sunshine matched Katya's mood as she and Paulette strolled lazily back to the dorm, stopping to study window displays. One window mannequin wore a pumpkin Villager cardigan and plaid matching skirt, just like her mom had in her shop. Finding the same sweater in a big city store that her mom had in her small-town store pleased Katya no end, like she belonged both places, too. This was turning into one of the best Thanksgiving's she'd ever had.

*\*\*\**

Back at the dorm, Katya stopped at her room to drop her coat and purse and kick off her shoes. Paulette followed her in and closed the door.

Katya looked at the closed door and knew Paulette was about to make a move. Did she want her to? A big lump filled Katya's throat. Yes. No.

"Can I put my arms around you?"

Katya nodded.

"We could just lie down on the bed. I won't do anything."

Katya nodded again. A warmth spread all over her body, in spite of the chilly room. Part pleasure, part fear.

Paulette lay down first and Katya lay in her arms, stiff and unsure. The height difference shamed Katya, as if she had great big feet; which she didn't. Shouldn't she be behind Paulette and cradling her? Not the other way around.

When Paulette stroked her arm, a sudden tingling in her inner thighs surprised her. Katya tried to enjoy the moment, to feel it, to let it please her. But fear and a flicker of shame made her sit bolt upright, and only the shame remained.

Paulette sat up, too. She took Katya's hand and said, "That's okay. I'm scared, too, but it was nice for a little bit, wasn't it?"

"I don't know." She thought she might cry; but if she did, it was because it *did* feel good, and she didn't want to admit it. Paulette seemed to understand. Katya had to know, "Do you feel ashamed? I do."

"I push bad feelings away. Somewhere down deep I know that this is how I was meant to be, no matter what the world tells me. So, I give myself permission."

Katya turned to her. "I wish I did. All I feel is confused."

Paulette sighed. After a few moments of sad silence, she said, "My mom doesn't know about me and girls. I think my dad suspects. His sister lives with a 'companion' they call her. Your mom?"

"My mom?" The very idea made Katya sweat. "No. My mom doesn't know a thing. I didn't know a thing until I met you," she said with more heat than she intended. She raised her hands palms up, elbows bent. "It would kill her to find out. I can never let her know. She's all I have. I could never hurt her that way."

A voice and a knocking came from the hallway. "Katya. Katya. You've got a phone call."

Katya and Paulette looked at each other, frowning. "What the heck?" Katya said.

She opened the door to see Mona's friend, the one who hadn't gone home for the holiday, standing there. "What?"

"You've got a phone call. Didn't you hear it? It rang about a million times." The girl was a good match for Mona. They were both hard to like.

Katya followed the girl down the hall. She went in her own room without a word, slamming the door behind her. Katya wondered if she had seen Paulette on her bed.

\*\*\*

"Hello?" Katya said as she picked up the receiver at the end of the hall.

"Hi, honey, how are you?"

"Mom. Is something wrong? I didn't expect you to call."

"No nothing's wrong. I just wanted to hear your voice. Are you all alone?"

"No, I'm not alone." Katya scrambled through her brain for a story. "A bunch of us went to a diner. It was fun."

"Did you have turkey?"

"I had grilled cheese and tomato soup. Not as good as yours, though." The lies just flowed out of her like a stream. Her guilt mixed with relief that she could hide the truth. "What about you?"

"Well, yes. I did have an invitation from that cousin in Cedar Rapids. You know the one. But my throat is sore and I stayed home to rest. I wrote you a letter. I had soup, too."

"That doesn't sound like much fun. How are you?" Katya pictured her mom in her old chenille robe with the worn spots, the one Katya used to slip on if she got cold watching TV. Her mother felt close, too close, like she knew all about Katya's day.

"Well, it would have been more fun with you here. But I get to see you soon. It won't be long until Christmas."

"I can't wait to see you." That part was true. "How's the store?" Katya was on safe ground now.

"Really busy."

Keep her talking about the store. "That's good." She remembered the sweater in the window. "I saw one of those orangey Villager sweaters like you had in stock."

"They're sold out. I had to order more."

"That's great, Mom." Katya's pleasure for her mother was genuine, no matter what else hadn't been.

Silence descended. Katya tried to think of more to say, but all she could think about was that she hadn't told her mom the truth. She quarreled with herself. She didn't have to tell her mom everything. She didn't live at home now. But still guilt gnawed at her insides.

After they hung up, Katya's mood had changed. Her mom's voice had made her want to turn back the clock and make today not have happened. That way, she would still be the same Katya her mom loved.

## CHAPTER THIRTEEN
Anna

December's sales surpassed November's in Anna's shop. The Christmas rush kept her too busy to count the days until Katya came home. And now it was the afternoon of Christmas Eve and today was the day.

Anna's eyes swept her shop where red and green dresses hung crookedly from their hangers, and ropes of pearls littered the glass counter top. The scarves that had hung from a small Christmas tree now lay on top of each other beneath it.

The few hours before closing had brought in a flurry of customers. All of them left happy except for the Baptist minister's wife. Squirrel Face said, "I can't imagine how these little scraps can cost so much." Anna rang up handkerchiefs, the cheapest thing in the shop, and smiled a real smile. Squirrel Lady didn't matter today. Nothing could spoil Anna's happiness. Katya was coming home.

She itched to close the shop so she could get to the train station. She straightened shelves, buttoned dresses, and emptied the fitting rooms. When the last blouse hung from its rack, she headed to the cash register to ring out the day. One last customer stepped inside and wiped his feet. The last customer was Dave.

Dave smiled and the right side of his mouth crooked up further than the left, giving him the lopsided smile that charmed her every time.

"Merry Christmas," she said.

Dave's eyes darted around the store. "The place looks great."

"Thanks."

He cocked his head back at the changing rooms and mouthed, "Anybody back there?"

When Anna shook her head, he said, "I thought I could pretend I'm shopping for Fran. Put some stuff on the counter."

Anna fumbled in the display case and pulled out black leather gloves, a green wool scarf, and some white mittens. Each time she put something on the counter, she wanted to touch Dave's hand.

Like a reminder of her guilt, the delivery buzzer sounded in the back, making her look sharply in that direction. "I'll have to get it." She hurried to the storeroom.

When she unbolted the alley door, Charlie's dad, who owned the hardware store next door, held out a package. "For you and Katya."

What if he saw Dave? What if he saw a guilty look in her eyes? Her hand shook as she reached for the package. With a forced smile she said, "Tell the family Merry Christmas."

The man raised his hand in farewell and closed the door with a clunk.

Anna hurried to lock it, trying to lock out her worries at the same time. When she turned, Dave stood behind her and off to the side, just out of view—she hoped. He must have followed her back there. He reached for her, put his arms around her and kissed her, a kiss that tasted of coffee and tenderness.

And she kissed him back, wanting to melt into him, to smell him, and listen to his heartbeat and feel the whisper of his breath.

She ran her fingers over the sandpaper tweed of his overcoat. The sweet scent of Old Spice greeted her as she burrowed into his warm, solid arms.

After a moment, Dave pulled back and fished around in his pocket. He handed her a box from Henson's Jewelry. "Merry Christmas."

Anna tugged at the red ribbon and it untied itself. Inside, a gold heart watch hung from a clip studded with stones. Dave said, "When you look at it, remember sometime we'll have Christmas together. Every day together. No more sneaking around."

Anna laughed and a few tears escaped her eyes. "Wouldn't that be wonderful?"

Dave took the watch from the box and pinned it to Anna's smock, his hand brushing her breast. A wave of desire shuddered through her.

"It's beautiful. Thank you." She pulled a handkerchief from her pocket and wiped her nose. "Your gift is in my desk. I hoped you'd stop by." She hurried out front and returned with a book tied with a red ribbon just like the one on her package.

Dave tugged off the ribbon and read aloud, *The Story of Swing.*

Anna knew he loved the bands of the forties, the bands of their youth like Glenn Miller, Harry James, and Benny Goodman.

"This is great, Anna. I'll enjoy this."

She looked into his eyes and fingered his lapel. Dave put the book on a brown card board packing case and covered her hand with his.

"We won't see each other while Katya is home, so I just wanted to see you one more time before Christmas."

Anna pulled away her hand to run it through Dave's hair, going just a bit gray right by his eyes. She touched the gray part. She took her hand from his hair and raised her new watch to read the time. "I hate to ask, but maybe you should go. I need to finish closing before I pick up Katya."

Dave laughed and said, "That watch is supposed to mean time together, not time to go." He didn't move, but leaned down to kiss her one more time.

Anna couldn't resist. She kissed him back and then straightened and pulled herself away. She gave his lapel a tiny shake that said she meant it, he had to leave.

When they turned to go back out front, her Saturday stock boy was standing at the door to the storeroom. "Sorry," he said. "I just came to pick up my check." Anna noticed the boy looked at Dave while he talked to her, a look that said they knew each other, and maybe something else. She wasn't sure what.

"Of course." Anna willed her face not to turn red. She left Dave standing in the middle of the storeroom.

Dave improvised. "Those gloves on the counter will be fine." Then he squeezed past the boy and Anna and went out front to wait.

Anna wrote the check for an extra twenty-five dollars. What she had intended as a Christmas bonus now looked like a bribe. How could she have not heard him come in? Shame set her cheeks on fire in spite of her efforts to stay calm.

Avoiding her eyes, the young man thanked her and slipped back out the front door as quietly as he'd come.

Anna took her place behind the counter and looked at Dave. "He acted like he knows you."

"He tries to make trouble at the Majestic sometimes. Don't worry about him, he's just a kid with a bad attitude."

"I think he saw us kiss."

"I doubt it." Dave picked up the black leather gloves. "I'll take these."

Dave paid, and she put the gloves in a small bag and handed it to him. His fingers hesitated as he took it from her. "Bye," he said. "I'll call you."

Anna mouthed a kiss, and Dave left her shop to go home to a wife whose only cheer came from a bottle.

*\*\*\**

Back in her office, the calculator handle scraped and released time after time as she closed out the cash. When the accounts were settled, Anna locked the money in the safe, traded her smock for her blue coat and hat, and pulled on her favorite black gloves. She realized they were just like the ones Dave had bought for Fran.

## CHAPTER FOURTEEN
Anna

Anna arrived at the station to find Katya waiting outside on her suitcase. Her daughter waved, the smile on her face as wide as she was tall.

Anna parked, got out, and ran to throw her arms around her daughter, hugging her hard. "Oh, I've missed you so much." She released her. "Look at you and your short skirt." When she saw Katya's unsure look, Anna said, "It looks great. Shows off your legs." And Katya smiled.

***

On the ride home Anna wondered if her daughter could read in her eyes that just minutes before she had kissed a married man. What would Katya think? Would she judge her? Turn against her? Anna couldn't bear that.

***

Brown sugar ham, fluffy mashed potatoes with creamery butter, and mint-seasoned peas filled their dinner plates. Only the bubble lights on the Christmas tree and red taper candles lit the room. In the background, Bing Crosby sang about a white Christmas.

Katya took a big bite of a Pillsbury crescent roll and talked with her mouth full. "What did you and my dad do for Christmas before I was born?"

Anna choked and reached for her water. She recovered, swallowed, and took a deep breath. "We got together with our neighbors. You know, Dave Frank, the man who runs the Majestic, and his wife Fran. They lived in the other half of the duplex on Hillside with their little boy." With mention of Randy, the memories came rushing back. She closed her eyes and took a breath before she said, "The little boy died." She didn't say how.

\*\*\*

Sleep came easily most nights for Anna, but tonight memories kept her awake. She had met John Simms, who was just back from the war, when he came into Younkers dress department in Des Moines where she worked. When Anna had tried to help him find a dress for his mother, he asked Anna her name, was she married, what kind of music did she like. His eyes crinkled up when he smiled a crooked smile, a smile that made her insides go all soft.

Instead of a dress, he bought Anna a tuna sandwich and a chocolate malt that tasted better than sirloin steak and champagne.

A wedding soon followed, and a job offer brought them to Weaver. John managed a construction crew, and Anna kept house. The young couple next door, the Franks, became their friends, the men exchanging war stories, the women talking of recipes, and fashion, and the Franks' little boy.

Then one day a terrible twist of fate destroyed both the Franks' world and Anna's own happy home. The lives of the two couples in the duplex on Hillside Avenue were never the same.

\*\*\*

John left her several weeks before Anna discovered she was pregnant with Katya. She cried that John was not there to share the joy of a child. Although Anna knew his leaving had nothing to do with her, it still hurt that he left without a word.

Where she had been robbed of her happy marriage, she had been given a daughter so special it felt like Anna's own life began the moment Katya's did. Mothering her was a joy.

## CHAPTER FIFTEEN
Dave

Christmas morning, Dave stayed in bed and wished the day away. Wished he could jump right into tomorrow. When that didn't work, he got up to face a hung-over wife. Christmas morning looked just like every other morning in Dave and Fran's house.

He stuck his feet into his corduroy slippers. Cold air chilled his right toe where there was a hole. In better days, Fran would have noticed the hole, and a new pair of slippers would be waiting under the Christmas tree wrapped in red paper. He should have bought some himself, but never got around to it.

"Coffee," he said aloud. *Coffee. Strong coffee and eggs scrambled not too dry with bacon done just this side of crisp, and toast with butter covering every inch.* He stuck his arms through his plaid wool bathrobe and looped the ties around his middle as he scuffed into the hallway. Fran snored behind the closed door of the room they used to share.

In the kitchen, Dave switched on the Crosley radio on top of the refrigerator. Burl Ives assaulted his ears with *Holly Jolly Christmas.* "Oh, God." He quick fiddled the dial to find Handel's *Messiah.* "For unto us a child is born, unto us a Son is given, and . . . duh, duh, hmmm. Hmmm." He sang along where he could remember the words, and hummed where he couldn't. He hadn't majored in music for nothing.

Within thirty seconds the coffee perked away. He clambered around for the frying pan and took bacon and eggs from the nearly empty fridge.

A few minutes later, Fran's hoarse "Good Morning" interrupted the bacon's sizzle. Dave turned to greet her, and her gray face shocked him like it did every day. When he married her, she had

had skin soft as feathers, and hair that shone like stars. Alcohol had turned her skin pasty and her hair limp. He couldn't bear to look her in the eyes. He said, "Merry Christmas," to the wall above her head.

He moved the bacon around the pan while waiting to see what she'd do next. Out of the corner of his eye he saw her pour a cup of coffee and open the cabinet where she kept the whiskey. There it was, what he waited for: *clink,* the sound made when the bottle touched the lip of the cup. That *clink* sounded louder in his ears than the *Hallelujah Chorus*, and it made him cringe. But he didn't blame Fran for drinking. He looked for ways to ease the pain, too.

Dave did a double take when Fran opened the cabinet again and took out, not the whiskey bottle, but two plates. She grabbed silverware from the drawer and set the table. *Hallelujah!* It was all he could do to keep from singing it, but he didn't want to scare her off.

As she folded and placed napkins by the plates, she said, "Smells good."

"Thanks."

"You want me to make the toast?"

"Great." Fran's cooperation stunned him. She wasn't going to make this morning as difficult as he had expected.

\*\*\*

"Did you get a card from your sister?" Dave asked as he spread strawberry jam on his toast, the knife making a familiar scrape. Conversation with Fran was like talking with an old friend with whom you had quarreled, both of you pretending you weren't uncomfortable.

"Yeah, her usual rambling."

The two of them laughed together at that, and Dave relaxed a little. Fran's sister tried to be some fancy society lady. She called rich people in her little town by their first name, when in fact, she didn't know these people, Fran and Dave didn't know these people, and they probably weren't all that rich anyway.

The light moment vanished when Fran rose like she just remembered something, bumped the table, and set the dishes rattling. Her coffee cup in hand, she shuffled over to the cabinet, and Dave clenched his teeth waiting for the *clink*. He didn't hear it because she took the whole bottle in her arm, cradled like a baby, and left the room.

Dave finished off his eggs, which had lost their flavor, gathered up the dirty dishes, and set them to soaking in the sink.

The sun shone in through the kitchen window like a beacon inviting him out of the house and away from Fran.

He shaved and showered, put on his favorite stretched-out, holey blue sweater and brown corduroys worn to a shine. The suits he wore to work made him look like the boss, but during the off hours when no one but Fran saw him, he just wanted to be comfortable. He traded his slippers for army boots and left by the back door.

Sitting behind the wheel of his Buick, he saw the gloves he bought for Fran and the book Anna had given him, forgotten on the passenger seat. The book made him want to drive by Anna's house.

As he passed her bungalow, it looked snug and warm. Anna and Katya would be inside doing what? Getting ready for church, maybe. He sighed, drove on past, and wondered where to go next. Then he knew.

\*\*\*

No one else had come to the cemetery on Christmas morning, a day that celebrated the birth of a baby not mourned the death of one. The solitude pleased Dave. He pulled off to the side and parked. With only the shining sun for company, he got out, hands in pockets, his eyes focused on the angel that guarded a small grave.

Crouching next to it, he picked off dead leaves and sticks, and patted the miniature space. "Hope you're nice and warm, little fella'."

This was the only spot where Dave lost himself in memories of Randy, the way he loved to run, his toddler steps beating soft on the grass, his silky hair sticking up like a baby bird. His small son laughing and showing perfect tiny teeth. That merry laugh echoed over the graves and made Dave smile even while his eyes misted over and a sob choked him.

"I love you, my boy. My only sweet boy." And then he covered his eyes and sobbed until he thought his heart would shatter. He coughed, cleared his throat and breathed deep and long.

He rose and strode quickly back to his car.

Lazily, he drove out of the cemetery and, from habit, took the road to the Majestic. In the harsh sun, his pride and joy could have passed for a bowling alley; but he knew when a band let loose and the night's customers danced their hearts out, magic took over.

On that thought, he headed home to check on Fran.

In the first years after Randy died and Fran started drinking, Dave had convinced her to go to AA. And she tried, she really did. Broken promise followed broken promise, and still she drank. They gave up. Now they both knew what every day would bring.

\*\*\*

Dave came in the kitchen through the garage, hoping Fran wouldn't be in the room. When she wasn't, he tip-toed back to her bedroom, and opened the door a crack to see her sprawled on the bed. He stepped inside and covered her with a blanket. From the kitchen he took his book and a fresh cup of coffee and settled in the living room

Seeing the names of the big band leaders took him back in time. Those names and the music they played had inspired him to buy the Majestic. When the big bands went out of style, he got the crooners to come in, the local Perry Comos and Frank Sinatras. Then came the doo-wop groups and the Elvis wannabes, and now, what the kids called the surfing sound and the British invasion.

Providing a venue for whatever music pleased the public and giving them a place to dance to it satisfied him. But speaking for himself, he would always love the big bands.

A big crowd would come to the Majestic on Saturday while the holiday mood was still on them. College kids would grab a last chance at Christmas break before the long slog to spring.

*** 

When Saturday came, Dave pulled out of the driveway and away from his empty home life. His mood picked up every time he headed toward The Majestic,

He whistled as he checked the supply of potato chips, candy bars, and pop. He gossiped with Moe as his handyman swept and mopped. The hall seemed cavernous without a band on stage and a crowd of young pretty girls dancing with sporty young men.

In a few hours, the place would come to life and so would Dave.

## CHAPTER SIXTEEN
Katya

Katya hoped the quiet clatter of the train back to school would calm her. Relief and regret fought each other in her troubled heart. Lying to her mom about Paulette had put her on her guard the whole Christmas break. She'd never hidden anything from her before.

As the train chugged her closer to Chicago, Katya looked forward to seeing her new friends. Smiling funny Dottie, from whom she didn't need to hide things. Perfect Paulette, who—well, Paulette couldn't be described—and even crabby old Mona. Life would always have a Mona.

***

With a thud, Katya dropped her bag on the floor of her room. Dottie wasn't back yet, and it smelled cold and unused. She peeled off her coat, leaving it on the bed as she went looking for Paulette. Katya stood in the open doorway of Paulette's room, watching her take clothes from her bag and hang them on hangers, her movements as graceful as a dancer. Katya almost hated to interrupt her. "Hi."

"Hi back." Paulette looked up and beamed. "Wanna meet in the lounge in five?"

Katya nodded.

***

The lounge had three worn upholstered chairs and a mismatched couch. The side tables sported rings where soda bottles had rested without coasters. All the seating faced a medium-sized television, which Katya tuned to *Let's Make a Deal*, her heart wishing Paulette would hurry.

Monty Hall asked, "Let's see what's behind Door Number One." In synch, Paulette opened the door to the lounge wearing a devilish grin. She closed the door, came to Katya and kissed her smack on the lips. Katya gave a start and stiffened.

Paulette's face fell. "What? No good?"

"Yes. I mean I think so. You just surprised the hell out of me."

Paulette did it again, only this time longer and deeper and oh so sweetly. Katya's head swam with happiness.

Did the door open again or was that just Monty and a contestant?

\*\*\*

While stepping off the elevator a few days later, Katya and Paulette ran into Mona. She snubbed them, as stuck up as the queen of England.

The elevator doors closed and Paulette said, "What's up with her?"

Katya shrugged. "She's so weird." At the door to her own room, she left Paulette. "Talk to you later."

Inside, Dottie narrowed her eyes and said, "Close the door."

Katya shut the door and sat on her bed. "What?"

"Mona's been here." Dottie made a face.

"So?"

"She said she saw you and Paulette 'acting inappropriately' in the lounge. And there was something about Thanksgiving I didn't really get."

Katya said, "There was nothing to see. What did you say?"

"I told her to stop making up stuff."

"Thanks. She's just being a bitch."

"Katya, this could be bad. If it's true, she might report you. She's mean enough."

Katya turned serious. "You think she'd do that?"

"I don't know what that weirdo would do."

Panic gathered in Katya's chest. "Geez. We were just laughing and having fun."

"Whatever you did, you and Paulette better cool it for a while."

Katya threw herself back on her pillow and talked to the ceiling. "Okay, so we touched a little, not much. Okay, maybe more than a little. I don't remember." Beating her mattress with her fists, Katya said, "What's old Mona doing at art school, anyway? She can't draw worth a damn. I hate that bitch."

***

Over the next few days, Katya avoided Mona *and* Paulette. Katya thought her worst fears had happened when Mona came out of the drawing teacher's office and fixed Katya with a nasty smile. Her heart jumped, tears stung her eyes, and her deodorant failed her even while she faked not noticing.

When she passed the bathroom, tears won out, and she pushed through the door. A locked stall gave her the privacy she needed. With her head against the cold, graffiti-covered painted stall, she sobbed. Awful possibilities lined up in Katya's head: humiliation, dismissal, the loss of her dreams, and —worst of all— her mom finding out. Life without her mother would be like losing half of herself.

"Katya?" Dottie said from outside the stall.

"Yeah." Her friend's voice lessened her fears.

"Come out here, will ya?"

Katya unlocked the door and faced Dottie.

"I saw you come in here crying. What's wrong?"

Katya blew her nose with toilet paper. "I saw Mona. She came out of Clarkson's office. I think she ratted. If I get thrown out, I might as well be dead."

"It could be something else. You don't know she ratted."

Katya wiped her nose with the back of her hand, and Dottie handed her some toilet paper. "I know she did. I just know it."

***

Katya spent the day worried out of her mind, and she didn't sleep at all that night. The next day she got a note to report to Ms. Clarkson's office, which made her burn with fear.

61

***

Katya stood in Ms. Clarkson's wide-open doorway. She wished the woman would never notice her, but she did, and said, "Katya, come on in. Close the door, please."

Directly across from the teacher's desk, Katya sat down in a hardback chair like a criminal in the witness stand. The older woman folded her hands on the desk and looked steadily at Katya. When at last Ms. Clarkson spoke, Katya jumped. Her teacher smiled. "I'm not going to eat you up."

Katya wanted to smile, but her mouth trembled instead. She knew red blotches, the curse of nervous redheads, covered her face. Perspiration streamed down her armpits inside her turtleneck.

"I can see you are very concerned. Let me put you at ease." Her teacher spoke with a slight southern accent.

With every word, Katya breathed a little easier. When Ms. Clarkson finished, Katya grew limp with relief. She didn't know if her legs would hold her.

Ms. Clarkson stood up, a sign that Katya should go. When Katya followed suit and rose, her legs mercifully held her erect.

Katya's teacher reached out to shake Katya's hand and said, "Now I don't want it to be necessary to discuss this with you again, understand?"

Eager to agree to anything at all, Katya's head bobbed uncontrollably.

She must have shaken her teacher's hand, and left the office, but she had no awareness of doing it.

***

After classes, Dottie met Katya at the elevator. "So, what did she say?"

"I'll tell you in our room."

Katya shut the door, flopped down on her bed and lay back, pounding her feet and arms in abandon. Then she sat up with a grin so wide it made her cheeks hurt.

Dottie stared. "Tell me. Tell me. Tell me."

62

"Okay, so Miss Clarkson —don't you just love her?"

"Katya." Impatience filled Dottie's voice.

"Miss Clarkson said Mona reported something she'd seen at the dorm. 'We won't delve into what it was she said she saw,' something like that. She said they couldn't run the school on gossip, but just in case there was any truth to Mona's report, she would advise similar activities take place away from the housing and academic facilities of this school. And that was all."

"Whoo hoo!" The two girls laughed, relief flying out of them like butterflies.

When they stopped laughing, Dottie said, "So are you going to tell Paulette?"

Katya didn't want to think about that. "I don't know what I'm going to tell Paulette."

***

One night in early February, Dottie and Katya worked away at their desks sketching, erasing, and mumbling to themselves. When somebody ran down the hall yelling, "Hey, it's snowing!" they looked up from their sketchpads, smiled and nodded at each other, and hurried to the crowded elevator. Every Chicago snowfall, the girls headed outside, using the snowflakes as an excuse for a study break.

In the halos made by the streetlights, the flakes fell like feathers. At first nobody talked, silenced by the beauty of the snow. Then a couple of the girls twirled around laughing and trying to catch snowflakes on their tongues. Katya fell back and found herself next to Paulette.

In that husky voice Katya loved, Paulette said, "You've been avoiding me."

"I'm a coward."

"How come?"

Katya told her what Mona had done. "I know I—we—got by this time, but I'm scared. I never want my mom to find out. I'm sorry."

"Are you ditching me?"

Katya couldn't find words. Her friend's face went chalky, and the light in her Grace Kelly eyes vanished. Without a word, Paulette walked ahead to join the other girls. Half way there, she turned around and said, "You can't hide forever."

Katya watched her go, her cheeks burning, and wished she were dead. An enormous shiver rattled her body. Back in the dorm, she passed Mona in the hall and nearly spit in her eye.

But Katya knew Mona wasn't the real villain. Katya was her own enemy because she was spineless, too afraid of what might happen to be brave.

## CHAPTER SEVENTEEN
Anna

By February, the gray tweed and brown wool clothes in Anna's shop—so classy in September—hung on the sale rack like wallflowers at a dance, wilted and tired. The shop's dull windows and floors depressed her, too. The place needed a facelift, something clean and bright to welcome the spring's new fashions.

She had finished inventory. Spring shipments hadn't arrived. The time was right to make some changes. She brought paint and tile samples to the store and asked the customers for their opinions. The Baptist minister's wife, Squirrel Face, sniffed and said, "None of them appeal to me." Of course, they didn't.

Anna faked a smile. Then the woman disappeared into a changing room with size twelve slips for her size twenty hips. Anna's office phone rang, and she welcomed the diversion.

The voice on the other end said, "It's Dave."

At the sound of his voice, Anna's mood brightened. "Hi," she said, giving the little word as much weight as it could hold.

"Got an idea. I'm going to Omaha in two weeks. Can you make up a reason to go?"

"I would love to." She paused to think. "I'm redecorating. I could shop at the retail supply store." Afraid to say any more about the Omaha plan, she said, "Somebody's here now. I'll call you back. Bye, love."

Anna looked up to see Squirrel Face passing in the hall the office shared with the changing rooms. What if she had heard her call Dave "Love"? Would she say something about sin again?

Anna followed her out front. "Is the Hanes or the Maidenform better?"

"Neither of them is quite right, but the Hanes will have to do." Squirrel Face sniffed again, and gave Anna a penetrating look that could mean anything. This time Anna pinned her with her own look, a veritable staring contest. Squirrel Face lowered her eyes first, paid, and left.

***

Anna called Dave back. "Old You-Know-Who was here."

"Squirrel Face, right?"

"Yes, her. Anyway, about Omaha, I can go if I can get someone to watch the store." Anna looked up to see her nemesis behind her again babbling about forgetting a glove. Was the old bat deliberately spying on her? The woman flicked back the stall's privacy curtain. "Here it is. I can't afford to lose these at the price I paid."

How did she get back in without ringing the bell?

Anna snarled at the closed door and put Squirrel Face out of her mind. Shannon, a young widow who lived with her parents and her two-year-old boy, liked to escape her sheltered life and fill in for Anna. When Anna called her, she welcomed the chance to work in the shop.

And Anna welcomed the chance to get away.

***

The shop door opened again. Sheriff Denison entered with Squirrel Face in tow. Her first thought was that she was being arrested, that Squirrel Face had heard her making plans over the phone. *You can't get arrested for adultery, can you?*

Anna stared wide-eyed and open-mouthed at the sheriff, waiting for him to handcuff her.

Instead of handcuffs, he held out a blue and black paisley blouse. Dirt smudged it and the tags were torn.

"I saw this . . ." the sheriff cast around for a word and settled on "item trailing from this woman's coat. Did it come from this shop?"

Anna, baffled, silently took the blouse and found the stock number she assigned every item. She held out the tag. "I can show you my records where there is a matching number."

Sheriff Dennison turned to Squirrel Face, "Do you have a receipt?"

Squirrel Face screwed up her face, flaming red now, and tears sprang from her eyes. She gave her head several short, fast shakes.

"Can you explain why it is in your possession?"

The short, fast shakes again.

"Did you remove this item from the shop without paying for it, Mrs. Beemer?"

She let out a sob like a bark.

The sheriff turned to Anna. "Is there somewhere where she can sit down?"

Anna went to her office and retrieved a straight back chair.

Squirrel Face sat. A too-small coat encased her fleshy body. The woman who aroused worry and anger in Anna now gave rise to a cleansing wave of pity. *What a sad life this woman must lead.* Dave was right. She was pathetic.

"She has clearly stolen this item from your shop. Do you want to press charges?"

Both heat and cold rushed through Anna's body, a strange disorienting sensation. Now was her chance to quiet this woman, to return to her the frightened and guilty feelings she gave Anna. But now that the opportunity was here, Anna felt no satisfaction. She would feel vindictive and petty to punish this unloved woman.

Anna didn't look at the woman when she spoke, she said her words to the sheriff. "No, no charges. I just want her to know that one time she told me sin was everywhere, and implied that I had somehow sinned. I felt judged. But now, now that she has clearly sinned, 'Thou shalt not steal,' isn't that how it goes? I am not going to judge her. I feel sorry for her. She can keep the blouse. I'll write it off." And Anna turned her back on the two of them, leaving them alone while she went to bury her head in her hands in the office.

It was only noon and the day felt twenty hours long already. Anna took a deep breath to restore herself. She had taken the high road, but not entirely for the best of reasons. Now she had insurance that if the woman did know anything about Anna's affair with Dave, she wouldn't broadcast it. After all, how would it look for the Baptist minister's wife to be exposed as a shoplifter?

## CHAPTER NINETEEN
Anna

The morning of her drive to Omaha, Anna got up early, her mood swinging between joy and dread.

Although old Squirrel Face wouldn't gossip now, no matter how much she knew or pretended to know, the dynamics of the situation, the deceit and ugly remarks sickened Anna. Her stock boy had seen her and Dave together, and maybe Charlie's dad had seen Dave behind her on Christmas Eve. Had other people seen things over the years? Had Shannon? Had Katya? The possibility panicked Anna.

And panic had forced her to make an agonizing decision.

She clicked on her bedside radio only to hear the Righteous Brothers' song about losing that loving feeling. The music hurt her heart.

She snapped the radio off and got dressed.

***

Instead of the new Interstate, Anna took old Highway 6 to Omaha. Farms sprinkled the gentle hills. Shabby bungalows in need of paint sat across from big new houses, shining in the morning sun. The sun tempted her to forget her worries, but forgetfulness wouldn't come.

When Anna and Dave spent time together, she barricaded all her guilt in a corner of her mind. Lately, it kept finding a way out.

Trying to push her thoughts away yet again, Anna turned on KOIL, the pop station Katya liked. A British duo sang about going to pieces and wanting to die. Were deejays conspiring against her this morning? Again, she snapped off the radio.

Soon the Dodge Street sign appeared, and the city traffic surrounded her, demanding all her attention.

***

Anna spied Dave in the hotel lobby before he saw her. When she walked up behind him and blew on his neck, he whirled around. Anna laughed and poured all her love into her smile.

He grabbed and hugged her. "Hey, lady, do I know you?"

"No. I just saw you and couldn't resist."

Dave took her elbow like she might escape and steered her to the elevator. When the doors closed, he said, "Am I glad to see you." His crooked smile proved it.

As soon as Dave locked the door to their room, they were in each other's arms, kissing, grabbing at each other's clothing. Dave tried to lift her sweater over her head while she tried to unbutton his shirt. At cross purposes, they both flung their own clothing to the floor and Anna backed, naked on to the bed pulling Dave along, still kissing him. They made love once fast and hard, and then again, slow and easy.

Then they lay silent in each other's arms. Anna thought they were like an old, happily married couple. Only they weren't. The conversation she had decided they must have ate away at her heart. She feared losing her nerve.

***

From the restaurant atop the Mutual of Omaha Building it was hard to tell where the lights of the city stopped and the stars began. Anna savored the rare public appearance with Dave, the two of them unafraid, like all these other dressed-up people.

She studied each couple. Were any of them like her and Dave, one of them married to someone else? Was it the plump and pretty lady with the short bald man, studying their menus? Or maybe the gray-haired man in the plaid sport coat with the younger woman? Or maybe she and Dave were the only cheaters here. Did they look guilty, wearing their guilt in their eyes, on their shoulders, in the way they held their heads?

They ordered and sipped drinks and made small talk.

"I had to go all last weekend without a Hershey's delivery. People aren't happy when they can't get their candy," Dave said.

Anna had her own complaint. "The store looks like Good Will. The only fall clothes left are the ones people brought back after Christmas. Maybe I should just give them away."

They talked of everything but what Anna needed to talk about while eating steaks and baked potatoes, the steaks as tender as the butter melting in the potatoes. When the waiter took their plates and brought them coffee, Anna chose her moment. Her chest felt empty, not like her heart had stopped beating, but like she had no heart at all.

"Dave. I have to tell you something." She set her coffee cup into its saucer with the smallest of taps, but kept her hands on it.

"You want to break it off, don't you?" Dave didn't look at her.

Now her heart slammed back into place, filling her chest so that Anna thought it might burst. Tears stung her eyes like bees. She nodded, sniffing, the tears finding their way down her cheeks. She looked directly into Dave's plain, handsome face. "How did you know?"

"I just had a feeling. Something in your eyes." Dave took her hand off the coffee cup. "What's changed? Why now?" His confusion stuck needles of pain to her heart. She felt mean knowing she was hurting him.

Sobs worked their way up Anna's throat. She took her purse and left the table before she made a scene. In the lobby by the elevator, she locked her arms tight across her chest, looking out at the night, at the cold, clear beauty of it, wishing darkness would swallow her and whisk her flying through those stars until she splintered into a thousand pieces in some other universe.

\*\*\*

Back in the room, Dave said heatedly, "Don't drive home now. It's late and you're upset. Why don't you wait until morning? We just got here."

71

Anna just kept crying and packing and shaking her head. "I have to go, Dave. If I stay, I might change my mind."

Dave grabbed her, a little roughly, but his touch soon turned gentle, his hands on her arms like a safe haven she was forced to leave. "Then stay. Please stay."

It took all her courage to button her coat and tie her scarf around her neck. She was suddenly calm. With a voice as flat as the Nebraska prairie, Anna said, "Good bye, Dave," and opened the door.

# CHAPTER TWENTY
Dave

*What just happened here?* Dave stared at the door by which Anna had walked out of his life. He wanted his hot stare to ignite it in flames. When he punched the wall next to it, he hurt his hand; but a satisfying kick overturned the arm chair, and it lay helpless and defeated. He wanted to get roaring drunk and forget he ever met the woman.

He wanted to chase her and beg her to come back.

A whooshing sound came from the bed as he sat down on it hard, out of furniture to abuse, and out of the urge to abuse it. "Shit." He flopped back on to the sheets still tangled from their earlier lovemaking. The image of Anna, so much more voluptuous unclothed than she appeared to be dressed, ambushed his imagination. He covered his face in an effort to hide from the mental picture. A crackle of static brought the radio to life and Dave found what he was looking for.

"This is Stretch Wilson bringing you late night jazz. Here's Dave Brubeck with the unsurpassed 'Take Five.'" Maybe the smooth sounds would relieve the pain in his gut, the anger surging through his head, the helplessness threatening to bring him to tears.

*Music soothes the savage beast* or something like that.

The telephone sat next to the radio and Dave saw the button for Room Service. He pushed it and ordered a double whiskey and today's *World Herald.* While he waited for the drink, he tossed his tie on the floor and flung off his shoes, which landed next to the overturned chair. If only memories could be so easily disposed of.

He'd focus his thoughts on business, not on Anna. He had come to Omaha to find a replacement seat for the Majestic. He wouldn't let personal affairs interfere with business.

\*\*\*

When Dave opened the door to Room Service, the waiter saw the overturned chair and general mess. "Everything okay, mister?"

"Just got dumped. That ever happen to you?"

"Plenty of times, sir." He turned to go.

"How does it make you feel?"

The guy nodded at the chair, lying sadly on its side, and said, "Like kicking the furniture." He turned to go again.

Dave said, "Wait," to stop him, and handed the guy a twenty. Way too big a tip, but he didn't feel like being sensible. He could tip whatever the hell he felt like tipping. Placing the drink next to the radio, Dave climbed on the bed to sit cross-legged. He spread the newspaper out in front of him, open to the For-Sale ads, and scanned for floor-mounted wooden auditorium seats. He'd found a few that way over the years. If only a happy outcome to his personal life could be found among the ads, some secret solution, printed neatly: "All wishes granted. All problems solved. All broken hearts mended, just . . ." and the magic answer would be printed right there.

He found neither chairs nor consolation in the For-Sale ads, but tomorrow he could hit a couple of antique shops in the Old Market around Howard Street, another source for used commercial furnishings. He folded the newspaper carefully, and then flung it across the room, missing the chair by a mile. He wished he'd thrown it harder so it whacked against the wall.

The sheets still smelled of Anna's perfume—Emeraude—as he tucked himself under them, undressing at the same time. He threw his pants and socks on the floor. That smell in the curve of her shoulder, lingering on her clothes, reminding him of comfort and delight and bliss.

"Shit. Shit. Shit." Swearing brought satisfaction. He would not think of Anna. He'd let the music and the whiskey feed fantasies about some beautiful blonde, one he'd met in the war, a Frenchwoman.

In some village, he couldn't remember the name—maybe he'd never known it—he and some buddies, dirty and parched from two days' march, had walked into a French bar where three girls sat at a table drinking wine. The blonde one caught his attention right away. Her eyes were blue and filled with sadness. France had been ravaged, and the people looked worn out.

An old guy smoking a cigarette sat at a beat-up piano, just doodling on the keys. Dave walked over to him. "'Sentimental Journey'?" Dave didn't know French, but the French loved American music, that much he knew. The old guy nodded, put out his cigarette, and played the opening bars. Dave gave him a smile and a thumbs-up and put a few francs in the tip jar.

When he turned back to look at the blonde, she was watching him. Putting down his gear next to the piano, he went to her and asked her to dance by holding his arms in the dance position. She rose, staring into his eyes the whole time—she was medium height, very slender, food was scarce, but her slight figure was lovely. Her skin shone clear as a summer sky, her lashes thick and dark as the chocolate he passed out to the street kids. She wore signature red French lipstick.

They danced slowly, closely. Gratitude filled him just to hold a woman, to feel her womanly shape against him warm and snug. She rested her cheek on his shoulder and the sensation took away his soldier loneliness. Dave sang quietly into her hair. She didn't move at all, except for her feet following his lead. The music and motion joined them. When the song ended with the beautiful word "home," the place every soldier longed for, Dave knew that in those few minutes during the ugly war, he had experienced perfection.

In his memory, he looked down at the blonde to say *"Merci"* and her face had turned into Anna's.

*Great. Just great.* Anna even stole his fantasies. He tossed back his drink and turned out the light, the radio still on. Music had been his consolation so many times. When he didn't make the high school football team, he found solace playing first trumpet in the swing band. He still remembered the fingering to "Ciribiribin."

In college, when the fraternity he wanted hadn't rushed him, he made friends in the music department. A piano major named Mary stole his heart for about a semester.

World War II came and he thought serving in an army band might save him from getting shot at, but many was the time he had to put down his trumpet and pick up his rifle.

And that time in France with the blonde and the piano and "Sentimental Journey."

In Omaha, in the hotel bedroom, Glen Miller's "In the Mood" filled the darkness, and Dave said to the radio, "A very *bad* mood," and switched it off.

***

Harvey's Antiques in the Old Market had three floors of junk, all displayed without plan and decorated with a thin layer of dust. Old china baby dolls sat next to coffee grinders which sat next to vintage evening dresses. These items perched on old ice boxes and wardrobes with carving so elaborate it threatened to come alive. Books, dress patterns (*don't think of Anna*), magazines and newspapers were tucked into cardboard boxes about to fall apart.

But no wooden auditorium seats. He had counted on something going his way on this doomed weekend.

Dave wandered amidst the merchandise, in awe of the sheer volume of it. He'd found a row of five seats, in near perfect condition, one time a few years ago. But that was a one-off. Never since.

Harvey, as weathered and neglected as his merchandise, appeared from behind a large headboard, and Dave asked if he might have some seats tucked away.

Harvey shook his head. "I hear they're pulling down an old theater in Kearny. I'm going out there midweek. Want me to keep an eye out for you?"

The possibility perked up Dave's mood. Maybe he'd take a ride out there today, himself, and save the weekend from being a complete waste. But he realized if he failed, he would feel even worse. Better to just let Harvey handle it.

"Sure," Dave said and thanked Harvey and left. He walked the streets of the Old Market and stopped in at a café for a burger. He toyed with the idea of sticking around to catch the band at the Royal Grove in Peony Park that night, but he couldn't get excited about it.

Instead, he went back to the hotel. Yesterday, he had entered a happy man. Today he packed up and checked out without replacement seats for the Majestic and without his best girl.

## CHAPTER TWENTY-ONE
Anna

The dark drive back to Weaver required all of Anna's focus because all she wanted to do was cry. She hadn't chickened out. She had followed her conscience, and done the right thing, which didn't feel right at all. It felt wrong wrong wrong.

The hurt she saw in Dave's eyes burrowed into her heart. How could hurting someone like that be right? But the world said it was what she should do. Loving a married man was wrong. Leaving him was right. How twisted and backward it all felt.

The glowing eyes of a raccoon smack in the middle of the lane reminded Anna she was driving. When she swerved to miss it, the car went off onto the soft shoulder and she momentarily lost control. She managed to bring the car to a halt and breath rushed from her in relief. She was fine. The car was fine. Everything was fine. But those eyes, the raccoon's eyes, had shone as accusingly as Dave's. For the merest second she had thought they were Dave's.

Soon she was back on the highway. She drove carefully, attentively, well within the speed limit. The sound of Dave's voice pleading her to stay repeated in her ears, but she willed it away and concentrated on the road. The voice returned, "Now? You're going to drive home now? At least stay til morning." She had left because her will was weak. He had nearly convinced her to stay; and if she had stayed . . . she didn't want to think what would have happened had she stayed.

Her mind on these things, her car drifted into the passing lane. A car she had not seen— there were so few on the road this time of night—laid on its horn. Anna had nearly cut him off. Panicking, she pulled her thoughts together, and steered back into the right lane. The car passed her, its tail lights growing more and more dim.

The glow-in-the-dark paint of a lodging sign for a Ramada Inn summoned her. You need a break, it said. You need to get off the road and get some rest, it scolded. Anna agreed with the sign. Two close calls had shaken her. She wasn't about to tempt a third.

\*\*\*

Pounding. Anna heard pounding. Was it her heart? No, it was outside her. She woke suddenly, rudely, from a hard, deep sleep. Where was she? What time is it?

"It's checkout time, ma'am. It's ten o'clock."

Anna blinked and squinted at the clock. Ten o'clock. She never slept until ten o'clock. She remembered. The raccoon, the honking driver, the sign for the Ramada. "Yes. I'm sorry. I overslept."

"Another half hour, ma'am. Then I have to clean the room."

The cleaning cart rumbled away from Anna's door and down the corridor.

\*\*\*

Back in Weaver, Anna prepared an evening meal of hamburger steak and an iceberg lettuce salad. *That's what life will be like from now on, hamburger steak and iceberg lettuce – pretty dull stuff.* She contemplated a life as dry and tasteless as her meal and tried to think of some consolation.

Maybe she'd pull out her old water colors. She could become an eccentric painter now that she was unattached. She could run around in a paint-smeared smock, wear a beret, and take up smoking.

On the top shelf of the closet behind the hat boxes, she found her smudged paint box. The well-used look of it made her smile. She sat on her bed and opened it carefully, like it might contain surprises. Her brushes were still in good condition. She had always taken good care of them. The tubes of paint were stiff and unyielding, but she could order more from Sears.

She carried the box into the kitchen, its contents rattling in a purposeful way. Leaving it on the table, she retrieved the catalog from the magazine rack in the living room. Back again at the table, she went to the index. Running her fingers down the "P" column she found, "Paint, watercolor," and her heart gave a little leap.

She hadn't sent in a catalogue order in years, but she remembered the steps easily. Tear out an order blank from the back, fill out the separate columns: item name, stock number, quantity, price, shipping according to the map of zones. It was all so orderly and preordained. She wanted her own life to have the same sense of tidiness and control. If only she could order the future she wanted. Quantity: one life Color: as bright as the rainbow Size: large and bountiful.

She addressed and stamped the envelope, and included a check. Licking the envelope's seal was like making a promise to herself. She would paint now, no more dreary thoughts of Dave. Her store during the day, painting during the evenings.

She went back to her now-cold dinner, took another look at it, and scraped it in the trash. From the frig she pulled out pork chops and onion, melted some butter in a frying pan and breathed in the ever-tempting smell of onions frying in butter. From her spice rack she chose rosemary—she never used rosemary—removed its lid and inhaled its strange, woody smell. She added the chops to the pan and seasoned them with salt, pepper, and rosemary. A small can of earthy smelling mushrooms and Anna had a dinner worthy of a budding artist.

The lively sizzle and rich smell restored her appetite. She savored every bite. Besides resuming her painting, Anna resolved to be a more adventurous cook.

***

After she had washed up, she carried her painting things to the couch. Several of her old paintings were in a manila folder, the paper stiff with age, but the colors still bright. A still life of vegetables, the carrots lumpy and lifeless, made her laugh. She'd start practicing with carrots. Sifting through several more fruit and flower sketches, Anna found a portrait of Katya about age six.

In the painting, her daughter leaned against a chair, her body long and graceful even then. Her hair tumbled across her shoulders. One bare foot crossed the other. Unlike the carrots, life and love breathed from this painting. When Anna got back into practice, she'd make another portrait of Katya the age she is now. On some special occasion, she'd give her both paintings.

Another memory floated up to the surface of Anna's mind. Mr. Andrews, her high school art teacher, had praised her work, making her feel talented and important. She had lived for art class and fantasized about him in bed at night, and in math class – which bored her silly. One night, she decided she was going to kiss him. She savored the idea, turned it over in her mind, and made plans how she would do it.

The next day she thought about the kiss all day. She didn't even tell her best friend when they walked to class together or ate lunch. After last period, she had gone to the art room on the pretext of picking up her painting.

When she got to Mr. Andrews's room, he was switching out the displayed paintings for new ones. "Oh, hi, Anna. Did you come for your painting?"

"I thought I'd take it home tonight."

"Let me get it for you." They both walked to where her painting was hung. Her plan was working. When he turned to hand it to her, that's when she'd do it. A sweet, gentle kiss on his lips. He handed her the painting, and she was about to take it and follow through on her plan, when in walked the math teacher. Her heart dropped into her stomach like a stone. Her chance was blown, and she'd never again have the nerve.

"Hey, Irwin, ya wanna shoot some baskets?" The other teacher saw Anna and said, "Oh, sorry. You're busy."

Anna looked at the other teacher, then at Mr. Andrews, as she took her painting. *Irwin? His name was Irwin? Ugh..*

"Thanks," Anna said as she took the painting and left the classroom. Mr. Andrews lost his dreaminess when Anna learned his name. The name didn't fit her fantasy. By week's end she had a crush on a football player who asked her to Homecoming.

Anna shook her head at her own young foolishness. Imagine if she'd gone through with the kiss and the other teacher had seen them. That outcome would have been very different.

*** 

When Monday came, Anna went into her shop bright and early. Her heart might be in pieces, but for the first time in years, her conscience was clear. Constant deceit was wearing, like Chinese water torture. She also felt ancient.

Would she grow old alone? Katya would be way out in Hollywood or New York or wherever they made movies. Would Anna end up wearing the print dresses she stocked for the church ladies, her ankles swollen in sensible shoes, and having her hair tinted blue? Was that the price she would pay for a clear conscience?

She heard the bell sound from out front and put on a smile for her first customer of the day. When she saw who it was, she grabbed a countertop to keep from stumbling in surprise.

"Anna, can we talk?" Dave asked.

"We can, but it won't make any difference."

"Please come back."

The invitation in his eyes tempted her. His strong, familiar voice made her weak.

"I'll leave Fran. I will. Just let me prepare her."

Anna closed her eyes. "Dave, that's all I ever hoped for. I still do. Remember Fran was my friend, too. Her problems sadden me, too. I'm not heartless."

Dave reached for her.

Anna didn't shrug his hands from her arms, but she didn't move in for an embrace, either. "Come back and tell me when you have left her." Sadness thickened her voice.

She watched him leave, and then crumpled onto the stool behind the cash register. *It was too hard, having to reject him twice.*

# CHAPTER TWENTY-TWO
Anna

Spring arrived in March and stayed. Birds sang like drunken sailors. Lipstick red tulips and daffodils as yellow as butter dotted brown yards. The townswomen shopped for pastel Easter dresses and bright casual clothes, eager to shed coats and boots. They loved the shop's new peach paint, European tiles in black and white, and the shiny ebony countertop by the cash register. When they stopped to study the vintage black and white fashion photos Anna had hung, she knew they liked them, too.

Anna had also freshened her own look. A new auburn tint, a little like Katya's, covered her hair's gray streaks, and a shorter style looked hip. Or so her customers said. She couldn't bring herself to say that word.

*\*\*\**

One day, Anna was making a deposit at the bank when an unfamiliar male voice greeted her. "Mrs. Simms?"

Anna turned to look at the man and a scene from a year ago popped into her head. Anna had chaperoned Katya's Senior Trip Day to Springbrook Lake. On the return bus ride, she had shared a seat with the guidance counselor, Neal Slater, the senior class sponsor. They talked about Iowa lakes, and she hadn't seen him since.

"How's Katya?" Neal asked.

"She just got an internship at a movie studio in California for the summer. She's so excited and I'm so nervous." Anna cringed. "Hollywood."

"Oh, she'll be fine. She's a good kid."

"I suppose." Anna glanced at the clock. She had to get back. "Nice talking to you."

That evening while watching *The Donna Reed Show* and polishing her nails, Anna's phone rang. Since the breakup with Dave, her phone hadn't rung much. She answered, careful not to bump a nail, "Hello?"

"This is Neal Slater."

Anna didn't remember him at first. But then, the afternoon's conversation came back to her. "Oh, yes, the bank."

"And last year's Skip Day."

"Right."

"Would you like to go out sometime?" He rushed on, not waiting for an answer. "Saturday night. Maybe take in a movie."

The invitation made her think the man could see her through the phone, curlers piled on her head sausage style, her once-pretty chenille robe now bald in spots. She put a hand up to her curlers and made a face when she bumped a nail. "Well, let me think. When? Saturday night? Well, yes. Yes, that would be fine." They talked some more and then said good-bye.

*Fine*? Did she say *fine*? Not *nice*? Or *I'd like that*. But *fine*?

Donna Reed's problems no longer held Anna's attention. Should she have said yes? She still felt like she belonged to Dave. It would take practice, this not thinking first of Dave. She hadn't seen him since their February breakup. When he walked down Main Street, he always walked on the side across from her shop, like if he passed her shop, he'd catch a disease.

When at first Dave had called to coax her back, it had been hard to resist. "Dave, please, please don't call anymore. I don't want to hang up on you, but I will if I have to." He stopped calling, sparing their breakup that final insult.

Still, when the phone first rang tonight, a tiny part of her had hoped it would be Dave.

## CHAPTER TWENTY-THREE
Dave

One April afternoon Dave came home before the evening show and found Fran on the floor. She clenched her arms around her middle like she was trying to hold it in. At first his heart raced, thinking she was dead.

He knelt by her. "Fran? Cookie?" The old nickname slipped out.

"My stomach's burning up." Fear made her hazel eyes as big as quarters. "Help me, Dave, please."

Dave had already hauled the phone off the end table; but he had been clumsy, and the receiver went flying across the floor. He let it lie while he thumbed the phone book, its pages shaking in his hands. *Hospital. Hospital. Damn it, where is hospital?* At last it appeared right where he had already looked. He turned the open book down and hauled the receiver back in by its cord, got control of the phone book and receiver and dialed the number. It rang twice. *Answer.* Two more times. *Answer, dammit.* His mind focused laser-like on making that happen.

"Malcom County Hospital."

*At last.* "This is Dave Franks. I need an ambulance right away. You know where I'm at? My house. 437 Meadow. Yeah, behind the Lutheran Church. I'll stand outside."

He hung up and stroked Fran's damp forehead. His own was just as damp.

"Now I'm going to move you to the couch. Then I'll stand outside and wave down the ambulance. Okay?"

Fran nodded, her eyes glittering with pain and fear.

As he lifted her shrunken body on the couch, she said, "I'm sorry, Dave. Maybe I'll just die. That would solve everything."

*Solve what? Her alcoholism? Their futile marriage?*

". Shhh. Don't talk like that. The ambulance will be here soon." He put her down gently, adjusted a pillow under her head, and covered her with the gold afghan.

Fran's lips compressed, and she squeezed her eyes shut.

Dave heard the wail of the siren not far away. He hurried to the front porch to wave them down.

\*\*\*

Sedation gave Fran relief the first three days in the hospital, and her stomach healed a little. Drinking had worn away the lining and only time and rest and a bland diet could fix it.

On the fifth day of Fran's hospitalization, Dave brought her wildflowers. There was no reason not to be nice to her. He didn't love her anymore, but he had stayed with her, and she had nobody else.

\*\*\*

In a perfect world, he would never have cheated on his wife. In that same unspoiled world, Anna would never have had an affair with a married man. She wasn't the type. Alone, together, they created their own world. He should have known one day it would have to end, no matter how imperfect the world turned out to be.

The night two months ago when Anna drove away from the hotel in Omaha, confusion had made Dave miserable. He'd invented excuses for her. She's tired. Sick. Something's wrong with Katya. With the shop. He'd refused to accept her decision.

Recalling his desperate attempts to win her back embarrassed him now. He tried to hate her and not himself. When the ballroom's heating system broke down, he was almost grateful for the distraction and worked to harden his heart. She acted stuck up until you got to know her. Her daughter always came first. She drank too much coffee. He crossed the street rather than walk in front of her shop, hoping to hurt her feelings. But he knew his heart would never harden to her. If she would take him back, he'd go back in a minute.

***

At the door to Fran's room, Dave stopped when he saw a nurse holding Fran's hand as his wife whipped back and forth, trying to break free. "Easy. Easy," the nurse said. Another nurse appeared with a syringe held skyward. Alarmed, Dave backed out of the way. The second nurse gave Fran the injection and she quieted. To Dave, the first nurse said, "It's the alcohol withdrawal."

***

After a week, the hospital released Fran with a fistful of prescriptions, diet instructions, and pamphlets on AA. In spite of her alcoholism, Fran had always tried to keep up her appearance. Now, without makeup, her hair greasy and matted, her dress wrinkled and buttoned crooked, she looked old and withered.

Why hadn't he thought to bring clean clothes from home? He tried to remember what her favorite clothes were; but because he avoided looking at her, he had no idea.

## CHAPTER TWENTY-FOUR
Dave

Poached eggs and dry toast, that's what Fran was eating when she said, "Tonight I'm going to AA."

Hope flashed through his brain like found money and vanished just as fast. Dave wanted to think AA would help, but they had been down that road before. And it ended right where it began.

But he was wrong.

Over the next few weeks, country music as much as AA helped Fran stay away from alcohol. Country twang became the soundtrack to Fran's sobriety. If she worked in the yard, an RCA portable nestled between a bag of potting soil and her starter petunias, and Patsy Cline sang about being crazy. Eventually Fran added chicken soup and applesauce to her menu. Her cheeks turned rosy and her body rounded out. By the second week in May, she had gone a month without drinking.

Dave brought home a bouquet of daisies to mark the day. She deserved an award. She had gone to two or three AA meetings every week. He had seen her bedroom light on late, as she read instead of drinking. He'd never known her to read before, but now she checked out three or four Daniel Steele's every week.

No one else would encourage her —she had no friends — so Dave felt responsible to give her support. It was the decent thing to do. He thought about working on his relationship with Fran, resurrecting their long dead marriage, but the idea only made him tired.

As he pulled into their driveway, daisies on the seat beside him, he wondered if Fran had the same thoughts. There was a time, when they were first married, that they could practically read each other's minds; but now, he had no idea what happened inside her head.

Dave entered the house through the back door into the kitchen where Fran stood at the stove stirring spaghetti sauce. Johnny Cash growled out a song from atop the radio. Dave liked Johnny Cash just about as much as he liked Burl Ives. Fran turned to him, and he gave her the daisies. She accepted them with a surprised look, but no smile.

The lack of a smile puzzled him. In the month since her hospitalization, they had been cordial. Not exactly relaxed, but definitely not cold. "Congratulations on your month milestone." He waited for a response.

"Thank you." Wordlessly, she put them in a vase and on the table, which was already set for dinner.

Questions popped up in Dave's head, the worst one being has *she started drinking again?*

"Sit down, Dave."

"Is it time for dinner?" He could hear the phony cheerfulness in his voice, and disliked himself for it.

"I just want to tell you something." She covered the sauce, put down her spoon in the spoon rest, and turned to face him, her arms bent. She gripped the counter on either side of her, as if she needed support.

Puzzled, he sat down at the table, the dishes and the flowers between them, and waited for Fran to continue. The flowers made his nose twitch. Fran's face gave him no clue as to what she planned to say.

"I want a divorce."

The words lay between them like dead fish. Dave could not have been more surprised if she had said she had a lover. And then he knew. She *did* have a lover. Without being told, he knew she did, and it hit him like a blow to his midsection. A big lump rose into his chest.

He opened his mouth to ask her who and when, but she spoke first. "I'm with someone at AA."

He stammered. Finally, he managed words. "I don't know what to say."

"To be honest, we've been together for years."

The news made him grateful he was seated, because otherwise, his legs would have collapsed. His mouth opened but nothing came out.

"We made the decision together to quit drinking."

The irony did not escape him. For years he had been hiding an affair from Fran— wanting to leave her but not having the heart— when all along, she had been having an affair, too, and now she was leaving him. Like some sick joke.

He pushed his chair back with such force, the vase of daisies tipped over and water spilled all over the table.

* * *

Dave sat in his car clenching the steering wheel, shell shocked. "What a waste," he said, shaking his head. *All those wasted years.* His face burned hot with frustration.

It certainly wasn't a perfect world. No siree. Miles from it.

## CHAPTER TWENTY-FIVE
Katya

Katya wadded up another piece of paper and slammed it into the trash can. "Damn!" Art school had taught her to swear.

"It's the pits, isn't it?" Dottie wadded her paper and trashed it, too.

"We'll never get this stuff done at this rate."

Piles of wadded paper lay in drifts at their feet. Katya stood to stretch and caught a look at herself in the mirror. She looked like a mad woman. Her hair went every which way thanks to the pencil she poked in it like a pin cushion.

All evening Dottie had crammed one Milky Way bar after another in her mouth. Chocolate smeared her cheeks and sweatshirt, and crumpled candy wrappers mixed with the crumpled sketch paper on the floor.

Katya bent down near Dottie's desk and picked up one of her crumpled sketches. It crackled as she straightened it. A turtle with crossed eyes and a goofy smile made her laugh. "This is good. I like this guy."

Dottie took the page from her and studied it. "Really? You think so?" Her eyes searched Katya's to see if she meant it.

Katya smiled. "He's great. Does he have a name?"

"Flapjack?" More of a question than an answer. Dottie stared at her creation.

"Flapjack? I love it! Dottie, stop messing with him."

Katya's roommate sighed. "I've been looking at him so long, I can't tell anymore."

"Well, I can. Now leave him alone. What else do you have to do?"

"I have to write a story with him as a character." Dottie screwed up her face. "I don't have a clue."

"Think about what would surprise people." Katya sat on her bed.

"Easy for you to say."

"Make him the unlikely hero or something."

Dottie's face lit up. "That just might work. Thanks. So, what are you working on?" Dottie reached for one of Katya's discarded sketches.

"The sportswear entry. We have to have one formal, one sportswear, and one lingerie. I'm trying to design an outfit for golf, but I don't know the first thing about golf, let alone what somebody would wear." Katya shrugged.

"So, why'd you choose it then?"

Katya laughed. "I don't know. I thought it would impress people."

\*\*\*

During the last week of project deadlines and final exams, the girls walked around with blank faces, their minds turned inward. Tension bounced off them, each girl in her own little bubble of worry.

Then, *poof,* it was all over. Projects were handed in. Final exams were finished. The girls, one by one, came out of the elevator grinning and humming. There was nothing left of the school year but the awards dinner. Katya floated in a sea of relief and joy.

CHAPTER TWENTY-SIX
Katya

The girls dressed in their art school best for the awards dinner. Sheaths, heels, up-dos and eyeliner. Clouds of Chanel Number Five and My Sin hung in the elevator when Katya stepped on. Paulette squeezed into the back corner wearing a navy dress Audrey Hepburn would have been proud to wear. Katya pretended not to see Paulette and then felt crummy about it. The interminable elevator ride finished, and the girls marched through the lobby, high heels wobbling.

\*\*\*

Only an art school would use purple iris and red carnations together and get away with it. The gaudy flowers stood out like Peter Maxx illustrations against the crisp table linens in the Windsor Hotel party room. Ms. Clarkson's cherry pink shantung A-line added one more brilliant color to the mix, as she welcomed the students from behind the podium.

The waiters delivered generous plates of chicken a la king and iceberg lettuce drenched in Thousand Island dressing. Wicker baskets of rolls were emptied and refilled several times as the girls made up for the sketchy meals they'd had during exams. The excitement and the rich food sent the noise level to deafening heights as a hundred girls gossiped and giggled.

After cherry pie and ice cream, Ms. Clarkson took up her post behind the podium again. "May I have your attention?" It took several minutes for the buzz to settle to a murmur. She introduced the dean, who made a speech nobody listened to.

At last came the announcements they all wanted to hear, the award winners. To Katya and Dottie's amazement, Mona won Most Improved Student. Katya didn't know if the award referred to Mona's drawing or to her appearance. She had dropped several pounds, let her hair grow, and wore a flattering dress in black and white op art print. Loud applause and unladylike shouts made Mona blush, and she looked almost pretty. The two roommates shrugged and kept clapping as the applause continued so long Ms. Clarkson had to tap her spoon against her water glass over and over.

At last the commotion quieted down. The Animation teacher took the podium.

Katya could tell Dottie was nervous because she started making jokes under her breath. When the teacher said Dottie's name for the winner of Most Original Character for Flapjack, Dottie almost missed hearing the announcement. Katya had to give her a big nudge in the ribs. When Dottie realized what was happening, she nearly tripped on her chair as she stood up.

Dottie came back to her seat clutching the certificate close to her chest with both arms. She hadn't expected any prizes, Katya knew. Dottie had no idea how gifted she was. She leaned close to Katya. "Now it's your turn."

Katya crossed her fingers under the table for her formal dress illustration. In her design, sheer jersey gauze in midnight blue flecked with silver thread flowed over the body like a slinky second skin. A shockingly low décolleté used the jersey's draping quality to best advantage. And to save the design from plainness, the dress fastened with a long line of small covered buttons all the way down one side. Katya believed it had a chance at the prize.

When Ms. Clarkson announced the name of a girl who occupied the back corner of the classroom as the winner, Katya could hardly comprehend the announcement. Nobody knew this girl, who kept to herself; but when Ms. Clarkson projected her sketch onto the screen, it stunned everyone and applause thundered in the room. White tapestry teamed with black satin to create a design worthy of a Bond girl. The design so impressed Katya that she couldn't even be jealous.

She gave herself a pep talk. *Keep trying. Keep working. Don't get discouraged,* when Dottie's elbow nudged Katya's ribs. "It's you. Get up there."

Katya gave her a "what's going on?" look, and Dottie said, "Your golf ensemble. It won." Katya wanted to shout out loud. She felt a goofy smile plastering her face as she jumped up and nearly ran to the podium. Ms. Clarkson projected the outfit on to the screen and the girls reacted with, "Fun" and "I'd like that."

Katya's design featured a navy blue skort, a sleeveless shirt in small red and white checks, navy and white spectator golf shoes, and a yellow, red, and navy madras plaid jacket. She had never before used two patterns together, and the skort—though not her original idea—still surprised people. When she got back to her seat, she hoped she had remembered to say thank you. Ecstatic thoughts crowded her head. *I wish Mom was here. I'll have to call her. I won. I won I won I won.*

Close to the ceremony's end, the girls were squirming in their seats. Katya gave a quick look under the table and saw a rainbow of high heels that had been kicked off pinched feet during dinner.

Only one award remained, the coveted Best Overall Portfolio. Every girl secretly hoped her unrecognized talent would be noticed, and she would win. With that award on a girl's record she could have any career she chose.

Paulette won.

And Katya started the mad applause. She was the first to stand, and all the girls followed suit as Paulette bore herself to the podium like the princess that she was.

\*\*\*

Back at the dorm the girls traded their dresses for PJs, washed away their special event makeup, and let down their updo's. Laughter rang through the hallways. Stashed bottles and six packs came out of hiding. The Beach Boys and The Beatles blasted from stereos, and most girls left their doors wide open. It was party time!

Katya stood at the sink washing her face. When someone pushed open the swinging door to the bathroom, she caught a glimpse of Paulette's face in the mirror before Paulette released the door and backed out into the hall. Katya rushed over and pulled open the door. She regretted her behavior since she and Paulette had stopped being friends, and Katya didn't want to end the year on that note. "Don't go, Paulette. I just want to congratulate you. Best Overall is super. You must be thrilled."

Paulette paused, a watchful look on her face. After a moment, her face relaxed and she smiled. "I am. Thanks."

An awkward silence set in until Katya said, "We've got a bottle in our room. You wanna come join us? Half the hall is in there."

Paulette looked pleased. "Sure. Just let me get rid of this stuff." She nodded at her john bucket.

Katya returned to washing her face. She had resisted hugging Paulette because she still cared for her. She would always care for her, bur fear held her back; and she forgave herself for it. The price was too high. Even though she had ended her friendship with Paulette clumsily, the last night of the school year had brought her redemption. Her heart felt light as the whipped cream on Main Street Café chocolate pie.

CHAPTER TWENTY-SEVEN
Anna

"A picnic has to have fried chicken." That's what Neal claimed when he asked Anna to City Park the week before Memorial Day.

"Let me bring some potato salad. Fried chicken without potato salad is illegal in some states." Anna would use her mom's recipe. Her mother had always asked her to make the dressing when she was a little girl. Mayonnaise, a smidge of mustard, some sugar and vinegar. Easy peasy.

***

On Sunday, she and Neal spread his red-checked stadium blanket under a towering oak. Together they set out plates and flatware while the breeze fluttered the paper napkins and the birds provided the dinner music. A deep sniff of the cold fried chicken made Anna go *mmmmmmmm.* Neal smiled as he peeked under the foil over Anna's potato salad, and the butter on the bread gleamed in the sunshine. Neal pulled out a cherry pie and said, "*Ta dum.*"

Shoulder to shoulder, they leaned against the oak's scratchy bark. Anna sprinkled salt on a chicken leg and bit in, the flavor bringing back every picnic she'd ever been on: church picnics, family picnics, picnics alone with Katya, picnics alone with Dave. She gave her head a tiny shake to rid it of the thought.

Neal worked on a thigh. He put it on his plate and swiped his face with a paper napkin that made a soft crackle. "Good stuff, huh?"

Anna nodded, her mouth still around the leg. Their shoulders touched, his warm and hard from the basketball he played with the other teachers. Anna resisted comparing it to Dave's shoulder. Neal smelled nice, too, like Zest soap. A strong desire to kiss him surprised her and she was thankful he couldn't see her blush.

Above and around them the trees were almost leafed out, the daffodils and hyacinths still held their color, and the May sky shone clean and blue, as if it was as new as the buds on the bushes.

With a speed Anna had forgotten was possible, a black cloud marched across the perfect sky, thunder rumbled up from the depths, and rain pelted them, taking their breath away. Neal straightened. "What the hell?"

They scrambled. Anna grabbed the picnic basket, and Neal bundled the corners of the blanket into a rough package with food, plates and napkins inside. With the blanket jingling and rattling, they dashed for Neal's car.

Once inside, they caught their breath and then whooped and laughed like kids. Rain dribbled down their faces, beat on the roof, and gushed from the windshield. They sat in silence a while, just watching the rain. Then Neal pulled Anna to him and kissed the daylights out of her, and she kissed him back, a delicious kiss, better than fried chicken.

They paused to come up for air. "You taste good," Neal said.

"So, do you. I need another taste." And she put her arms around him and pressed her breasts against his damp chest. Anna's desire surprised her, but she liked it. Really liked it. Neal reached for her breast, and they both looked down to see her nipples peeking through her soaked blouse. Anna rolled her eyes, embarrassed in spite of what they'd been about to do. "Not here." Her voice had turned husky. "Let's go back to my place."

Neal gave his eyebrows a Groucho Marx wiggle. He took his arm from behind her and started the engine.

\*\*\*

Inside Anna's house, they dropped the messy picnic bundle on the floor, cutlery rattling, and made headlong for the couch. Anna hiked up her skirt and threw her panties aside while Neal whipped off his belt. He lay on top of her, she urging him on, desire burning in her. Neal hard and promising.

She ignored the feeling of cheating on Dave and lost herself in pleasure. And then, then at the crucial moment—nothing. Neal wilted. He kept trying but what had been there no longer was. He dropped his head on her shoulder. "Shit!!"

Anna lay there waiting. She had an outrageous urge to giggle. Should she say something? Should she sit up? She didn't know the protocol for this situation. Finally, not looking at her, Neal sat up and fixed his pants. She sat up, too, and retrieved her panties.

Anna gave him a sideways glance and stole a phrase from Katya. She smiled a little and said, "Bummer." Neal chuckled too and Anna took his hand. "No biggie."

"That's for sure," said Neal, and then they really did laugh.

"Look, let's forget this happened and have some coffee."

***

Anna brought in two cups and saucers and a pot of good strong coffee. In her mind, a strong cup of coffee could fix most anything, though she had never used it for this particular malady before.

She handed Neal a cup and took the armchair, letting him have the couch, the tray sitting between them like a line neither could cross. When her mind compared Neal's performance to Dave's, Anna tried to ignore it. Poor Neal ranked pretty low on the *Bandstand* scale. He had an uneven beat and was not good to dance to. The thought made her want to giggle again, so in defense she took a deep breath and thought of unpaid bills. She might slip out later for some office time.

Anna couldn't gauge the quality of the silence between them. She was working past the discomfort caused by Neal's non-performance, but men took this sort of thing to heart more than women did. She asked him his summer plans.

"Summers I work on my Ph.D. at Drake. Two courses a year."

"That's challenging. Good for you." Their small talk filled the strained silence.

Neal sipped his coffee, then set down the cup. "Yeah, they have a good program. I'll finish coursework this year and then I have to write my dissertation." He cringed.

Anna smiled. "Not looking forward to that?" She crossed her legs.

"Yes. No. I've heard horror stories." He shrugged.

Silence settled in again.

Neal broke it with a surprising invitation. "Why don't you come visit me in Des Moines? We could spend a Sunday together."

"That might be fun."

"Great. I'll give you a call." Then he drained his coffee cup, set it on the tray, and stood up.

Anna stood, too. Suddenly tired, she was glad he was leaving.

She walked him to the door and they kissed each other on the cheek. As she watched him climb into his car, she knew he wouldn't call. And furthermore, she didn't care.

With a sigh, she picked up the blanket with the picnic things inside.

# CHAPTER TWENTY-EIGHT
Anna

Anna carried the messy bundle to the kitchen and opened it on the floor. She considered that messy things were so much easier to clean up than messy relationships. Her lovely potato salad had made an unappetizing smear across the blanket's black and red checks. She scraped it onto a plate and dumped it in the trash. Potato salad messed up the leftover chicken, too. There would be no cold chicken for lunch tomorrow.

She gathered the blanket and took it to the basement to load in the washing machine. As she came back up, someone knocked on the back door at the head of the stairs. Pulling aside the curtain, Dave's eyes looked at her, steady and green. She had told him not to stop by anymore, but today, all rules were off. She smiled and let him in.

Dave looked her up and down. "Caught in the rain?"

"Yep," was all she said. She knew he wanted an explanation, but here he was at her door uninvited. It was his place to make explanations. "You want to sit? There's coffee."

"Sure." He pulled out a kitchen chair. He didn't take off his hat, as if he was unsure if he would stay or not.

Anna took the chair across from him and rested her chin on her hands. "So?"

"So, Fran's stopped drinking."

Anna blinked. And blinked again. It was hard information to take in. Then she smiled and sat up straight. "But that's great, isn't it?"

"There's more." Dave's voice had a wariness in it, and he readjusted his hat, still not taking it off.

"What?" Anna couldn't judge the gravity of Dave's remark. He sounded serious, like he might be dying or Fran might be dying or . . . she had no more guesses.

"She asked for a divorce. She's been having an affair for years."

Anna felt that like a smack to the forehead. She exhaled a short breath of disbelief. "What?" Goosebumps broke out on her arms, and the kitchen felt suddenly cold.

"I can leave her now." He paused. "Well, I guess she'll be leaving me. Anyway," Dave paused and put his hat on the table, "You and I can be together again."

Anna stood, went to the sink, and turned on water to wash the cutlery.

"Well, what do you think?" The smallest touch of impatience sounded in his voice.

Anna turned to face him and then, like a snake lashing out, she sent the wet dishcloth sailing across the room. It missed its mark and made a splat on Dave's shoulder instead of his face. Her heart pounded like thunder and she wanted it to pound harder and louder, she was that mad. "You waltz in here and without even asking me how I feel, just assume I want you back. Well, not so fast, buster. I don't know what to think. I've been working so hard at not loving you. I'm seeing someone else now."

Dave brushed off his shoulder while he nodded at her blouse. "Does the someone else explain that?"

She followed his eyes to her chest and saw the top buttons were undone and the rest were buttoned crookedly. Looking him in the eye she said, "Maybe," daring him to say anything, maybe even hoping he would.

Quietly, with a voice as cold as fried chicken at a picnic, Dave said, "I see." Then he picked up the wet dishcloth from where it had landed on the floor and put it on the table. He put his hat back on and let himself out the back door, shutting it with the smallest of clicks.

Anna turned back to the soapy dishwater. "Oh, crap. Crap. Crap. Crap." She smacked a fist down into the soapy water, and suds splashed her face, mixing with her hot tears.

# CHAPTER TWENTY-NINE
Katya

Katya's heart hammered like the bass drum in the Weaver marching band, but she put on her best smile as she stepped into the Cheshire Movies design studio for the first time. Just as she was hoping nothing would go wrong, she shifted her purse and knocked a container of stick pins off a cluttered table. The metal container bounced with a ping, and pins sprayed the floor.

The sewing machines on the side of the room stopped. Her stomach lurched, her eyes filled with tears, and she felt a blush climbing up her neck. Everyone, who just moments before had ignored her, now stared at her. She dropped to the floor and started gathering the pins, hoping everyone went back to their work.

The door squeaked open and Katya heard footsteps behind her. Someone got down to help her gather pins. She looked up to thank them, and her eyes nearly popped from their sockets. She was picking up stick pins with Lisa Graham, the movie star. She and Charlie had seen her in *New York Woman* at least three times. Katya almost said "Wow," and then stopped herself.

A short, chubby woman with gray hair in a Buster Brown style hurried toward them. "Lisa! Here, let me do that."

Lisa rose and went to a man in a wheel chair. Who was he? Why was he in a wheel chair? Then the gray-haired woman knelt down with an *oomph* and started gathering pins, and Katya forgot about wheelchair man.

"I don't know you, do I?" The woman continued to collect stray pins.

"I'm the new intern. I'm so sorry. What a lousy first impression." The woman's friendly voice stopped the near flow of Katya's tears.

"Don't worry about it. Don't know what pins were doing there anyway." The woman sat back on her haunches and held out her hand. "Hi, I'm Chubbs. I wasn't expecting you until tomorrow."

Rooting in her purse, Katya pulled out a rumpled, sweat-stained paper with directions to the studio and the name of her contact, Bambi Roosevelt. She studied the paper and saw the date: June 7, 1966. She showed it to the woman, who smacked her own forehead. "You're right. Sorry."

"I'm Katya Simms." The weirdness of having this conversation while kneeling threatened to make her giggle.

Chubbs made the effort to stand up. "I'm Bambi. I ask you; do I look like a Bambi? My parents must have had someone else in mind."

Katya wondered if she should laugh at the woman's remark, decided not to, and stood up, too.

The room was the size of a double garage. To the right, four women in smocks sat, heads bowed over the now-whirring sewing machines. A rainbow of fabric scraps littered the floor at their feet. Pincushions perched on their wrists like porcupines.

Mannequins stood at attention next to the seamstresses. Some had pieces of muslin pinned to them. Others wore unfinished garments, some with the skirt missing, some with only one sleeve.

Next to the seamstresses, pattern pieces covered pale pink satin spread out on a table big enough for a ping pong game. An artist's palette of fabric bolts rested in wall bins behind the table.

An oversized chalkboard, mounted next to the fabric bins, dominated the room. Titles headed three columns divided by horizontal lines. In the squares formed by the crosshatches were dates and scribbled notes: M's fitting, deliver to wardrobe, staff meeting.

Katya studied it. "What's that?"

"That's the Board." She capitalized the words with her voice. "It is our real boss. Check it every day for what is happening that day and what deadlines are closing in." Then she waved it away. "But we don't want to overwhelm you."

To the left, two illustrators sat on stools at drawing boards. The man wore bell bottoms and a shirt with flowing sleeves like a Spanish dancer. The woman had Twiggy short hair bleached white blond. The man in discussion with Lisa Graham sat kinglike in his wheelchair. Instinctively, Katya knew he was the boss. A thick crop of salt and pepper hair topped his tanned, chiseled face.

Chubbs found a spot for Katya to put her things. "I'm your supervisor, but you'll help everybody. Whatever needs to be done. I'll introduce you to Jerry when he's done with Lisa. Don't let him scare you."

Katya gulped.

"Jerry is head designer. He can sketch, but he is also responsible for orders and appointments and meetings with studio people, so sometimes you will help him. Sometimes you'll help the other artists. They'll explain to you the design as they imagine it. Your job is to read their minds, and make sketches from what they explain. Do you think you can do that?"

Katya gulped again. "I hope so."

Chubbs gave her a kind look.

With burning cheeks, Katya followed Chubbs over to Jerry.

"You're the one who knocked over the pins," he said.

Katya cringed. "Yessir."

"Know anything about sketching?"

"Yessir."

The man picked out some drawings from his stack. "Here, see if you can finish these off. Fabric swatches are pinned there." He pointed. He rolled away and then stopped and did a half turn, giving her a penetrating look. "What's your name again?"

"Katya."

He made an expression Katya couldn't read.

"Is that Russian?"

"Danish, I think."

Jerry turned to Chubbs, growled something, and wheeled himself over to the cutting table where the two of them talked in low tones. She hoped they weren't talking about her.

One of the sketch artists smiled at her. "Hi, I'm Marty. Here, we have an extra drawing board." He yanked out a table from behind some mannequins and hat boxes.

Katya's nerves settled down as she saw drawing pencils and pads. She could do this. All these designs needed was to have the fabric filled in on the clothing.

The rest of the day blurred into coffee runs, floor sweeping, drawing, hoisting new fabric bolts into the bins, more drawing. First, she was on her knees picking up pins, then everyone was gathering their belongings to go home. Jerry had his sport jacket on and his briefcase in his lap as he wheeled himself to the door. He stopped his wheelchair and turned it to face the room. "Lisa is so happy with the designs that everyone is invited to her house Friday evening for drinks and dinner." He turned again and was gone.

Katya looked around her at her smiling, chattering cohorts. The invitation had opened them up, and they looked human and approachable. Still, did the invitation mean her, too? She'd only just arrived. First day on the job and she's invited to a movie star's party? Couldn't possibly be true.

Marty looked at her and must have guessed her reaction. "What's wrong? Can't you come?"

"Does she mean me, too? I only just got here." Katya didn't dare wish that the invitation was real.

"She invited the studio. That means you. It means me. It means the seamstresses." He smiled his friendly smile.

Disbelief and happy bewilderment made Katya grin, too. Wow. She was going to a movie star's house. *Little old me from Weaver, Iowa. Oh my gosh, what will I wear?*

## CHAPTER THIRTY
Katya

Friday night came. Stars sprinkled the velvet sky over Lisa's pool, which shimmered in torchlight. A breeze fluttered the shadowy outlines of orange trees and sent their sweet tart smell into the night air.

Katya studied the other women and wondered if they all could tell her red lace mini dress was homemade. Their clothes all looked like they came from boutiques on Rodeo Drive. Not Chubbs, though. She wore baggy black pants, a sequined and shapeless tunic top, and a sparkly barrette in her gray hair. On her feet were her foam-soled work shoes. She looked like a munchkin in its best bib and tucker. "This is me dressed up. Take it or leave it," she said.

A solidly built black man over six feet tall joined them, and Chubbs gave him a kiss on the cheek.

"This is my husband, Elijah."

He took Katya's hand and kissed it. "Pleased to meet you."

Katya watched him kiss her hand, hypnotized.

"Are you new?" Elijah asked.

Katya couldn't speak. She stared first at her hand and then at Elijah. She had met so few black people, and a black man—who was married to a white lady—had just kissed her hand. No one had ever kissed her hand before. And she had never known a mixed-race couple. An overwhelming urge to giggle colored her cheeks and made her eyes pop.

With the greatest of efforts, she remembered her manners. "I'm Katya."

"Charming name."

"Thank you." She conquered her inappropriate urge to laugh.

Someone else caught his eye, and he wished her good luck and moved on. Katya couldn't look at Chubbs. She knew she had behaved like an idiot.

Chubbs patted her arm. "Don't worry about it. He always has that effect on women. He's a cameraman over in Studio 6. All the stars want him. He makes them look prettier than they are."

Katya appreciated that the pretty women liked Elijah, but he liked plain, eccentric Chubbs.

Before Katya recovered from her clumsiness with Elijah, Lisa Graham approached them. She didn't need any special cameraman to enhance her beauty. Katya wanted to run. All these famous people made her heart pound and her stomach cramp.

"Hello, ladies, I hope you're having a good time."

"Great party, Lisa, as always," said Chubbs.

Lisa thanked her and turned to Katya. "Didn't we pick up pins together a few days ago?"

Katya laughed and dipped her head. "That would be me."

Chubbs nudged her, motioned her glass at another cluster of people nearby, and left Katya with Lisa.

"Are you settling in okay? Don't let Jerry scare you."

"That's what Chubbs said." No clever remarks would come to mind. Katya thought she sounded like a robot.

"He's really a sweetheart, he just likes to sound off sometimes."

Katya couldn't think of a thing to say.

A waiter passed and Lisa motioned him over. "Here, let me get you a drink."

Standing so close to Lisa set Katya's body to tingling all over in the most unsettling way. *I must be star struck*. Katya feared she might faint, but steadiness returned just in time.

"Great dress. Where did you get it?" Lisa said.

Katya realized Lisa had spoken. "You think so?"

"Absolutely. Most redheads wouldn't dare wear red, but it looks great on you."

"Thanks. I made it." She wouldn't have needed to add that last part, but she wanted to impress this woman in some way other than spilling pins.

They chatted about Lisa's clothes for her new movie, and then she moved on to her other guests, and Chubbs came back.

"The band is setting up on the back patio. Shall we go have a listen?" She turned to show the way without waiting for an answer.

Katya followed, but stole a glance at a laughing Lisa, now chatting with another cluster of people. As Katya passed Lisa's back, Lisa turned and smiled, and Katya's stomach jumped right up into her throat and back down again.

*** 

Elijah asked his wife to dance and Katya smiled to see Chubbs rest her cheek on his chest, practically on his stomach, with closed eyes and a blissful smile on her face. Katya wondered if she would ever feel so devoted to someone. Marty, the sketch artist who set up her drawing board came toward her. "Want to dance?"

When the band switched to "The Girl from Ipanema" and Marty did a cha cha-like step, Katya laughed aloud as she tried to follow him. She soon got the hang of it and *chalypsoed* right along with everybody else. When she heard "The Twist," familiar from art school dances, she put Marty to shame. They danced until the band took a break, and the buffet opened up.

The buffet table gleamed like something from a movie about royalty. A flower arrangement the size of a small tree rose from the center. Silver platters and hot dishes surrounded it, twinkling in the light of more torches. Roast beef, ham, and fried chicken.

Cheeses and fruit. Salmon, shrimp, and caviar. At least she thought it was caviar. A mountain of hot rolls spilled out of a wicker basket.

Another smaller table held a crystal bowl, big as a beach ball, filled with chocolate mousse topped with whipped cream.

Katya had stopped trying to take it all in: the beauty of the California night, the scent of orange trees and the ocean, flickering stars like distant candles, the music a soundtrack of *bossa nova*, the setting a palace. She was Alice and this was Wonderland.

Katya's dream world had her hovering somewhere in the clouds. A nearby "Son of a bitch!" followed by the crunch of metal meeting concrete landed her right back on Earth. She turned to see her boss Jerry overturned in his wheelchair, his torso resting awkwardly against one arm. Jerry's hand and wrist protruded from under him at an unnatural angle.

# CHAPTER THIRTY-ONE
## Katya

On Monday, Jerry showed up at the studio as usual, only his wrist was in a cast and his temper was in a huff. He commandeered Katya to do his sketching.

For the next two weeks she fulfilled his every whim. He aimed his grumpiness at her as if it was her fault he had broken his wrist. She didn't snap back.

"Fuller there." Jerry pointed with his cast-laden hand, the tips of his fingers peeking out like dull teeth. His pointing technique was inexact and Katya took a guess as to what he wanted. She sketched in more fullness of the skirt below the hipline, and that seemed to please him.

"Yes. That's it." As he pulled his clumsy arm away from the sketch, it knocked over his coffee. Katya quickly grabbed the sketches so that they were only slightly damp on the edges. In fury, Jerry closed his eyes and swore under his breath. "This damn cast. Now they'll have to all be redone."

Katya showed him how she had saved them, knowing *she* would have to redo them if he wanted another set. He was immoveable. "No, they'll have to be redone."

Chubbs hurried over. "No, Jerry, look, they're fine." Chubbs carefully wiped away the coffee that stained the edges. "Nothing got on the figures. It's just around the edges."

Reluctantly, he agreed that they could still use the drawings. No sooner had the desk been cleaned and the sketches laid out again, when Katya knocked over the pencil holder. The pencils, tacks, stamps, and clips rolled around the desktop. They didn't hurt the sketches, but one more mishap sent Jerry over the edge. "Dammit, girl. Watch what you're doing."

It was enough. It was too much. She had a temper, too. She had feelings. The stupid, arrogant man had been riding her all week. Get me coffee. Fuller here. Lower there. Where's my jacket? Get that phone.

Katya slammed down her pencil and headed for the ladies' room, tears streaming down her cheeks, a sob rising unchecked from her throat. When she reached the door, she rushed in and slammed it shut with a good loud bang.

Jerry was punishing her for his accident, when it had been his fault. The wheel got off the sidewalk and stuck in damp ground. He should have asked for help. But no. He wheeled it back and forth until it dug in, got unbalanced, and dumped him on the ground.

She was just the intern here. The errand girl. All this responsibility wasn't part of the bargain. All this pressure. She sniffed loudly, blowing her nose, hating her blotchy face in the mirror.

"Katya? Katya, let me in." Chubbs knocked on the door.

"I'm not going back out there." She was mad at the world, even Chubbs.

"Let me in." She meant it.

Katya unlocked the door. Chubbs darted around it and closed and locked it again. She patted Katya on the back. "I don't blame you, honey. He's been in the worst mood."

"And he's taking it out on me."

"He's taking it out on all of us."

Katya wiped her eyes and leaned back against the sink. "I like the work. I really do. I love it, but he's so bad-tempered all the time. He makes me so nervous."

"Look, it's almost lunch time. You splash some water on your face. I'll go talk to him."

"I don't know. He makes me so mad."

"Come on, this will pass. It's just the way things go sometimes. Now get presentable and come on out." Chubbs shook her fist, not to threaten but to show toughness. "Let's stick together."

Katya splashed cold water on her face until its color turned more normal. When she opened the door, an empty studio greeted her. Everyone but Chubbs and Jerry had gone to lunch.

Chubbs called her over. Embarrassed but not sorry, Katya gave Jerry a steely look.

"Look, Katya, you're doing good work."

Jerry's praise surprised her.

"We're working on deadline and operating on a short fuse. That's just how it is. How about I take you and Chubbs to lunch? Chubbs, call for a car, will you please?" That was the first time Katya ever heard him use the word *please*.

\*\*\*

The car stopped at the curb in front of Chasen's green awning. On the outside walls, either side of the door a fancy script spelled out the name, the C like a fat swirl. Katya saw men in Nehru jackets and women in A-line mini-dresses she was sure came from Carnaby Street. Did she look okay in her bell bottoms and fringed shirt? The driver got Jerry settled in his chair and they dove into the sea of beautiful people.

On the inside, Katya said, "Goodie, goodie, goodie." On the outside, she tried to keep her cool while she followed Chubbs and Jerry. Mirrored and paneled booths lined three sides of the famous hangout. A buzz of talk hit her ears. People laughed, ate, drank, and smoked, clustered around the booths like bright busy birds. They talked with their hands, waved at acquaintances, and gestured to waiters. Her heart sang, *Look at me, I'm at Chasen's.*

The maitre d' gave Jerry a familiar nod. "Your regular booth, Mr. Simon?"

"Sure thing, Gus."

Katya sank into the corner booth, its red leather softened by use. From her corner, she could see the whole room. When Elizabeth

Taylor disappeared into a back room, Katya's mouth fell open. She shut it fast before people noticed.

Jerry studied the menu. Three other actors whose faces she recognized, but whose names she couldn't remember, sat just next to them. Off to the right, Lisa Graham smiled and nodded at two men, looking entirely at home. The sight of her doubled the tempo of Katya's heart.

"So, what are we hungry for?" Jerry looked her in the eye. "I recommend the Lobster Newburg."

Katya looked at Chubbs, who agreed with Jerry. "Sounds good to me."

Katya followed her lead and said the same thing. She'd never tasted lobster. The only seafood she'd ever had was tuna from a can and fish sticks at Friday school lunches. Supposing she didn't like it? Supposing she had an overpowering urge to spit it out?

"And a bottle of wine, I think."

When the waiter came, Jerry took care of the ordering, Chubbs waved at some people she knew, and Katya stole looks at Lisa.

When the waiter left, Jerry turned to Katya. "I think you should stay on at the studio."

Katya narrowed her eyes. "You mean today?"

"No. You tell her Chubbs."

Katya, completely at sea, looked at Chubbs for help.

"Jerry wants you to stay on when your internship ends."

Had she heard right? "You mean not go back to school?"

Jerry interrupted, even though he asked Chubbs to speak for him. "You'd learn ten times as much here as you would back at school. Plus, we'd put you on salary. I can't keep up with the work with my arm like this. Marty and Pam are busy with the Godwin movie. So, what do you think?"

"Give her some time, Jerry. I'm sure she didn't see this coming."

Katya was about to speak when Lisa came to stand by their booth. "Who's working on my wardrobe with the three of you here?"

Katya tried to act normal, but her insides jumped up and down. Lisa talked with Jerry and Chubbs about design details while Katya felt first like an insider and then like a dunce. Before Lisa left, she turned to Katya. "Are they treating you well?"

Katya and Chubbs exchanged a look, remembering what had brought them to the restaurant. I'm catching on." Chubbs and Jerry laughed and Lisa left with a wave and a "Gotta run."

Jerry returned to their earlier conversation. "Well, think about staying and let me know by the end of the week."

Katya finally found her tongue. "Look, you don't even like me. You shout at me, you get impatient. Why do you want me to stay? Why would I *want* to stay?"

Again, Jerry looked at Chubbs to speak for him. "That's just his way. Don't let him bully you."

"And what about when his arm heals? Then what? Just throw me out?"

"No, we can use another sketch artist."

Katya's mind would not work. Too much. Too fast.

During the conversation, their food had been delivered, but Katya hadn't yet tasted it. With her mind on things other than food, she put a bite of the creamy sauce in her mouth. The unexpected flavor washed over her, rich and nutty sweet.

"So, what do you think?" Chubbs nodded to Katya's plate.

Katya took another bite, put down her fork, and covered her full mouth. "I'll never eat fish sticks again."

\*\*\*

Later, on the way out to the car, Chubbs whispered that Marty might be leaving. She put a finger to her lips and Katya nodded.

The afternoon passed without anybody knocking anything over, and the clock read five thirty much sooner than Katya expected.

# CHAPTER THIRTY-TWO
## Katya

Katya waited for her bus on a bench beneath an orange tree, relieved the day had ended. The extremes had worn her out. She put her head back on the bench and closed her eyes.

"Do you need a ride?" A familiar voice made her eyes fly back open to the welcome sight of Lisa Graham in a white convertible.

"I was waiting for the Number 12."

"A convertible's more fun." Lisa patted the passenger seat and reached over to open the door.

Happy anticipation rose inside Katya like helium, erasing her exhaustion with giddiness. She climbed in and let the beautiful car surround her in luxury.

They rode high above the ocean on roads that hugged the cliffs and made Katya grip the door handle. She was relieved when Lisa pulled into one of the overlooks and stopped the car.

When they got out for a better look, Katya went too near the cliff's edge. Her stomach flip-flopped and she grabbed the guard rail. Lisa put her arm around her to steady her. "Easy. It takes some getting used to."

*She had fallen down a rabbit hole far bigger and stranger than Alice ever did.* The ocean pushed in and over and around the craggy shoreline, spilling over itself, churning foam, and then drawing back out for yet another sweep inward. The distant horizon beckoned her. The same blazing sun that set over the rolling hills of Iowa, set here over the dazzling California water. It felt familiar and brand new at the same time.

Lisa's touch sent a shiver from Katya's throat down to her belly and lower, a feeling as unstoppable as the ocean's waves. Her stomach flip-flopped for a different reason; and before she could stop herself, she turned to Lisa and kissed her full on the mouth. Their lips met softly, carefully, like tasting something strange and sweet. Then Katya lost herself in the kiss, deciding this was a taste she liked even better than Lobster Newberg.

When their lips parted, Katya looked away, shy at her forwardness.

Lisa laughed her golden laugh. "Let's get back in the car before we fall over the edge."

Katya thought she'd fallen over some barrier already. "I've never done anything like that before."

"Are you glad you did it?"

Katya nodded, her cheeks burning.

Seated again in the luxurious vehicle, Katya had to come to terms with what she'd done, making the first move and not being ashamed. She would have to get used to her new self, the one that did things like kiss a movie star. As they watched the sun go down, they talked.

"The most exciting things in Weaver were the football and basketball games. I don't think I missed one game in all my high school years. I always went with my friend Charlie."

"It sounds fun. Did you enjoy it?"

"I did. Just part of every week, week after week. Kinda like the waves."

"My town in Oklahoma only had summer baseball. At least that's all I remember. I used to go to the games just for something to do. And to drink Cokes. I must have downed gallons of Coca Cola in my youth."

"Not anymore?"

"I kind of lost my taste for it. It was a lot harder to lose my mountain accent. I took endless voice lessons before I learned to use my lips."

"Say something for me in mountain."

Lisa laughed, thought a moment, then cleared her throat. Her voice came from down in her throat. Her lips barely moved. "Ahm gwano warsh that thar dawg."

Katya smiled. "You're exaggerating."

Lisa smiled, too. "Maybe a little."

Katya told her about Jerry's offer, about how she didn't know if she should drop out of school. It was all so confusing. And, shyly, she said how much she missed her mom. "We're really close, but I've haven't told her about . . . you know."

"Liking girls?"

Katya nodded. "I'm afraid she'd hate me."

"It's hard. The world doesn't like people like us very much." Lisa started the engine and put the car into reverse. "We'd better head back. You look worn out and I've got an early call. Can we get together again?"

Doubt crept into Katya's heart. She didn't know if she had the courage to go to the scary place this might take her, but she had to find out. She nodded. "Yes."

***

That weekend Lisa drove Katya along the coast to her Monterey beach house, a sweet little bungalow of a place. They walked the beach at sunset, kicking the warm sand and dipping their toes in the foamy trail of the waves. Lisa collected wedge shells and sand dollars, teaching Katya the names. Gulls dive-bombed hapless fish while the orange and pink sun dropped to the horizon.

They sat shoulder to shoulder on a beach blanket of purple French terry, watching the sun disappear. Lisa put her arm around Katya's shoulder and pulled her down on the blanket, turning to kiss her, caressing her arm and then her breast. Katya only hesitated for a moment before relaxing and letting the pleasure wash over her like the surf.

When Lisa's hands began to stray elsewhere, lower, to places where Katya hadn't imagined hands might go, she stiffened and drew back. Although the beach was deserted, Katya felt like she was on display.

"It's okay. No rush. Not until you're ready." Lisa pulled her hands away and rubbed Katya's back, helping her to relax. When the sun finally dropped, they went inside for ham sandwiches and beer. Pale blue and mauve walls, like the inside of shells, made the little house a calm retreat. The royal blue and purple furniture pleased the artist in Katya, soothed her taught nerves, and put her in a dreamy state.

When Lisa put Tony Bennet on the stereo, and he sang about leaving his heart in San Francisco, Katya realized she'd left her reluctance on the beach. She turned to Lisa. "I think I'm ready now."

***

The first time had left Katya with the knowledge she had crossed a line. Into sexuality. Into adulthood. Into a scary place. And she couldn't ever go back.

# CHAPTER THIRTY-THREE
Anna

The plane engine's steady hum lulled her into a happy doze, and Anna smiled at nothing and no one. Clouds floated by like gentle giants outside her window on TWA's flight to Los Angeles.

Without warning, the plane shuddered, and Anna was wide awake. She grabbed her armrest with tensed arms. The pilot made an announcement about turbulence and everyone taking their seat. When she looked around, no one else looked alarmed, so she relaxed a little. But she kept a grip on the armrest just in case.

As if by arrangement, when they entered California's skies, the flight smoothed out and sunshine glinted off the wing. The stewardesses picked up the last of the coffee cups. Passengers snapped their seats into upright position. And Anna's ears popped as the plane made its descent.

*** 

Anna took the steps down from the plane's door with care. The time change made her feel off kilter, having left Omaha at noon and arrived at about the same time. When she reached the bottom, looked up, and saw Katya's shining face above the rest of the crowd, everything about Anna's world felt right, three hours out of sync or not.

She quickened her pace, and she watched Katya maneuver to the front of the crowd. Laughing and hugging, Anna pulled back to look at her beloved daughter. "You look great!" *But older. More experienced.* Something about the set of her shoulders, a knowing look in her eyes. Anna wondered why.

"How was the flight?" Katya picked up her carryon as they made for the baggage area.

"A little bumpy for a while. Scared me, but then it was okay."
Everything was okay, now that she was with her beloved daughter.
Anna's heart soared.

"Well, it's all smooth sailing for the rest of your trip." And her
tall daughter hugged her again.

Katya explained that she had come by bus, but that they should
take a cab back to her apartment to make room for the luggage.

As they stood in the taxi rank, Katya talked and talked about
plans. Tomorrow they'd go to the Farmer's Market with Marty and
Pam. Then tomorrow night Chubbs had invited them for dinner.
And Sunday maybe they'd go to the pier.

Anna knew she wouldn't remember all Katya said. Just the
sound of her daughter's voice put a glow in her heart. A yellow
cab stopped, loaded them up, and they began the ride. Palm trees
lined the streets like upside down rag mops, just like in the movies,
but not at all like the big shade trees in Weaver. She was a stranger
in a strange land.

***

Katya gave Anna her own bedroom, a tiny closet of a room with a
twin bed, bedside table, and chest of drawers, all in yellowish fake
wood. Cheap and plain, Anna thought, but she knew her daughter's
apartment made her proud, so she said she loved it. And she did
indeed love the showy pink bougainvillea outside the window, so
much more exotic than the zinnias and marigolds in Weaver's
yards.

For dinner, Katya introduced Anna to pizza delivery. Within
half an hour of Katya's phone call, a boy in a red and white uniform
knocked on their door, pizza in hand. "I've seen the commercials
on TV. Kind of exciting to happen for real," she told her daughter,
who smiled a proud smile. Katya even had a bottle of cheap wine
to accompany it. "To celebrate your visit."

They ate the pizza on the couch, which had a frilly shawl, the
same color as the bougainvillea. Katya had thrown it, as if by
accident, across a couple of stains. "Wardrobe was going to get rid

of it." Orange and red pillows, bright as kisses, livened up a beige chair.

After the pizza, they turned the TV on low, and Katya talked over it. "Mom, I've got a real job at the studio."

"You mean when you graduate?"

"No, I mean now."

Anna had to consider the impact of the offer. Surely, Katya didn't mean now. This summer. "You're not going back to school? But why?" The unexpected news hit Anna's chest like a shock wave.

Katya didn't answer right away. "Jerry says I'll learn ten times as much here as at school. And it's a job like this that I'm going to school to get, isn't it?"

This was news Anna had not been prepared for. It felt all wrong, as wrong as if Anna's shop sold groceries; but somehow, she knew Katya had made up her mind.

She wanted to argue, say how much she loved giving her the opportunity to go to art school. Katya's quitting hurt like the rejection of a gift. But she could tell by the steady look in her daughter's eyes, the relaxed set of her shoulders that Katya had already moved past the decision. Anna knew her words would only stir up conflict. And that was the last thing she wanted on this trip.

# CHAPTER THIRTY-FOUR
Anna

Just as Katya promised, Marty and Pam came by Saturday morning in Marty's blue Mustang convertible, a piece of sky on wheels. When they got to the Farmer's Market, families in shorts, black men dressed in robes, rich women in mini dresses and big sunglasses, and several of what Katya told her mom were hippies, in fringed leather vests and bell bottom jeans, all crowded together, the variety of people as rich as the selection of produce.

The food stalls spread on for what seemed like forever. "Look at these oranges, the strawberries." Anna's voice sounded amazed even to her own ears. The fruit and vegetables were piled high on tables and in bins like treasure. Tomatoes as red as blood, tart smelling oranges, fruit the shape of the stars. The abundance left Anna's head spinning.

Not only was the produce a far cry from the potatoes and apples in the Weaver Grocery, the merchants were nothing like plain featured Mrs. Ham, who had been behind the single cash register as long as Anna could remember. These men and women were Mexicans and Asians talking languages that rattled Anna's ears. Her senses were on overdrive.

Katya must have read her mind because she put an arm around her mother and laughed. "How are you doing, Mom?"

"This is wonderful, Katya. You come here every Saturday?"

"Well, every one so far."

"Aren't you lucky?" Anna didn't really mean it. Waves of strangeness assaulted her. In spite of the sunshine, the happy throngs of people, and the colorful surroundings, Anna's mood kept shifting from sheer pleasure to frightened isolation. A pang of homesickness turned her thoughts to her shop, and she wondered what customers had stopped by this Saturday morning—or afternoon, by now.

They met up with Marty and Pam, whose wicker baskets overflowed with peppers and onions and cheeses. "Marty loves his Mexican food," Katya said.

Marty grinned. "We had to introduce Katya to tacos and quesadillas. Now she can't get enough. Are you up for a Mexican lunch, Mrs. Simms? They have great food here."

Anna shrugged. "Why not? I'm game." She gave Marty her best smile. Katya did have nice friends. In spite of their worldliness, they were warm and genuine.

They sat at a battered round wooden table with a stained red umbrella. Anna picked up her taco, which Katya had ordered for her, and the innards spilled out the ends. She juggled it to keep it under control, but it defied her. She looked around to see if anyone had noticed how messy she was, when Marty said, "Don't worry about being neat. Part of the fun is the mess."

He wiped his face and hands with a wrinkled napkin, and put a slice of something pale green on her plate. "Try that."

Anna cut off a little piece and carefully placed it in her mouth. She waited for the taste, and as she chewed, a wonderful nutty creaminess spread across her tongue.

"That's an avocado."

Anna covered her full mouth with a cupped hand. "Delicious."

From behind Marty, a lovely voice said, "All of Cheshire Studios is here today."

As if on cue, all four heads swiveled around.

"Not quite all." Pam stood to hug the beautiful woman. "Hello, Lisa. We're showing Katya's mom the local color. Mrs. Simms, this is Lisa Graham."

Anna nodded, still chewing. *Oh my god, the first time I meet a movie star and my mouth is stuffed full.* She looked to Katya for help, only Katya looked nervous, her lips stuck in a stiff smile.

"What are you shopping for?" Marty asked Lisa.

She held out her empty basket. "Just getting started. What looks good?' She looked at Anna for an answer.

Anna, still chewing, swallowed and made them all laugh when she said, "Everything!"

"I better get started then." Lisa turned to go, but came back after a few steps. "Look, since you're showing Katya's mom around Hollywood, why don't you all stop by my place for lunch and a swim tomorrow?"

Marty and Pam bobbed their heads and smiled. When Anna looked to Katya for her answer, fear flickered across Katya's eyes.

"Mom, do you want to?" Katya sounded as if she hoped Anna would say no.

"Well, darling, it's up to you. You're the boss."

Pam and Marty said, "Oh, come on, it'll be fun."

Katya looked out-numbered. "Sure." She didn't sound so sure.

\*\*\*

Back at the apartment, Katya took a swim in the tiny pool while Anna napped.

She woke up two hours later, thinking about the movie star she had met this morning, the movie star that made her daughter nervous. *Probably because she was so famous.*

"Mom, are you awake?" Katya tapped the bedroom door.

Her daughter opened the door and threw her lanky frame on the bed next to Anna, the sign she was ready for some girl talk.

"What did you think of my friends?"

A watchful look on Katya's face puzzled Anna, but she let it go. "They must think a lot of you to show me such a nice time." Anna wanted Katya to open up, especially about the movie star.

Katya didn't take her bait.

"And brunch at Lisa Graham's. *La di da.*"

"She came from someplace even smaller than Weaver." Katya looked down and then back up. "We need to start thinking about tonight, Mom. Chubbs is going to pick us up at 6:30."

\*\*\*

127

Anna dressed in her sleeveless black dress and pearls, which made her feel plain. That's what somebody wears when they don't know what to wear. And her skirt was too long, too. Everybody here wore them above the knee. "I love your dress, Katya." Her daughter wore a beige mini dress with bands of black and teal. "I feel like an old frump. My skirt is way too long."

"Mom, you know you're beautiful. But you should shorten your skirts. You have nice legs."

"Not too bad for a forty-five-year old?" Anna lifted her skirt and did a little wiggle.

"Don't get sassy, Mom."

***

"I can see where Katya gets her looks." The black man kissed Anna's hand and she blushed.

*So, Hollywood people really kissed hands, just like in the movies.*

"Elijah, behave yourself," Chubbs said.

Chubbs led them into the open and airy house. Abstract paintings in red and yellow, green and blue, covered white walls. Some of the paintings looked taller than Katya. A weirdly shaped and shiny black sculpture sat on top of a marble pedestal. Compared to her house in Weaver, this was more like an art museum.

Anna leaned into Katya's ear. "Wow."

"I know. Something, isn't it?"

African rugs hung from the walls. In lighted glass cabinets were other sculptures that looked so old they housed the wisdom of centuries, and some so finely chiseled Anna could feel the wind blowing the drapery of their clothes. Gold glistened on the Emmys for cinematography and other awards that filled one end of the cabinet. Chairs shaped like boomerangs and low-slung couches sat scattered around on wall-to-wall white shag carpeting.

Chubbs led them through this eye-popping display to their back patio, three levels of slate tiles. There were couches there, too. *Upholstered furniture out of doors. What next?*

A white-coated Mexican stood behind a bar on wheels.

"Have a Cosmo," Chubbs said. "Jose makes the best Cosmos."

Anna did. It tasted like rubies would taste if you could drink them.

The four of them got comfortable on the soft cushions, and Elijah entertained them, referring to the lead lady in his current movie. "'No, Elijah. My left side. My left,' as if it made any difference." And everyone laughed. The pleasant chatter, the view of the green hills, and the scent of lemon trees on the breeze seduced Anna, who began to understand Katya's desire to stay. Weaver could be lovely, too; but it also had scorching summers and arctic winters.

Jose appeared and announced that dinner was ready.

They took seats around a glass-topped table, their wine glasses already filled. Elijah raised his glass. "To the Iowa town that sent these charming ladies to California. What's the name again?" He turned to Katya.

"Weaver."

"To Weaver," he said. They raised their glasses and repeated the toast.

The meal passed in a blur of refilled wine glasses, platters of tiny shrimp and salmon tender as butter, pearl-sized potatoes sprinkled with fresh parsley, and a salad of tart lettuce with frilly edges. Jose passed and cleared and poured, never making a sound.

Their host and hostess told tales of the Bayeux Tapestry in France and Machu Picchu in Peru. *How did her daughter know such people?* People who visited storybook places and lived in a house straight out of the Sunday paper.

Elijah looked around the table and then rose. "Why don't we have coffee and dessert inside? It's getting chilly out here."

From a boomerang chair, which was more comfortable than she expected, Anna glanced at a clock shaped like a sun. Nine-forty-five. She stifled a yawn and thanked Jose for the coffee while longing for bed. In spite of the coffee, Anna was unable to stifle a second yawn.

Chubbs caught her. "Oh, dear. We've worn you out. Why don't I run you and Katya home?"

\*\*\*

Next morning, Anna woke to the smell of coffee.

"Want some breakfast, Mom?" Katya asked through the closed door.

*Breakfast in bed?* "Sure."

"Comin' through." Katya opened the door with her elbow while carrying a tray. "Don't move a muscle."

On the tray sat a bowl of strawberries from the market and a croissant that smelled like perfume. Katya arranged the tray on Anna's lap, and brought in a pot of coffee. Scratches dulled the plastic plate and one of the fork's tines bent up higher than the others; but to Anna, it felt like the Ritz.

Anna munched, warmed by her daughter's company. Katya sat cross legged on the foot of the bed, stealing strawberries. "Oh, Katya, I think Hollywood is too much for me." Laughing, she used an expression she hadn't used in years. "Too much of a muchness."

Katya cocked her head. "Aren't you having fun, Mom? You seem like you are."

"It's just overwhelming for a small-town girl like me."

"I still get that feeling sometimes. Mostly it feels like this is the place for me. You were the best thing about Weaver for me. You and Charlie. Otherwise, I was always a fish out of water."

Now Anna cocked her head. "How do you mean? You seemed content to me."

"I don't mean anything you did. I was happy in Weaver, thanks to you. Only now I'm happier here." She stretched out her long arms. "Hollywood seems boundless."

130

Anna let it pass. The whole wide world called to Katya. A simple mom couldn't compete.

"Movie stars. Houses like magazine pictures. People who have been to France and South America. Farmers who speak foreign languages. And to think, all I wanted to see in California was you."

## CHAPTER THIRTY-FIVE
Dave

Worry clouded the young woman's eyes as she sat alone in her car on the road's shoulder. Dave stopped and rolled down his window. "Do you need some help?"

"I'm out of gas, and I'm going to be late for work." A hopeful look replaced the wrinkle.

"I could go get some gas to get you back to the station." Dave noticed the young woman's clear skin, dimples, and bright eyes.

He drove into Weaver and brought back a full gas can. He pulled his car onto the curb in front of hers, and she got out of her car and introduced herself. "I'm Shannon Jackson," and she held out her hand for Dave to shake.

"Sorry," he shook his head. "My hands have gas on them." As he poured in the fuel, and before the nervous lump in his throat grew so big, he couldn't speak, he said, "My name's Dave Frank. I run the Majestic. Would you like to go out sometime? I only have Monday nights off, but we could see a movie."

The young woman hesitated, blushed prettily and, nodded. "Okay. Sure. That'd be fun."

As she climbed back in her car, he asked, "Where do you work?"

She started her engine and checked her rear-view mirror. "I'm filling in for Anna Simms at her shop. She's in California visiting her daughter."

*Shit.* The very last answer Dave expected. *Now you've gone and done it.* If he had known she had a connection to Anna, he never would have asked her out.

She pulled away with a wave and a smile.

Dave sat in his car a moment before starting the ignition. *Hell, why shouldn't he ask her out?* Anna had turned him away. So, why did he feel guilty?

Because he missed her. This time could have been theirs if things hadn't gotten so mixed up. He turned defensive. Bucked himself up. If Anna didn't want him, he'd find someone who did. Living the rest of his life alone appealed to him about as much as living with an alcoholic.

# CHAPTER THIRTY-SIX
Anna

Anna closed her eyes as she sat in a lounge chair covered in blue and white ticking next to Lisa Graham's pool. The feathery soft breeze, the mellow warmth of the sun, and the scent of citrus, combined with the laughter of Lisa, Katya, Marty and Pam splashing in the pool. Just like last night on Chubbs' patio, Anna understood how this life appealed to Katya.

A crack of lightning startled Anna, and she opened her eyes to an evil-looking sky. Rain drops pelted her skin. *Looks like California weather can change as quickly as Iowa's.* Anna remembered the doomed picnic with Neal.

Yelps came from the four in the pool as they clambered out and under the overhang of the pool house. As Anna rushed to join them, she caught the face of an Asian woman peering out at them from the main house, giving Anna an ominous foreboding. A shiver ran down her arms.

"Come on inside," Lisa said. "I've got robes for everyone." She passed them out like candy, while Anna guessed at how much they cost. Then they sprawled on the sofas and chairs like sheiks in a tent.

The blue and white theme continued inside the pool house. Deep-cushioned couches surrounded a white marble coffee table about five feet square. A blue Persian rug covered white tile floors. At one end was a white marble bar; at the other, an open kitchen with stainless steel appliances and two glass bistro tables. Potted palms made a screen between the kitchen and the main room.

Toss pillows in shades of yellow, like patches of sunlight, dotted the window seat that looked out on the pool. The rain kept on and gave Anna the feeling of being stranded on a luxury island.

Lisa's hospitality and warmth struck Anna as genuine. She had expected Hollywood people to be phony, but no one she had met had been.

Lisa said, "Marty, you be bartender. Katya, let's find some munchies."

Marty hummed and whistled as he clattered and measured, surrounded by bottles and aluminum bar things.

At the other end of the room, Katya and Lisa laughed and talked while they made snacks.

Anna watched Katya from the cushiony couch. She could just see her through the palms. In Iowa, guests always asked to help with food, so she padded towards the palms in her bare feet. As she got close enough to see through the leaves, she saw Lisa move in close to Katya and kiss her on the mouth.

Katya pushed her away roughly. "Don't. Not now. Not with my mom here."

Anna's skin moved. She backed away, unsure if Katya had seen her. She padded toward the door and pretended to study the rain while her mind tried to wrap around what she had just seen.

A kiss, a push, some angry words. Katya hadn't wanted the kiss, but she hadn't wanted it *now*, with Anna there. Did that mean, had Anna not been there, she would have wanted it? And if she wanted the kiss, then what did that mean?

The rain beat down, and so did the words in her head. "Not now. Not while my mom's here."

Marty tapped her shoulder. "Martini?" Anna took the glass. She felt like a snoop. After all, she had looked through a thick screen of palms. If only she hadn't. Then she wouldn't have seen, and she wouldn't have to think about what she had seen.

She knew now why Lisa's invitation made Katya nervous at the Farmer's Market. Gulping the martini, she went back to the couch just as Katya brought out the food. The little scene in the kitchen repeated in Anna's head like a stuck recording. As the unaccustomed alcohol took effect, she heard herself raising her voice to drown out the inner voices. "Katya, I didn't tell you. I've been seeing Neal Slater."

Katya took a seat on the couch across from Anna. "You mean Mr. Slater from school?"

"Yes, he's the one."

Lisa took a seat beside Katya, and Anna had to bite her tongue to keep from railing at her. *You're corrupting my daughter. You pervert. You . . .* Anna didn't say it, she just nailed her with a look and kept drinking the martini. The more she drank, the less miserable she felt. The room turned hazy as Anna finished off the drink in one big gulp. She turned to Marty. "These are delicious. Could I have another one?"

Katya said, "Go easy, Mom, Marty's martinis are pretty strong."

"Don't you worry, Katya. I'm just fine." Anna's focus was a little off.

Marty handed her the second martini. She took a sip.

The others talked movie talk. Opening nights. Deal rumors. Who was dating whom?

"Did you hear me, Katya? What I said about Neal?" Anna heard the slur in her own voice. Her voice had a will of its own, its volume raised more than Anna intended.

Everyone stopped talking and looked at Anna.

"Yes, Mom, I heard you. That's good. He's a nice guy. Is it serious?"

Pam held out the cheese plate to Anna, who gave her head a quick shake. "No. Not serious." She swallowed another big mouthful of martini.

The movie talk resumed. Anna tried to concentrate on it, but it kept slipping away from her like wet soap. She heard herself talking again, even louder this time. "I used to see someone else, too. I never told you." She wanted to hurt Katya. To match her shock for shock.

"That's good, Mom. I'm glad you're going out."

"That's not what I mean." Anna couldn't stop talking.

"Mom, those martinis are pretty strong. Maybe you should slow down." Katya came towards her and took the nearly empty martini glass from her hand. "Let me make you some coffee."

Anna crumpled. The whole room spun around and she thought she might throw up. She cried and wailed. "I saw you. You and Miss Fancy Movie Star. Her acting so nice all the time. I saw what you did." When Katya put her arm around her mom, Anna shrugged her off.

***

Back in Katya's bedroom, Anna awakened to see herself covered with the pool house robe, her bathing suit still underneath. Her regular clothes were in a heap beside her, a reminder of where she had been, what she had done. Shame hit her smack in the stomach, not just shame about what she had done, but shame for what she had found out about Katya. She pounded the bed once hard with her fist.

A memory of two women teachers who used to live in Weaver came to her. One taught elementary school and one directed high school chorus. They used to shop together at Anna's store. Then an ugly rumor spread through the town that shopping wasn't all they did together.

They left Weaver suddenly, mysteriously leaving two vacancies in the school's faculty and a trail of bewildered townspeople behind them. At that time, the tale was so ugly, so preposterous, that Anna hadn't believed it. Now, she was forced to consider her daughter in light of it.

Or she could run. Disappear. She had never behaved so badly in her life and to think she had done it in front of her daughter's friends. She threw back the expensive beach robe—hating it now— and pulled her bag from the closet. She would leave tonight.

"Mom?" Katya's voice was tentative.

Anna didn't answer. *Just let me get away. Away from this city. Away from unwanted knowledge. Away from my daughter.*

Katya came in anyway. "Are you okay, Mom?"

Anna flounced around the room in a way that she hated when she saw women do it on television, but she couldn't help herself. She didn't answer.

"Mom, please, talk to me."

Anna refused to look at her daughter and kept packing.

Katya took her by the shoulders. "Mom, talk to me."

A look hot as fire shot from Anna's eyes. "What about? About your *friend*? About how I shamed you in front of all your friends? About how I said things I should never have said. Saw things I wish I had never seen." She stopped shouting. In a small voice she said, "I saw you and that woman. I saw you. I don't know what this means, Katya. Tell me what this means." Hot tears flooded her cheeks.

The color drained from Katya's face. Anna could barely hear her.

"I can't tell you, Mom. I can't."

Anna kept on in a lost voice. "I know now why a fancy movie star is so nice to a young girl. Why she makes you nervous when you think I'm not watching. I'll bet you're staying because of her, not because of a job. You're scaring me, Katya. I'm losing you."

Katya's mouth trembled.

"I'm leaving and I'm never coming back. California doesn't agree with me. And I don't like what's it's done to you."

Katya started to cry, too. "Please, Mom. Don't go. I want you to stay. I want us to talk about this. We always talk about things."

"We can't talk about this. I just don't understand what's happened to you."

"I want to be your little girl again, but I can't. I want you to love me the way I am now."

"I don't understand the way you are now. I'll never understand the way you are now." With that, she broke away from Katya's hold on her shoulders. Amid her hastily packed luggage Anna found the two small watercolors of her daughter, the old one and

138

the new one. She crumpled them and threw them on the floor. "Here, these were supposed to be a present, pictures of my precious daughter. Ha! That's a laugh."

Anna left Katya crying on the couch. Riding in the taxi, she felt scooped out, baffled. Maybe she'd get lucky and the plane would crash.

***

The plane didn't crash. Anna arrived as the sun rose. She drove to Weaver, went home, and slept.

Midafternoon, she stood on the sidewalk in front of her shop, looking through the window to see Shannon behind the cash register talking to a man, a familiar and handsome man. Her heart knew him by the way he stood, the way he threw his head back when he laughed. She watched them finish their talk with a private look that excluded her. The man turned to leave, opened the door, and came face to face with Anna.

"Hello, Dave," she said so softly she wasn't sure she'd said it aloud.

## CHAPTER THIRTY-SEVEN
Dave

All day Dave fretted about the painful meeting yesterday with Anna. He had felt like a condemned man when he looked out the window to see that she had returned early from California.

When she said hello, he thought his heart would stop or jump out of the top of his head. As if that memory wasn't enough to torture him, wouldn't you know tonight of all nights when August's heat and humidity were so thick he could spread it on bread, the night Dave had asked Shannon to come to the ballroom, the damn AC compressor would conk out just before the crowd showed up? The AC unit, a big, old, and ugly beast he babied to keep running, failed at the worst times. He'd have to reset it.

Dave shut the door to the Green Room and changed into work pants, catching the right pants leg on the toe of his shoe. "Damn," he swore. He took off the other shoe before he stepped out of that leg. Then he caught a look at himself in the mirror. No pants. One shoe off. One shoe on. Face sweaty. *Look what dating a twenty-three-year-old woman is doing to you.*

Groaning, he sat down on a hard-back chair, took a breath, took off the other shoe, and put on his stained workpants.

The unpaved parking lot behind the ballroom smelled of dust, and the late afternoon heat seared the top of his head. Now, where was the reset button? He wedged his body into the space behind the unit, a space about half as wide as he was.

From that position, which put a cramp smack in the middle of his back, he could just about see inside. He stuck his hand in and searched around, scratching his knuckles. *Could he electrocute himself?* He felt the button. He pressed it and waited. Nothing. Maybe he was off center. Maybe if he moved his finger, raised himself up, and pressed again. He nearly shouted with glee when the unit burst into its noisy thrum.

When he relaxed his tense body, he cracked his head on the building behind, sending a needle of pain down his skull. "Shit."

***

The band played "Stardust," the strobe lights swirled over the heads of the dancers, and Dave thought the place looked pretty good in the dim light. He wanted Shannon to like it. Waiting for her to come, he scanned the crowd and glanced at the door repeatedly, like a guilty man.

Just then she came in looking cool and happy, her dimples flashing. She wore a pale pink dress over her slightly plump figure. Dave smoothed down his hair, checked that his suit coat was buttoned, and walked over to her.

Tiers of seats lined three sides of the dance floor. Dave found a vacant one for Shannon, and stood beside her making conversation until the vocalist, sounding almost as good as Tony Bennett, sang "Stranger in Paradise." Dave asked Shannon to dance.

Shannon's soft body felt warm and good in his arms, but her rhythm was off. She was always just slightly behind the beat, so that he felt like he was playing catch-up with the song.

"What do you think of my place?" He looked down into her face, the skin smooth as cream.

She smiled into his eyes. "Oh, I've always liked coming here. I used to come on Saturday nights in high school."

Dave cringed and looked up. Of course, she'd been here before. Why hadn't he thought of that? He was probably the manager, then, too, and she was a fresh-faced teenager wearing a white dress.

He cursed himself. If he was going to date her, he would have to stop all this mental arithmetic about ages.

"I used to come with my husband before he was killed. He was my high school sweetheart."

*Was that a wistful look in her eyes?*

Dave cringed again. He hadn't thought the place might bring back painful memories for her. The song stopped, and he asked her if she wanted a Coke, wishing his place had a counter and stools like they had in Clear Lake at Surf City Ballroom. The Majestic only had a concession stand.

They danced several more dances, and the band took a break. When Shannon went to use the pay phone to check on her two-year-old son, Eddie, Dave went to the Green Room to touch base with the band, The Swing Kings.

They were a friendly bunch, joking and passing around a bottle of whiskey. Normally, he would have accepted a drink, but not tonight. "Maybe after we close. Got a lady friend here." They all smiled and patted him on the back. "Jail bait, huh?" "Robbing the cradle, are you?" Dave grinned, but said nothing. The teasing irritated him. He wanted to tell them to shut up.

Shortly after the break, Shannon had to leave. Dave walked her to her car, wondering if he should kiss her as they stood, or through the window after she got in the car. How clumsy to reduce kissing to a decision. Shannon was tempting with her pink skin and bright teeth, shining eyes, and killer dimples. He went ahead and kissed her as they stood next to the car, and she tasted as fine and soft as the summer night.

Sweet as she was, he was glad to see her drive away. The evening had been trying from the beginning, from the moment the compressor cut out, through the trial of dancing a half beat behind the music, to the kidding from the boys in the band.

He stood and watched her car's tail lights, the tension in his back melting away. He took off his suit jacket and tossed it over one shoulder. When he walked back into the ballroom, he felt so relieved, so giddy that the evening was over, he decided being a single, middle-aged man who ran a ballroom with a lousy air conditioning system was just about the best thing a man could be.

\*\*\*

The next morning, he made the call he hated to make, to Johnson's Heat and Air. He would replace the compressor.

When Ed Johnson came, he talked for over half an hour about brands of air conditioning units. Like Dave cared. At last, Ed shut up and installed the new compressor. It took him all of eighteen minutes.

While Ed sat in the driver seat and figured on his clipboard, Dave stood in the sun, sweating and waiting for the bill. In spite of Ed's runaway mouth, he did good work and charged a fair price. Ed handed him the bill, Dave wrote a check, and the man drove off, gravel crunching under his wheels.

Taking refuge in his office, Dave basked in the blast of cool air coming through the air duct. He pulled the overflowing air conditioning file from the drawer and added the bill to the stack.

Thinking back on last night and his relief when Shannon left, Dave decided he wasn't going to ask her out anymore. The age difference hounded him.

As if he had conjured her up, the phone rang and Shannon's girly voice trilled in his ear. She told him what a good time she'd had last night. "I'd love to do it again sometime."

Dave agreed that it was fun. What else could he say?

Shannon rattled on. "Next Sunday my mom wants you to come for Sunday dinner. You could meet Eddie, you know, get to know the family."

Dave's heart sank. *Shit.* He wanted to go meet the family about as much as he wanted to buy a new air conditioning unit. "Uh, well."

"Oh, come on, don't be shy."

"No, really."

"We eat about one o'clock. Do you like roast beef?"

He said yes, he did like roast beef, but . . .

"See you at one o'clock then." And she was gone.

Why hadn't he spoken up? Now things were going to get complicated. He'd been a perfect coward.

***

Sunday came much sooner than he wanted it to. To make things worse, it was a gorgeous summer morning as he dressed and redressed. It's as if the shining sun, the breeze in the trees, and the singing birds were trying to seduce him into enjoying the day. He did not want to enjoy the day with Shannon and her family because he knew, in the future, he did not want to *be* with Shannon.

First, he put on a white short-sleeved shirt and tie. Too serious. Off came the tie. He threw it on the bed, and unbuttoned the top buttons of his shirt. Nah. Now he looked too plain. Maybe a blue shirt. He shrugged off the white shirt and threw it on top of the tie. He tugged a blue and white striped shirt from a hanger, buttoned it up, and tucked it in. Black belt? Brown belt?

***

Dave pulled his Buick into the driveway of Shannon's parents' farm, and parked next to their aging Chevy Bel Air. A big old elm tree shaded the uneven sidewalk to the back door. All the buildings, from the crooked barn to the vintage house, sported fresh coats of paint like dressed up aging women.

Shannon stood at the back door with her little boy in tow. Her yellow dress made her as pretty as the marigolds in the flower beds flanking the door. Eddie buried his head in her dress, one eye peeking out at Dave.

A little boy. He'd had a little boy once. Now he'd be how old? Dave started to do the math and then stopped himself, but not before he realized his son would have been closer to Shannon's age than Dave was.

Shannon brought him through the kitchen where her mom was tending to several steaming pots on the stove, and introduced them. "I'll be out to help in a minute, Mom." Then Shannon took his hand and pulled him through the dining room, where the table was set with the good dishes and a vase of garden flowers.

The flowers—especially the flowers—caused his heart to sink right down into his shoes.

Shannon continued on into the living room where a man sat reading the Sunday paper, his face hidden until Shannon said, "Dad?"

The man lowered the paper. "I'm Sam." He put aside the paper, and rose to shake hands. His rough hands had a good strong grip. Dave had known that he and Shannon's dad were about the same age, but the truth hadn't hit until now. The reality shamed Dave, like he'd broken some rule no one had told him about. Shannon went back to the kitchen, and Dave wanted to run out the door and leave this whole scenario in his dust.

Instead, he did his best to make conversation. "How's the corn looking?"

"Good. Got plenty of rain. It'll be a good year."

Dave nodded and scoured the recesses of his brain for another topic.

Sam saved him by speaking up. "Shannon says you run the Majestic. Mary and I used to go there when we were dating." Dave wondered absently if Sam danced half a beat behind the music.

"Hasn't changed much." This was awkward, as painful as a splinter.

Dave sighed with relief when Shannon came in to call them to the table.

*\*\*\**

Eddie sat in his high chair chatting happily to himself, a bib with a train on it tucked up under his chin. When everyone bowed their heads, even little Eddie, Dave quickly followed suit. Shannon's dad said a short prayer in his plain farmer voice and the family chimed in "Amen."

Shannon's mom passed Dave the potatoes. "Help yourself." She had kind eyes.

Then came a roast beef cut in chunks so tender they fell apart, carrots, and onions browned to a caramel color from having been nestled against the roast, and gravy as smooth as silk. The warm rolls smelled of yeast, and when he spread one with butter, he wanted to lick his fingers. Shannon's grandmother probably drank from these very same tumblers at this very same table.

No one talked during the sacred ritual of passing the food and filling the plates. No one except Eddie, who sang to a bread roll as he munched it, crumbs decorating his cheeks.

Serving spoons clinked against bowls, forks against plates. Through the open windows, Dave could hear the breeze sighing through the elms in the green yard. The clean, high, whispering beckoned Dave. He wished he could escape into those branches dancing with the sky. The lace curtains fluttered like a lady flirting.

He felt the connection of this family with generations of farmers who had done exactly what they were doing, sharing the bounty of their land. These were good, plain people. They humbled him. They made him feel like running a ballroom was a silly thing to do.

"This is a wonderful meal, Mrs. Edelman," Dave said.

She nodded her thanks. "Just call me Mary." She gave him a smile, her face still flushed from cooking.

"How do you find the bands that play at the ballroom?" asked Sam.

Dave explained about the flyers and pamphlets and word of mouth among the ballroom owners. Dave could feel Shannon watching him, taking the measure of how he got along with her parents.

Sam said, "Seems like an interesting line of work. How'd you get into it?" Sam cut another bite of roast and put it in his mouth.

"I always liked music. When I was overseas . . ." Dave paused mid forkful of potatoes.

"You fought in the war?" Sam drank from his tumbler.

Dave nodded.

"My brother was killed at Anzio. Were you there?" Sam's expression said he wanted Dave to have been there, to have been connected to his lost brother.

Dave felt unexplainably guilty that he hadn't been at Anzio. He shook his head.

"I kept farming. Farmers were exempt. Essential occupation." Sam talked to his plate.

Talk came easier. Mary talked about her garden, how much trouble she had keeping the rabbits from her lettuce. Eddie entertained by virtue of his pink cheeks, curly hair, and sweet nature. The child was so obviously adored by his mother and grandparents and not yet aware of the tragedy life had dealt him with the death of his father.

Finally, the last deviled egg was consumed, the last mouthful of potatoes and gravy enjoyed, and Shannon and her mother cleared the dishes. Dave made a small effort to help, though he sensed that here a man helping with the dishes would not be considered a compliment.

The meal ended with cherry pie covered in ice cream, and watery coffee, the way the farmers liked it.

Mary shooed Dave and Shannon away. "Sam and Eddie will both need their naps. You go on out on the front porch. I'll join you when I get the dishes done." The first time Dave had observed the habit of farmers napping on the floor after dinner, he had been amused. Now he knew to expect it.

Dave followed Shannon out the little-used front door, which squeaked when she opened it. A swing swayed with the breeze on one end of the shiny gray, slant-floored porch. The swing creaked as he and Shannon pushed it together. They caught a rhythm that had escaped them on the dance floor.

The swaying elms, their sweet breeze, the sight of cornfields stretching endlessly across the road with their promise of a plentiful crop, and the mellow day all seduced Dave just as he had feared. He almost let himself relax until Shannon said, "I think my parents like you."

Dave's senses stood to attention. He could feel Shannon pulling him into an association he resisted. "They're friendly people." He hoped the remark had been neutral. He didn't want to be rude, but he didn't want to encourage her, either.

"Eddie, too."

She wasn't going to give up.

"He's a real cute kid."

Dave sensed that Shannon read his resistance. He felt her withdraw like a flower closing up at night. She got out of the swing and went down the few steps to stoop by the red impatiens, tugging at some weeds.

Dave remained in the swing thinking that what she needed was a young man, a man equal to this family, a young man with the heart to be Eddie's father. Dave knew he was a flawed man. He'd spent too many years living with an alcoholic wife he cheated on. He'd seen too much to ever again match the youthful hunger for life he saw in Shannon's eyes.

With a start, he looked up to see Mary come out on the porch, her forehead damp from the heat of the kitchen. She sat down on the top step and held her face up to the breeze. Dave could see she'd been as pretty as Shannon in her younger days. He wondered how soon he could escape this family that made him feel left out of some warm secret.

He realized Mary was talking. "Why don't we have a look at the garden? I'm sure we could find some strawberries to send home with you. Shannon, go get something to put them in."

Dave and Mary walked around to the side yard, the grass lush and green at their feet. There the garden basked in the sun, orderly as a quilt. She pointed to a row that was just black soil. "I picked all the peas and canned a dozen quarts. The tomatoes are still coming on." The plants were tied up on two by fours with white strips of cloth. Fat red fruit hung warming in the sunshine, threatening to drop off the vine.

Shannon appeared with a used paper bag which Mary claimed. She dropped her dish towel on the ground and knelt on it as if in homage to the earth, while her hands searched around under the plants for the biggest, ripest berries. When the bag was three quarters full, she stood, rolled down the top, and handed it to him.

What the hell was he going to do with strawberries? It was enough. He wanted to get away. There was too much good will here. He'd become too solitary a man. These people were good, but they weren't for him. Their sincerity, their earnest wholesomeness irritated him. He wanted to leave before he said or did something hurtful.

The three walked around to the front porch again, and there sat Sam in the swing, his hair mussed from his nap on the floor.

Before anyone could suggest anything more, Dave spoke up. "It's time I'm getting back to work. I need to be there when the band arrives and check on supplies in the concession stand." He felt like he was explaining too much, and they would guess he was making excuses. He stopped. "Thanks for a delicious meal." He turned to look at Shannon, who came to stand beside him. As he walked to his car, she followed.

He climbed in. She stood at his open window. "I hope you had a good time."

He wasn't going to kiss her just because he didn't know how not to. "It was great. Thanks for everything," He started his engine. He turned the car around and gave Shannon one last perfunctory wave before driving away. Pain and puzzlement showed on her face as he watched her from the rear-view mirror.

And Dave felt as old as the hills.

## CHAPTER THIRTY-EIGHT
Katya

Sweat beaded on Katya's upper lip as she forced a smile at the young man sent over by Costumes. She didn't want him to know this was her first solo assignment. As he modeled a red jump suit, which Katya had to transform into a space warrior uniform, she talked to hide her nervousness. "So, how long have you been in movies?"

"This is my first, and if I have to wear stuff like this, it may be my last."

She laughed. "Just think of it as Halloween."

She led him to her sketching desk. "I didn't think I'd like working on a space movie, but I'm getting into it." And she showed him some sketches. "These are for the warriors, like you. Let's try out these extra pieces."

Katya talked as she pinned some muslin epaulettes to his shoulders, trying to put him at ease. "These and some cuffs will be made of silver cloth." She put the cuffs around his wrists.

Chubbs came over to have a look. "Good so far, but it needs more. Maybe a silver lightning strike on the front? We could stencil something with silver paint. On the boots, too."

"Oh, I like that."

When the young man left, Katya went to The Board, secretly proud to see her name beside the title *Lightning Man*. She crossed off "Fitting cuffs and epaulettes" and added "Accessories to Wardrobe" on the August 25th square. That's the date Jerry had given her.

\*\*\*

Together, Katya and Chubbs chose silver lame left over from an evening gown as the best fabric for the uniform additions. Katya worked closely with the head seamstress all afternoon. The woman didn't smile often, and her voice had an edge and a harsh accent. Her presence made Katya's mouth dry, and she dropped things.

But the woman's knowledge of sewing won Katya over. Her suggestions about cutting the cuffs on the bias, and using Pellon to stiffen and stabilize the fabric gave Katya confidence in her design. The silver fabric, by itself, crawled as she pinned and cut it, but the Pellon would keep it under control. The woman's spiky manner unnerved Katya, but the seamstress could teach her a lot.

By 5:30 Katya's stomach growled uncontrollably. Boy, a Main Street burger would taste good right now. "Is there a good burger place around here?" she said to nobody in particular.

Marty piped up, "Joe's is just around the corner. I wish I could go with you, but I have an appointment."

Katya turned to Pam. "You want a burger?" It could be a chance to get to know Pam better. She sometimes felt that Pam didn't like her much.

Pam looked up from her sketching and shook her head. "Can't." That was all. No explanation.

Chubbs took some pins from her mouth. "I could go for a burger. Elijah has a dinner meeting, so I need to eat someplace."

"Great," said Katya.

"Just give me ten minutes to come to a good stopping place."

\*\*\*

As they walked leisurely to the burger joint, Katya confided in Chubbs, "Sometimes I don't think Pam likes me."

"She's a bit of a strange one, but she's talented and works hard."

Katya let it go. You couldn't choose your colleagues.

Inside Joe's, Cheshire employees wearing blue shirts with the studio name, sat at the counter stools. Secretaries and bit actors filled all but one of the blue plastic-covered booths. Katya and Chubbs snagged the last booth in the back. The menu sported ketchup-stains, just like the menus at Weaver's Main Street Café.

"I wonder if the burgers are as good as those back home." She studied the menu. "Oh, and malts. I'm going to have a chocolate malt." Her stomach growled in appreciation.

"Sounds like you might be a bit homesick." Chubbs wiggled, getting comfortable. The plastic on the booth squeaked with her movements. Finally, both were still.

"Only for the burgers."

Chubbs closed the menu decisively. "I'll have what you're having." She paused, and then went on. "Your mother is charming. You must have enjoyed her visit. Seems like you two are close."

Katya opened her mouth and closed it again. Her stomach stopped growling and started cramping. "Maybe we used to be, but we had a big fight, and she left early. I've been worried about it ever since."

Chubbs forehead wrinkled. "A fight?"

"She may never talk to me again." Katya set her jaw so she wouldn't cry.

"What on earth did you fight about?" Chubbs' short hair flicked across her face when she turned suddenly to face Katya.

Katya hesitated. "I'd like to tell you, I'd like to tell somebody, but I'm afraid you'll react the same way she did."

Chubbs look mildly perturbed. "Now I really have to know. Did you shoot somebody?"

Katya shook her head. "No, no shooting."

"Well, what then?" A hint of exasperation entered Chubbs' voice.

Katya stared at the table. "You're not going to like it."

"Just say it, for Pete's sake."

"She saw me with somebody." Katya said it softly.

"Yes?"

"A movie star." Katya played with the salt and pepper shakers, twirling them around. They clinked against each other and she put them down solidly. She didn't look at Chubbs.

"So?"

Katya whispered. "An actress." The salt shaker fell over with a clatter. Katya set it back up and put her hands in her lap and looked at them.

Chubbs stayed silent. Katya raised her head to see Chubbs' eyes, to read her reaction in them. They registered about a thousand unreadable emotions.

"We were, well, kissing."

"Oh." Chubbs' eyebrows shot up. "Yes, she wouldn't like that, would she?"

The silence stretched out. "So, you're . . .?" Chubbs didn't finish the question.

Like talking to Dottie about Paulette, talking to Chubbs about Lisa was a relief. "I guess so. I sure didn't know it in Weaver. I didn't even know there were people like that, like me."

"It's not that unusual in Hollywood. People hide it, that's all."

Katya gave her a sad smile. "I wish this had stayed hidden from my mom."

"Can you tell me who?" Chubbs paused. "You can trust me, but I understand if you want don't want to tell."

"I don't think I should. Maybe some other time."

Mercifully, the waitress delivered their food and gave them something with which to occupy themselves. They ate in silence, dipping fries into ketchup, slurping their malts.

Just about the time Katya thought they had said all there was to say on the subject, Chubbs said, "You know being married to a black man doesn't sit well with some people, either."

Katya took a slurp from her malt and set it down. "I admit I was speechless when you introduced Elijah as your husband."

"We lost some friends over it. You'll find that the people that matter will stick by you."

Slowly, sadly, Katya shook her head. "I don't think my mom will."

"Give her some time." Chubbs patted her hand in a motherly fashion. "Why don't you write to her?"

## CHAPTER THIRTY-NINE
Anna

August deliveries filled Anna's shop with new fall merchandise that reminded her why she loved clothes. Soft creamy wools in heathery plaids the color of chocolate and pumpkin, apples and holly. Matching sweaters in leaf tones so pretty they almost crackled.

She hummed the Beatles' song about how yesterday troubles felt far away as she dressed the window mannequin in a Pendleton jacket. A matching violet skirt and sweater got placed front and center. The glass countertop was the best spot for gloves and scarves in argyle patterns. Even the classic print dresses that Anna found dull, but sold steadily as church and club dresses, looked appealing when they were fresh and new.

She continued to hum the song about troubles staying, so true in Anna's world. Dave was divorcing Fran and dating Shannon, when he should have been with Anna. Katya had turned California girl and become part of a glittering world Anna didn't understand and didn't want to. The people that mattered the most to her no longer felt the same way about her. Her store remained the one constant in her life, and she would give it all her devotion, all her passion.

\*\*\*

Married women, not their daughters, had always been her store's clientele; but Anna wanted to get the daughters shopping at her store, too. She hoped a late order for mini dresses and A-line skirts, like she'd seen in California, would come in time for back-to-school splurges with summer job money.

Anna toyed with expanding the size of the store. She could turn the musty little vacant office next door into a lively place where giggling high school girls could stop on their way home from school, dump their books, and try on clothes. She'd call it The Attic or something clever. If Katya were here, she'd have some ideas. Maybe she'd write a letter to ask her. Maybe not. No, definitely not.

While the mood was still with her, Anna made notes in her office. She sketched a new sign, and then sketching reminded her of Katya, and she crumpled the sketch and threw it in the trash. She forced her thinking away from Katya and back to plans. She could knock out the west wall or put an arch between the stores. Add a rack or two of fringed hippie shoulder bags, and pierced earrings. All the young girls were getting their ears pierced.

Come spring, she'd bring in prom dresses in the new brights, not the timid pastels of the fifties. Hats? Would she have room for hats? Easter hats would be fun, some Jackie Kennedy pill boxes and even a wide brim or two.

This daydreaming convinced her the store could fill the hollow places in her life.

Anna tore the list off her notepad and thumb tacked it to her bulletin board, right smack in the middle so it covered up bills to pay. A glance at her watch showed the afternoon had passed checking in new stock and daydreaming. She only had an hour to close out the day's sales.

\*\*\*

Anna concentrated so completely on her calculations that when an explosive blast slammed her desk into her belly like a poltergeist, she jerked and screamed. The store's foundation shifted. For a moment, absolute silence existed, and then dust and glass and plaster rained down. She remained rooted to her chair. Bits of plaster sprinkled the account books open on her desk.

When the worst of it stopped, Anna pushed back her chair to stand, but her legs threatened to collapse. Was this a bad dream and would she soon wake up?

Her legs grew steadier and she turned to the hallway, fearful her joints might not work. The dressing curtain lay in a heap on the floor. She stepped over it, although it was too late to save it from damage, and looked into the store. There, right there between the Hanes hosiery display and the rack of Bobby Brooks knits sat a green Ford Fairlane, the shop door attached to its front bumper like some outsize ornament.

As Anna clung to the doorframe, she wondered if her heart had stopped because no reassuring beat sounded in her chest. She felt outside herself, watching her movements.

In the window, a mannequin's top half, the one wearing the new Pendleton jacket, had been knocked clean off. The head and torso lay staring at the ceiling next to the cash register. In her confusion, Anna admired the violet shade of the jacket as it lay there without the skirt. Window glass continued to tinkle down, a delicate sound out of place in the destruction, like snowflakes on a trash pile.

She looked over at the white-haired woman behind the wheel of the car and thought absently that she had sold her the dress she was wearing. Just when she thought she was going to faint dead away, a man's voice brought her back. "Anna, are you okay?"

She nodded hesitantly and recognized the voice of the druggist next door. He helped her to a chair. "Sit there," he said, and she was glad to.

At first, she was oblivious to her surroundings; but soon voices shouted back and forth, and people moved in and out through the debris. Someone brought her a glass of water. She sipped it gingerly as she came to grips with reality.

Pointlessly, she said, "What happened?"

Sam Dennison, chief of police, spoke up. "It's old Mrs. Carson. She probably just stepped on the gas instead of the brakes. It happens. And not just with old people."

"Is she okay?" Anna wanted to know.

"She has a cut on her forehead. Mostly just fright. They'll take her to the emergency room."

Firemen helped the lady from her car and to the ambulance waiting outside.

"What time is it?"

"Going on five thirty." A small crowd had gathered out of nowhere. They must have been there awhile, but she hadn't noticed them before. The quiet late afternoon had produced more gawkers than Anna thought occupied the whole of Main Street.

Sheriff Dennison continued to talk to her. Anna tried to concentrate. "We'll rope off the entrance, but you'll need to get a contractor in here to see if there are any gas leaks or fire hazards. We usually call Wilmer Freeman and his son. Okay if I give them a call?"

Anna nodded, not entirely sure what he had asked.

***

It seemed to take hours, to board up the gaps where windows had been, to sweep up the plaster, glass, and broken jewelry. By seven, the police told her to go on home, they'd keep an eye on it overnight. Anna was glad to be excused.

All the things that had given Anna her life force—her daughter, Dave, her store—especially her store because it was going to be her salvation—they were all gone. Was all this some punishment for being an adulterer all those years? For raising a daughter who . . . Anna couldn't finish the thought.

Nothing anchored her. Like a ghost, she walked the block to the café and sat down in a booth, wondering if she had plaster in her hair. Only a few solitary souls occupied scattered booths, like checkers on a board near game's end.

She ordered black coffee and a hamburger with fries, although she rarely ate hamburgers. Having one made her feel like Katya was there. The waitress brought the coffee right away, and Anna gulped it down. It moved through her veins, making her brain feel less squashed.

When she raised her head to signal the waitress for more, Dave's green eyes met her own. In the same way that the accident at her store had seemed unreal, so did Dave's presence. He headed toward her booth. He was real all right.

Her eyes soaked up his worn, handsome face. A stray lock of hair flopped down on his forehead, and she wanted to push it back in place.

Dave stood next to her booth, his hand so close she wanted to take hold of it and feel its warmth. Until that moment she hadn't realized how much she needed comforting. "I saw what happened to your shop."

Anna shrugged and sighed. "One minute I was closing out the books and the next minute, a Ford Fairlane parked in my store." Her laugh was sad.

The waitress came with the coffee pot. "Coffee for you, too?" She said to Dave.

Dave looked at Anna, his look asking if it was okay to sit down. Anna nodded. He sat down, and the waitress brought him coffee. "Are you eating?" she said.

Again, Dave looked at Anna, and again she nodded. The waitress handed him a menu, but he handed it back. "Just give me a burger."

Dave reached Anna's hand. "Are you okay?"

"I'm exhausted. I don't even know how I feel. Empty. I feel empty. What will I do, Dave? I just unpacked the prettiest new things. I suppose they're all ruined now."

"You don't have to decide anything tonight."

Anna was quiet. The destruction of her store took all the fight out of her. Like the dust settled in her shop, defeat descended on her.

Their burgers came, and they ate without conversation. Silverware rattled behind the counter as the waitress counted out place settings. Snippets of conversation drifted to them from the couple near the window. Steaks sizzled and snapped on the grill, sending their tempting aroma out into the restaurant.

Anna's burger tasted so good she could have eaten another one. Instead, she ordered peach pie and more coffee. Who knew catastrophe made a person hungry?

As Anna finished her pie, Dave said her name quietly. "Anna, I know this isn't the right time, but I never see you. There's never a right time, and I really want to talk to you."

Through Anna's emotional fog, she considered his face and his request. "I thought we already talked."

"I was nosy. What you and Neal did is none of my business." Then, contradicting his own words, he said, "Are you still seeing him?"

Anna had seen Neal on Main Street a few times, but he hadn't stopped in or called. That was just as well. Her feelings about him were as mixed up as a rack of sale clothes at season's end.

"You want the truth?"

"The truth."

"The truth is I don't know. I haven't seen him since I got back from California."

Another silence descended. Anna considered her present situation. She and Dave were alone together in public in Weaver for the very first time. During the years she had been with Dave she had imagined this moment countless times. Yet here they were without fanfare, weary and weighed down, but together. It wasn't like she had imagined, but it was good.

"Did you have a good time in California?"

Anna looked him square in the eye. "It started out great and then Katya and I had a big fight. I came home early. I don't know if she'll ever speak to me again."

"You and Katya? You never fight."

"Well, we did this time."

"What about?"

159

"I can't tell you, Dave. I can't tell anybody."

Dave's lips settled into a thin tight line. Anna knew he wanted to say something but decided not to.

"You aren't going to call Katya about the store?"

Anna shook her head and stared at the table. Before Dave could ask her any more questions, she asked him one. "What about you and Shannon?"

Dave's eyes engaged hers. "I don't want to be with Shannon."

"Then why did you take her out?"

"I helped her when she ran out of gas. I was still pissed about you and Neal. She was there. She was sweet and pretty. I asked her out."

"She's a very nice young woman."

"That she is. But she is just that. Young. She's too young. She wants a father for her little boy. I don't blame her, but I've had a little boy. I've lost a little boy. I don't want to go down that road again. She needs somebody young, and I hope she finds him." He paused. "You look like you could fall asleep at the table." Dave's voice was gentle.

"I'm beat."

Dave spoke very quietly, but Anna heard every word he said. "Can I come home with you tonight?"

Fatigue made her face hurt, but there were no words she would rather have heard. "I'd like that."

\*\*\*

Dave trailed a finger up and down her arm as Anna lay naked next to him. "What are you going to tell you-know-who?"

"I don't have to tell him anything. He has no claim on me. Have you talked to Shannon?"

"I haven't called her since she had me to their house for dinner. And she hasn't called me." He stopped, then started again, "Why won't you tell me what you and Katya fought about?

160

"I just can't, that's why." She rolled away from him, got out of bed and put on her pajamas. Barefoot, she walked into the bathroom for a glass of water.

When she got back in bed, Dave's eyes were closed and he softly snored. Thoughts about Katya haunted her, tortured her. If her customers knew the truth, it would be worse than if they knew about her and Dave. Was it legal, what Katya did? Could she be arrested? And did this mean she would never hold a sweet, soft grandbaby? No handsome son-in-law? No family holidays together? What did the future hold for them both? It was too awful to think about.

She'd never tell Dave. She'd never tell anyone.

CHAPTER THIRTY-SEVEN
Dave

Getting back together with Anna gave Dave a sense of urgency in ending things with Shannon. He couldn't rest until he had called off their messy situation like a gentleman, although Shannon might call him something else altogether.

Seated in his office at the Majestic, he dialed her number and her mother answered.

"Oh, hello, Dave. We enjoyed having you over on Sunday."

"Thank you, Mary. It was a delicious meal." *Oh, please, just get Shannon. I don't want to talk to her mother. She's too nice. I feel like a complete jerk. Just let me talk to Shannon.* He prayed to the god of breakups.

At last, Shannon came to the phone, her voice full of sweetness and hope.

"Could we meet for coffee in half an hour? I need to talk to you." Dave tried to discourage her hopeful tone.

"Sure, Dave. Is anything wrong? You sound funny."

*She's not going to make this easy.* "I just need to see you."

"I'll have to bring Eddie along. Mom is about to leave for circle."

Dumping the girl with her baby present made Dave sweat. "Yes, that's fine." He had no choice but to agree, not if he wanted to get this over with.

*** 

Dave waited for Shannon in the café. He didn't really want coffee, but he ordered it anyway. He was nervous enough without it. When it came, he raised the cup, blew on it, set it down without drinking, and then repeated the motion. The hair on the back of his neck bristled as he saw Shannon entering the door wearing jeans and a shirt, her hair less neat than usual. As she got closer, he could see a small food stain on the shirt tail. Clearly, she hadn't been expecting to meet anyone today.

Dave realized they sat in the same booth he and Anna had only the night before. His guilty conscience made him think Shannon might know. But that was ridiculous.

Eddie was fussy, squirming and whimpering. Shannon said he needed a nap.

"I'll try to be short." Taking a deep breath, he began, "Shannon, I think you are a beautiful, lovely young woman . . ."

"But." Shannon said. Her face turned a blotchy pink. She knew what was coming. Eddie's ratty teddy bear bunched up against the toddler, face out, its eyes staring accusingly at Dave. Dave tried to look away from them, but they held his gaze against his will.

Eddie whined and snuggled into his mother's arms. He did look tired, even feverish. His little face was flushed, and his eyes looked glassy.

"I don't think I'm the man for you."

"You just don't like me."

Dave could see her lower lip tremble, and her eyes cloud over. Apropos of nothing, he noticed the waitress deliver a plate of eggs to the adjoining booth. A flirtatious exchange took place between her and her customers, and she laughed, pleased with herself.

He made his voice purposely flat to arouse as little emotion as possible. "I don't like the difference in our ages. You deserve someone young. You need someone young."

Eddie squirmed and fussed and Shannon shifted him in her arms. She put the teddy bear on the table, and Dave felt released from its scrutiny. Shannon spoke to Eddie more shortly than she usually did, "Sit still." Then she returned her attention to Dave. "What if I want *you*? My parents like you. Eddie likes you."

Dave wanted to be honest with her. He had waffled enough times and it just brought more confusion. "Shannon. I don't have the energy or desire to raise a child. My own child died years ago

163

and I do not want to be a parent again. I am not being harsh to hurt you, only to make you understand how completely I do not want it."

"You don't love me because of Eddie."

"Shannon, you are putting words in my mouth. Let's just end this now. You can blame me and put whatever construction on my behavior that you choose, but this must be over."

Shannon looked so unhappy, so supremely hurt and miserable that Dave wanted to comfort her, but he steeled himself. Eddie had fallen into a restless sleep on her breast. She looked like a lovely, heartbroken Madonna, and Dave felt like a worm.

"Yes," Shannon said, her head nodding with determination. She was visibly willing herself to stay calm.

Dave's gut knotted. There was more to say, and like what he had already said, this, too, must be put out there. Shannon had to know. "There's more, Shannon."

She looked like she was going to be sick. Dave hated himself for doing this to her. It's what he meant by her family's goodness irritating him, which sounded like a feeble excuse.

The waitress paused at their table with the coffee pot held aloft ready to refill their cups. Dave shifted his eyes to her, gave his head a tiny shake, and she moved away, her coffee pot leading the way. "Before I dated you, I was with someone else for a very long time."

"You mean your wife?"

"No, Shannon, I don't mean my wife."

"Who then?" Her voice had become hard and impatient. Dave was glad, he felt it right that he be punished.

"It's someone you know."

"Is this a guessing game?" Her eyes flashed at him.

In spite of Shannon's innocence, she was no fool. He couldn't weasel her. "It's Anna Simms."

"You mean from the shop?" Her nose wrinkled as if she smelled something bad.

Dave didn't answer. How many Anna Simms were there?

"When I asked you out, I didn't know you had any connection to her."

"Were you seeing us at the same time?"

"No. We had stopped seeing each other months before. She was tired of the deceit, and I felt like I could never leave my wife, even though she was an alcoholic. I knew she drank because she blamed herself for the death of our son when he was a little younger than Eddie. He was run over right in front of her."

Shannon's face paled. Her voice grew soft. "Oh, Dave. That's terrible." She looked down at her own sleeping cherub, and Dave could see tears shining in her eyes.

"When I asked you out, she was seeing somebody else. But none of that really has to do with us. I just wanted you to know my history. My wife stopped drinking and she left me for a man she met at AA. And yesterday there was a freak accident at Anna's shop. Have you heard about that?"

"Mom heard about it from neighbors."

"I ran into Anna, we reconnected and well—that's the way it is now."

Shannon looked like a Mack truck had run rough shod through her heart, just like the Ford Fairlane had done to Anna's shop. Wordlessly, she gathered her purse and Eddie's stuffed animal. The teddy bear had been lying on the table face up, staring at the ceiling.

Because Shannon's arms were full, Dave said, "Can I help you?" She didn't answer, just left him alone and rebuffed, no more than he deserved.

Dave heaved a sigh that could have moved mountains.

## CHAPTER THIRTY-EIGHT
Katya

In the days after the *Lightning Man* actor had visited the design studio, Katya and the seamstresses had cut and sewed and pressed so many silver cuffs and epaulettes that they never wanted to see the movie. When at last the accessories lay spread out on Chubbs' cutting table, the silver fabric twinkling, Katya took as much pride in them as if she'd designed a gown for Elizabeth Taylor. And, most importantly, she'd made deadline, August 26, a Friday. And then she could celebrate her first success with the weekend.

Like precious jewels, she packed them between layers of tissue paper in long tailor's boxes. Tomorrow she would deliver them to the set.

Fabric scraps and threads littered the floor. Scissors and tape measures lay everywhere but where they should be. Rumpled sketches, broken pencils, and used tissues cluttered her desk. She tidied it all and left for lunch, satisfaction making her walk tall, her full six feet.

Before she reached the door, Katya heard Jerry call her name, and he didn't sound happy.

She balked, turned around. "Yes?"

"Get in here." Jerry made one of his skillful three-point turns with his chair and disappeared into his office.

Katya gulped and gulped again. What? Why was he so mad? Her project was finished. He liked the work, he'd said so. What could be wrong at this late date? She felt the heat rise in her face and her heart pound like the bass speaker on a stereo.

"What?" Her voice shook as she stepped into his office.

"Wardrobe just called. They've been waiting for you for two hours. The boxes should have already been delivered."

"But they're due tomorrow. It's on The Board."

"According to them they were due two hours ago. Are they ready?"

"Yes." Katya nodded her head repeatedly, as if the more she nodded, the sooner he'd stop berating her.

"Then get them the hell over there. I thought I could count on you."

*****

Katya scuttled from the room like a scolded servant. She tried to put the lids on the boxes, but her hands were shaking so badly they wouldn't work.

"Here, let me do that," Marty said.

Katya was so glad to see a friendly face. "Marty. I know I put the correct date up there. I know it."

"It's too late to argue now. Just come on. Pull yourself together. I'll help you. You get these lids on and I'll get the push cart."

In wardrobe the warriors milled about in their unadorned jump suits. Shame filled Katya's heart that she had arrived late and was the cause of the delay. The wardrobe mistress met them. "You're just lucky there has been an electrical problem on set. I think we can still make it in time."

"Can we help?" Katya asked, eager to make up for any trouble she'd caused.

"Just get out of the way." The woman didn't even look at her when she said it. She and two assistants worked furiously, lining up the warriors, and fastening the accessories.

Marty and Katya turned the pushcart around and left as quickly as possible.

*****

They walked half a block without talking while Marty struggled with the squeaking cart. "Will he fire me, Marty?" She dreaded returning to the studio. She dreaded the accusing glares of her coworkers. A late delivery affected the studio's reputation, and she was responsible. When she had dreamt of working in Hollywood, her dreams had never included days like this.

"I doubt it. He needs you. We all do. Just next time confirm the date of a meeting a few days in advance."

Katya returned to the studio and endured the shame. She kept her head down all afternoon, glued to sketches for the movie's victory banquet. Tension charged the air, replacing the usual buzz of work and gossip. The day could not end soon enough.

***

The next morning Jerry called Katya into his office.

*Oh, shit. Not again. Haven't I been punished enough?*

"How did it go with wardrobe?"

"Okay. Marty helped me. They were late getting started anyway because of electrical problems." Katya stopped, then added lamely, "That's what she said."

"You got lucky. From now on, call and confirm all deadlines a few days in advance."

Katya nodded. *Please stop. It's enough. It will never happen again. I'll call a million times.*

"Now, get back to work."

## CHAPTER THIRTY-NINE
Anna

Anna took her mail from the battered old mail box, and a blue envelope fell to the street. She stooped to pick it up, brushed off the dust, and saw the address written in large, loopy handwriting. Unmistakable handwriting. Katya's handwriting. Postmarked California, two days ago, September 20. Anna's heart hiccupped and stopped.

She carried the mail inside, pretending to be calm. Pretending that the letter held no power over her. She prolonged the decision to open it by leaving it until last.

Dampness formed under her arms and on her forehead. In slow motion, she removed the rubber band from the newspaper and spread it flat, noting the headline, the county fair next week. Then carefully, she slit the envelope of her bank statement. Nothing new. Water bill. Same.

Then she held the blue envelope in both hands, turning it over and wondering if the letter would make or break her day, her life, her heart. She fingered it as if touch could read its secrets. Tears stung her eyes as she pressed it to her chest.

Inside that envelope, Katya might say that the actress meant nothing to her. The thing was a one off, a youthful experiment, a stupid mistake. There might even be an apology and a plea for forgiveness. A promise that nothing like that would ever happen again. Or it could say other things. Things she didn't want to hear.

Anna could cling to her hopes as long as she didn't look inside the letter. She carried it to the bedroom, where she propped it against the mirror, unopened.

\*\*\*

Setting up a temporary store became Anna's urgent task. All day she moved stock from the old store to the one around the corner. The grueling work left her feeling like the car that hit her shop had hit her, too. She loaded the rack with clothes, wheeled it down the bumpy block and around the corner, unloaded it, wheeled it back to the old store, loaded it, down the block, and on and on.

By late afternoon, lint and dust covered her pants and shirt. Her hair style had gone wrong sometime around noon. She was too pooped to pop, as her mom used to say. Never had she been so happy to get home. Off came her pants and shirt and on went her favorite old bald chenille housecoat and soft pink slippers.

Thoughts of the letter weren't as easy to get rid of as her dirty clothes. Would the letter say that Katya was . . . well, the way Anna feared? Katya and a woman. Anna forced herself to think about it, even though her stomach tightened and her eyes squeezed tight shut. Never. Never. Never.

She swept the picture right out of her mind. Weary with the effort, she padded to the kitchen to see what was for dinner.

Leftover tuna casserole in a Corning ware dish would have to do. A little melted butter might bring it back to life. She put it in a clean dish, dotted it with butter, and covered it with foil. While she opened the oven door, Dave opened the back door. "Anybody home?" He looked right at her.

Anna put her arms around him and her head on his shoulder. "Just this tired old lady." Dave's arms around her made all her worries go away. She drank in his Dave smell, as good as melted butter.

"You look beautiful to me," Dave said into her hair. He snuck a hand inside her robe to caress her breast.

Desire rose up in Anna that wiped away her tired pains.

He released her and loosened his tie. "Sorry, honey, I don't have very long. You don't have to feed me. I just wanted to see you for a little bit. Mind if I have a shave?"

"Go right ahead." But she didn't let him go.

"Oh, you make this hard, but a man's gotta work." He unwrapped her arms from around him.

As he headed for the bathroom, Anna said, "You can share leftover tuna if you want, but I won't blame you if you want something better."

"Sounds good to me," he said from the hallway

Anna made a salad, and when Dave came back, he set the table.

\*\*\*

It was after midnight when she felt Dave crawl into bed beside her. Barely awake, she snuggled into him and they finished what they'd started in the kitchen. Then they slept like spoons until morning. It was then he saw the letter.

He picked it up. "Is this from Katya?"

Anna nodded as she zipped up her slacks.

"Aren't you going to open it?"

She shook her head.

"Okay." He nodded.

Anna knew he wouldn't press. She also knew he really wanted to know why she didn't open it. She wanted to tell him, but she wasn't ready. She'd never be ready.

\*\*\*

Gloves, stockings, slips, bras, and panties were today's travelers. Anna packed cartons carefully and stacked them on a hand cart she borrowed from the druggist next door. The thing didn't drive easily. It caught on every bump in the sidewalk, rolling right, then left. At no time did the front two wheels agree on the direction they would take her. She fought it, argued with it, pleaded with it, and tried not to hurt anybody.

On her way to the new store, Anna saw Shannon and her mother walking her way, Eddie in his grandmother's arms. *Oh, jeez, what if the cart runs into them?* She started to sweat. She quickly looked away, then back. She couldn't pretend she didn't see them. Should she speak? Nod? Smile?

171

Cold steel was warmer than the look in Shannon's eyes. Anna did her best to be friendly, but her voice shook when she said, "Moving to a temporary store is harder than I thought."

"Good!" A wild flash filled Shannon's eyes.

Anna said nothing and Shannon went on, her face getting redder moment by moment. "I hope it's really hard. I want you to pay. You stole Dave from his wife before, and now you take him away from me." A bit of saliva flew from the corner of Shannon's mouth.

Anna blinked in bewilderment.

Shannon wasn't finished. "You don't know what it's like to raise a child without a father."

Anna knew her mouth was gaping like an idiot. And besides, she *did* know what it was like to raise a child alone, but saying so would be useless.

Anna looked at Shannon's mother for help.

The woman shifted Eddie to the other arm, put her left hand on Shannon's shoulder. "Shannon, come on, dear. Let's find Daddy."

Shannon shook off her mother's hand and, without warning, shoved Anna hard, so hard she fell against the cartons on the cart, which tumbled onto the sidewalk with a *thunk*.

Anna cracked her head on the push bar. As Shannon continued to rant, the hard concrete smacked her backside, "Ouch!" Her head hurt, her butt hurt, she knew she looked a fool sitting on the pavement, her legs outstretched, surrounded by gloves and bras.

Leaning against the push cart for leverage, she struggled to stand up. Perversely, the cart now moved with ease, rolling away from her to the curb and threatening to roll into the street. The druggist caught it. Anna sat on the pavement, her head in her hands.

A man arrived on the scene, talked to Shannon in a steady, firm voice, and took charge of her. Probably her father.

Then he knelt by Anna. "I'm so sorry. Let me help you up."

The druggist spoke up. "I'll help Mrs. Simms. You go with your family."

Shannon's mother threw Anna a helpless look and followed her husband, who had a firm grip on Shannon as he led her away. Eddie started to wail.

Passers-by stopped and picked up the pink and black undies, tucking them back into the cartons. They gave Anna and the druggist a wide berth.

He knelt beside Anna. "Come inside. You've got quite a cut there. I'll clean it up." Anna had been so caught up in surprise, that not until he mentioned it, did she feel the warm trickle of blood on her temple.

The druggist helped her to her feet and she limped inside, wanting to cry but lacking the energy. He guided her back to his office next to the bathroom. For a moment, he disappeared, and came back with a metal box, a red cross on its side. Inside, it held an impressive array of first aid items just right for a drug store. As he dabbed at her forehead with alcohol-soaked gauze, Anna winced.

"Don't think you'll need stitches. I'll put some antibiotic ointment on it."

The ointment smelled fresh and felt cool. The bandage he applied muffled the pain. Being taken care of felt so much better than being humiliated in the middle of the sidewalk. Could she ever go out there again?

The druggist lovingly repacked the first aid kit. "What on earth was that all about?"

"I wish I knew. She used to work for me."

"It sounded like more than work to me."

Anna didn't answer. Let the man think what he wants. Everyone would, anyway.

The druggist didn't ask again. Anna read in his face that he wasn't all that interested. She thanked him.

"If you feel dizzy, call your doctor."

Right outside the drugstore the editor of the *Malcolm County Tribune* waited for her with his notebook in hand.

*Great. Just great.*

"Excuse me, Mrs. Simms, can you tell me what the altercation was about?"

The two were old friends. What was with the Mrs. Simms stuff? "I'm sorry, Garson, it's a private matter."

"Was it about work?"

Anna nodded her head until it hurt. "Yes, it was about work." And as she turned to straighten the cartons, a photographer snapped her picture. She gave the photographer a look of pure disgust.

In the privacy of her shop, she closed the door, and locked it. If the whole town hadn't known about her and Dave before, they sure did now. She collapsed into a chair with a sigh as big as China.

Shame, guilt, humiliation all pressed down on her, heavy as her heart. She felt like a bad person, a thoroughly bad person who deserved all this pain that piled on her. She was an adulterer—or used to be—and her daughter was a pervert. First her store got destroyed, and now she got publicly disgraced like a witch in Salem. She covered her face with her hands.

Somebody banged on the door.

"Go away."

"It's me, Anna. Let me in."

Dave. Her hands shook and refused to grip the lock. Another try, and the knob turned. Dave swooped her into his arms. Babbling, she flooded him with tears. "There. There." He stroked her hair.

At last she had cried herself out, and with a solid grip, he led her back to the chair. She wanted to empty herself out and let Dave fix her.

Then reality intervened. "How did you know?"

"Moe told me. He was at the hardware store when it happened."

He handed her his handkerchief and she blew her nose. "I'm going to take you home and you're going to get into bed with a strong hot whiskey and some aspirin."

"I don't have any whiskey."

"I came prepared." He led her to his car, one arm around her like her very own bodyguard.

As Dave started the car he swore, "I never would have thought that sweet young woman had such a mean streak."

"She had the craziest look in her eyes."

\*\*\*

Like a magic potion, Dave's prescription sent Anna into blessed sleep. She woke with a headache and a sore behind, but a steely refusal to let Shannon's outburst change anything. Shannon wasn't the only one who could get mad. Just let one single person bad mouth her, insult her, be rude or unkind, and Anna would bad mouth and insult right back.

\*\*\*

The next day, Anna resumed her cart pushing, which hurt her back. Her resolve helped her ignore the pain. The druggist came out to check on her bandage, and she thanked him. The Sheriff, the same one who had come to her store after the car drove into it, stopped her and asked if she wanted to press charges.

"I just want her to leave me alone." She clenched her fists by her sides.

"You want to get a restraining order?"

"Nothing like that. Can't you just give her a warning?"

"I can do that." She could see he was relieved she wasn't going to make a big deal.

People looked at her with her forehead bandaged, talking to the sheriff, making more fuel for the gossip machine. Anna held her bandaged head high. Let 'em look.

Her sore muscles and aching head made her cut short her day. Around four o'clock she locked up both shops and went home, dreaming of a hot bath soothing her bruised back and steam melting her cares away.

But first another hard knock. Lying on her front step was the weekly edition of the *Malcolm County Tribune*. She picked it up like a dead mouse, hoping against hope that Garson had kept the story short and sweet. Would he repeat the things Shannon had said?

Anna gave the front page a once over. Not there, thank God. She spied it on the page three in the *Main Street* section. "Weaver's usually calm Main Street was disturbed by an altercation between the owner of Anna's Style Shop and her employee. The owner sustained a minor cut on the forehead. No charges have been filed." At least Garson had made it about work, even if the bystanders knew otherwise. And he hadn't named names, bless his fickle heart.

The article made the need for the bath urgent. Anna opened the taps full force. Utility bill be damned. Water shot from them in fat streams, splashing and pounding. She peeled off her clothes and left them on the floor where they fell. Moaning and purring, she slowly lowered herself into the filling tub. Wisps of steam evaporated, taking her worry with it. The water's heat soaked deep into her bones.

# CHAPTER FORTY
Katya

Katya had a headache the size of the back lot at Metro Studios. At least no one else waited for the bus tonight. Katya had the bench all to herself, yet it felt like the whole world knew she had botched the delivery to wardrobe. The strain of her shame and Jerry's fierce lecture still burned inside her. She wished she could talk to Lisa and unload all her troubles.

As that thought passed through Katya's head, Lisa drove up in her white convertible. The sight of the shining car, bright as a brass button, wiped away Katya's fatigue. She hopped in. "I was just thinking about you." She started to tell Lisa about her work fiasco.

Lisa didn't wait for her to finish. "I have news."

Katya noticed Lisa's flushed face. Her eyes gleamed like a happy cat. She pulled the car over to the curb and put on the hand brake. Then she looked Katya full in the face.

"I'm going to London." Triumph rang through her voice. She threw back her head and laughed at nothing in particular. Then she continued. "A spy spoof with guess who?" She clapped her hands together. "Shane Leonard!"

Lisa's excitement left no room for Katya's tale of woe. Katya swallowed her hurt and congratulated Lisa, who hopped from one London subject to the next. Katya barely kept up. She just smiled and nodded like the village idiot. The only part of Lisa's spiel that Katya understood was that a Carnaby Street designer would dress the movie, and Lisa had to leave next week for meetings.

"Next week? For how long?" Katya swallowed hard

"Six months, maybe longer."

"You're kidding."

Lisa shook her head.

"But what will I do? You mean we won't see each other for six months."

Lisa patted Katya's knee. "I'm afraid so." She paused and then went on, "Wait! I've just had a brilliant idea. Why don't you live in my house when I'm gone? Kim could take care of you."

Katya blinked, trying to keep up with the lightning pace of the conversation. Harsh words burst from her mouth. "No, Lisa, you wait. Just wait. Give me a minute to take this in." She hadn't meant to raise her voice, and Lisa's face looked like a five-year-old whose birthday party had been ruined. Katya lowered her voice. "It's just so much so fast. And I've had a crappy day. And I don't know if I want to live in your house. Kim gives me the creeps. She looks like a killer." It wasn't what Katya meant to *say*, but it was exactly how she *felt*.

Lisa did a double take and laughed, throwing back her head.

For a moment, Katya was puzzled, but then she joined in.

Finally, Lisa took a deep breath and let out one last giggle. "She is kind of creepy, but she's harmless. Believe me. She's just very protective of me. She and I go way back."

Now it was Katya's turn to act like a five-year-old. "But I'll miss you. Won't you miss me?"

Lisa's eyes turned soft, the way Katya loved. "Of course, I will, sweetie, but this is a great step for me. I've never made a movie with Shane Leonard before. This is what the movie business is like."

Katya couldn't think what more to say.

"Come on, why don't you come home with me, and you can tell me what made your day so terrible. We'll get Kim to fix us something to eat. I promise she won't poison you."

\*\*\*

While Lisa asked Kim to fix dinner, Katya studied the housekeeper. She looked like an Asian Hitler. She was short, the corners of her mouth turned downward, and the shadow of a mustache made her upper lip look dirty. Her hair had a Nazi flourish to it, plastered across her broad Mongolian forehead. Kim caught Katya looking and flashed her an evil look. Katya shuddered and looked away.

While Kim cooked, Katya and Lisa settled into the sitting room, a room that was new to Katya. Sheer blue-gray curtains covered one wall. Books crammed every inch of the shelves on the adjacent wall. Two wing back chairs, upholstered in a tapestry of Paris street signs, sat at right angles to each other.

Katya said she liked the fabric.

Lisa caressed the cushion she sat on. "Maybe one day I'll get to Paris and see all these signs for real. That's why I'm so excited about going to London. I've never been there, either." She paused. "But I'm sorry I got so caught up in my own news and you've had an awful day. What happened?"

They each took a seat in one of the chairs. Lisa kicked off her shoes and put her feet up.

As Katya explained, Lisa's brow furrowed. "But that's terrible. Who would deliberately make your delivery late?"

Katya shrugged.

At that moment, Kim appeared with two trays. She set Lisa's carefully on the side table next to her, and slammed down Katya's, threatening to send the hot plate into her lap.

The woman might behave like the devil, but she cooked like an angel. The scrambled eggs were light as meringue with sharp, fresh herbs that set Katya's nose to tingling. Next to the eggs, two pieces of golden toast shimmered with butter and strawberry jam.

They talked little while they ate, and soon Kim came to take away their trays and bring them coffee, which they sipped in silence until Lisa said, "Would you like to go upstairs?"

Katya grinned. "I thought you'd never ask." She set her coffee cup down and stood up, suppressing the urge to take the stairs two at a time.

\*\*\*

179

As soon as the bedroom door was closed, they hurried to undress themselves and each other. They tossed back the sheets and climbed in bed where they brought each other pleasure again and again. Katya was surprised at her own abandon, shouting and gasping, but in Lisa's hands she was powerless.

At last they lay in each other's arms, tired and spent. They caught their breath and Lisa talked about London. As Katya drifted off to sleep, she knew she would agree to stay in Lisa's house. Her dreams that night were of Katya and Lisa making love. Kim stood over them watching, her eyes glowing red.

The next few days, Lisa had meetings about London, shopping for London, and packing for London. Nights, she called Katya at her apartment and babbled endlessly about London this and London that. Katya started to wish that the whole city would just sink into the sea.

## CHAPTER FORTY-ONE
### Anna

Anna felt a pang each time she put a mark down sticker on a brand-new piece of merchandise. The violet skirt and sweater set, a personal favorite, had been showered with plaster dust. It looked insulted hanging on a sale rack.

The beautiful lingerie that had taken a fall on the pavement, thanks to Shannon, was thrown together in a bin and priced at a dollar a piece.

At least she could be grateful that Wilmer said the damage to the shop wasn't as bad as it looked. He could probably have the main shop open by mid-November, and a tarp would block off the new addition for a few weeks after that.

Anna's temporary store had nothing to recommend it. Only one small window let in any light. The ghastly green of the concrete block walls set a sickly atmosphere. The cramped and sad place would fit three times into her old store.

Anna feared no one would venture inside to buy her damaged merchandise. The article in *The Tribune* about Shannon's attack on her wouldn't encourage customers, either. Perhaps if she put a sales rack of clothes on the sidewalk in front, people would be tempted inside.

As she chose three tops from one rack, two skirts from another, and three dresses from her third, she forgot her fears. And then, to her surprise, the door creaked and a woman stepped inside.

"Can I help you?" Then she recognized the woman, as unexpected as if she had been the Baptist minister's wife. The woman was Shannon's mother.

"I'm not here to shop," Mary said. She pointed to one of the crooked hard back chairs and asked if she could sit down.

Anna nodded because she couldn't talk. Her tongue was stuck.

The woman heaved a sigh as sad as her eyes, which were red behind her smudged glasses.

"I came to apologize for Shannon." She paused, waiting for Anna's reaction.

Anna's tongue still wouldn't work.

"She's been unsettled ever since her husband died. Her dad and I have been worried sick about her. When she started going out with Dave, she seemed so happy, maybe too happy. She rushed into things. I don't think he made any promises to her, but she seemed to think he had."

Anna got her tongue under control and opened her mouth to speak.

Mary held up her hand. "Please let me finish or I'll never get this said." After a deep breath she continued. "Yesterday we took her to old Doc Martin, and he prescribed some pills. It's all so worrying and I don't understand it."

The woman started to cry. "And it was in the paper. I'm ashamed. My family has never been in a mess like this before. How can we go to church tomorrow? And she hit you. How's your head?"

"It hurts. And I've never been in a mess like this before, either. I hope the publicity doesn't ruin my store. I've had enough problems already what with the car driving into it. That makes twice me and my shop have been in the newspaper this year."

Mary looked up at her through red eyes, a tired smile on her face. "I wish it had never happened. Truly I do. You must believe me."

"I believe you." Anna realized they had errant daughters in common. If this woman's pain was half of what her own was, Anna felt sorry for her. "We can't control what our children do, and we get hurt in the process."

"Yes. That's right." Mrs. Edelman lifted up her glasses and reached under them to wipe her eyes with an embroidered handkerchief. "Well, that's all I wanted to tell you. I hope you don't get Shannon in trouble with the police, but I wouldn't blame you if you did."

"I won't do that. But I do want her to leave me alone."

"I'll try to see that she does."

"I know you will." The woman stood, and Anna said, "Thank you for coming. I know it wasn't easy for you."

Anna watched Mrs. Edelman leave, her steps heavy with sadness and the weight of parenting. She might be a simple woman, but she had a good heart.

## CHAPTER FORTY-TWO
Katya

Now that the accessories for the soldier's uniforms were delivered and the studio upheaval had blown over, designs for the principals in the movie occupied Katya. All the designs for the leading lady were finished except for the victory banquet costume, which had to look romantic and still futuristic.

Three sketches had that look: a white silk bodysuit, red chiffon harem pants, and a black satin caftan covered in red sequin lightning bolts.

Katya tucked those three drawings into her portfolio, along with a couple back up designs, for an all-important meeting with Jerry the next morning. She'd give the sketches a final once-over at home. After she closed the portfolio, she ran a hand over its coffee-stained cover, savoring the feel of it, a symbol of how far she'd come in a short time. She had confidence in these designs. With these, she'd put herself back into Jerry's good graces. She was sure of it.

After a quick trip to the ladies' room, she grabbed her purse and the portfolio and headed for the bus stop.

\*\*\*

Back in her apartment, Katya kicked off her shoes and left them lying where they landed. She untucked her blouse and changed into her oldest pair of jeans and a stretched-out sweatshirt. Ahhh. Comfortable at last, she headed for the frig and food. Katya slathered two pieces of bread with mayonnaise and slapped on some ham. Now work. She settled on the couch with her sandwich and her portfolio.

The caftan needed a headpiece. Would a large jewel placed Cleopatra-like in the center of the actress's forehead be too much? Katya flipped through the sketches, blinked, and flipped again. Her heart went into overdrive. She stood and looked around her, then at the spot by the door where she had put the portfolio when she got home. Nothing.

The only sketches in the portfolio were the backups. She was certain she hadn't carried the portfolio into the bedroom, but she looked there anyway. Under the bed she found dust bunnies and one of her mother's black jet earrings. Cradling it in her hand, she dusted it off and placed it on the bedside table.

But where were the sketches of the caftan, the harem pants, and the bodysuit?

Mentally, she retraced her steps when she left work. She knew she had put the sketches in the portfolio. She knew it as surely as she knew her own name. Where were they? Katya went back into the living room and flopped down on the couch. Her stomach hardened against the truth. Someone had taken the sketches. The idea sickened her.

Why would someone do that? Just like the accessories. Twice now someone had sabotaged her work, someone in the studio, one of her friends. It just *couldn't* be Chubbs or Marty. Could it be Pam? One of the seamstresses? An outsider? Katya bit her lip.

Then she shook herself. The meeting came first. She'd have to recreate the designs, and that could take all night. The clock on the stove said seven fifteen. Katya put on a pot of coffee and began.

At three thirty in the morning, she finished the designs. Her back needed a stretch and her eyes were dry as the Sahara, but she had saved herself. She closed her portfolio, crumpled onto the sofa, and fell into delicious sleep.

*\*\*\**

"Let's go with this one." Jerry pointed to the red chiffon harem pants with a low-cut, long-sleeved, tight bodice of sequin-covered satin. When he asked where the headpiece sketches were—sci-fi costumes always had distinctive headpieces—Katya remembered that she had had a red jeweled cap on the lost drawing. "We talked about headpieces, Katya." Jerry's eyebrows narrowed and he spoke sharply. "I hope I haven't made a mistake offering you this job. Maybe you're too young for the responsibility." He waited.

Katya understood the expression tongue-tied, although brain-tied would be more accurate. Her brain stuck between explaining the sketches had disappeared, which would sound like an excuse and a repeat of the warrior costume fiasco, or reassuring him that she wasn't too young. Her brain remained stuck and no words came out of her mouth.

Jerry gave her a disgusted look. "I want to see three by this afternoon." He turned away from her.

Katya felt the weight of Jerry's annoyance. For a second time, she crept from his office wishing the floor would open and swallow her up. Clenching her teeth, she went back to her desk, and slammed down her portfolio.

\*\*\*

The others in the studio had gone to lunch, but Katya worked through the break. She drew a line, another one, erased half an inch, shaded the curve, stood back, studied, and adjusted. She determined to have three choices that would restore Jerry's confidence in her.

With her kneaded eraser, she erased a tiny spot on the jewel to give it shine. The eraser slipped from her hand, bounced, and hid itself between Marty's filing cabinets. Katya crouched down to retrieve it and saw the torn corner of a sketch sticking out from a file drawer. A closer look showed Katya's initials on the corner. Why would her initials be on something in Marty's file?

She darted a look around to be sure she was alone and opened the drawer just enough to see the harem pants sketch. Her mouth fell open. The others were probably there, too. Should she take the sketches back? Leave them in place? The decision was made for her as two seamstresses came back from lunch. Katya closed the drawer, pulled her eraser from between the cabinets, and went back to her desk, her head a mess of questions.

Her concentration was shot, but there was no more time, anyway. Jerry wheeled in with Chubbs right behind him. Discussion of designs for a musical occupied them. He and Chubbs finished, and as he rolled past Katya he said, "Ready?" and rolled on into his office without waiting for an answer.

Katya followed him. A dry, chalky taste filled her mouth. She put the portfolio on Jerry's desk and said a silent prayer. Before she could open it, Jerry put his hand on it to keep it closed, and Katya's heart stopped with a great big "Uh oh."

"Sit down." Jerry nodded to the chair across from him.

Katya's back stiffened, and the hair on her arms prickled. Her eyes narrowed as she caught Jerry's gaze. She braced for a lecture.

"I saw you working on these headpieces earlier this week. Why didn't you have them with you this morning?"

His eyes pierced hers, and Katya squirmed, a mouse cornered by a cat. Heat crept in to her cheeks, and she sputtered. Nothing plausible came to her, and she was afraid to mention her suspicions. Again, her mouth just wouldn't work. Was Jerry going to fire her if she didn't explain? If she did explain, would he fire her anyway?

Jerry sighed and looked down at her portfolio. He opened it. "Let's see what you've got."

## CHAPTER FORTY -HREE
Katya

Friday night Katya moved out of her apartment and into Lisa's house. Lisa was leaving in the morning, two weeks after she had made her big announcement.

Katya carefully hung her few clothes and boxes of personal things in the vast guest room closet. Her homemade skirts and blouses looked sad and alone among the custom fittings, built-in drawers, satin-padded hangers, and soft lightning. She pushed them all to one end as if they were intruders, which is what Katya felt like. If she didn't disturb things, maybe Kim wouldn't disturb her.

She could hear Lisa's voice from her bedroom across the hall. When she wasn't giving Kim instructions on how to pack her supersize luggage, she was on the phone with her publicist arranging press conferences. Lisa laughed and said "darling" a lot. She sounded like Rosalind Russel or somebody like that. Katya had never seen this side of Lisa before. Would this new Lisa still like her?

Katya, feeling like a kid left out of the fun, crossed the hall to Lisa's room.

"Oh, there you are," Lisa said in the phony voice.

"Anything I can do?" Katya forced herself to sound cheerful.

Lisa put her in charge of shoes and handbags. While Katya placed butter soft pumps into satin bags, Lisa turned to her with a megawatt smile on her face. "Rona Barrett promised me a plug tomorrow night. Make sure you catch her show." She pointed at Katya, her long red-polished fingernail giving her command special emphasis. Katya wanted to give the finger a swat.

Another hour, and all of Lisa's luggage was snapped shut and lined up. Kim had gone down to her own room behind the kitchen, and Katya and Lisa were alone. An unaccustomed nervousness came over Katya. She had made a sketch of Lisa and herself as a going away present, and kept looking for the right moment to give it to her.

They both started to speak at exactly the same moment. They both stopped and laughed. Katya let Lisa continue. "I'm really beat, honey. I'd like to get to bed now." Lisa's tone made it clear that getting to bed didn't include Katya. Katya started to tell her about the sketch when the phone rang. Lisa answered it, waved Katya away, and yakked on in that voice that Katya had started to hate. Her heart shrank a little.

As Katya passed the line of luggage in the hall, she unlatched one piece. Its clasp *boinged* and whacked her finger with unexpected pain. Katya winced as she tucked the sketch inside. The moment reminded her of her mother's hasty departure and the way she had thrown her paintings on the floor. Later, when Katya examined them, she smoothed them out and admired her mother's work. She hadn't known her mom could paint. It was the excuse she needed to write and thank her, and she had done that. But her mother never answered her letter.

***

Saturday passed in a blur of Lisa's departure. She and Lisa managed a few quiet moments together just before the limo came.

"I'll miss you, K." Lisa kissed her briefly.

Katya wanted to cling to her, but held back. "I'll miss you, too. Call me every night."

Kim came to say the limo had arrived, and Lisa's face took on a whole new look, what Katya was starting to think of as her international-movie-star look, the star-that-rode-in-limos-and-had-London-press-conferences look. She walked taller, talked faster, strutted wider, and smiled bigger. She turned back to Katya, momentarily her old self. "I'll bring you a present." And she threw Katya a kiss.

***

Katya took refuge in her bedroom, closing and locking the door, the only insurance against Kim's appearance. She plopped down on the seafoam green bedspread, disturbing its perfect, placid surface, her hands behind her head, and contemplated the ceiling.

Tears made a sneak attack on her eyes, and Katya let them win. They rolled down her cheeks while Katya gave free rein to sobs. Her mom was gone, her girlfriend was gone, and someone at work had a grudge against her.

Katya longed to return to her Weaver days, days when she had stopped in at her mom's shop after school. They'd joke around, plan dinner, and Katya would do her homework in her mom's cubbyhole of an office, its single desk lamp lighting the small area in bright yellow warmth. Katya had felt safe there: taller, smarter, full of promise. She had wanted to make her mom as proud of her as she was of her mom.

Katya looked around at the opulent bedroom in Lisa's house, the very antithesis of her mother's office, and felt anything but safe and proud. She felt the weight of failing to earn her mother's pride, and actually accomplishing the reverse: making her ashamed.

She gathered up the pale satin bedspread, poised to wipe her nose with it, and then dropped it. She used the back of her hand instead, and sniffed.

In the bathroom attached to the bedroom, Katya splashed her face with cold water and wiped it with the green towel that perfectly matched the bedspread, being careful to rehang it exactly as she had found it. She took a deep breath, walked to the door of the bedroom, unlocked it and opened it wide. She couldn't cower in here forever.

***

190

Katya clenched the handrail as she went down the short, wide, crescent steps of the curving stairway. Each cold marble step came up to slap the bottom of her shoe before she was ready for it.

She sought the warmth of the room with the Paris chairs. There she felt welcome and safe, like she used to feel in her mom's office. She switched on a table lamp and scanned the bookshelves.

Right at eye level, the block letters on the spine of a bright red book caught Katya's attention. She pulled it from the shelf and opened it to the first page; but before she could start to read, a snapshot fell to the floor. Katya stooped to pick it up and was about to tuck it back into the book when she looked more closely. It was a black and white photo, its edges yellowed, of a tall American serviceman and an Asian woman. The woman looked like a younger, smiling version of Kim.

Katya turned to put the photo directly beneath the table lamp to see better when Kim appeared from nowhere, set Katya's dinner tray down with a crash, and leaped to grab the photo from Katya. "No!"

Katya, startled, jerked her head to look at Kim as she quick-stepped out of the room. She had seen something in Kim's eyes she never expected to see: fear.

# CHAPTER FORTY-FOUR
Katya

Mid-September Jerry assigned Katya to an upcoming musical. Picture hats, feather boas, and showy corsage designs made Katya forget all about red warrior costumes and victory banquet designs. The hat and boa ideas had come together effortlessly, but the fabric flowers disappointed her. She wanted fun and beautiful. She got sad and limp.

Three bolts of green chiffon, in three different shades, lay nearby for inspiration. Eraser crumbs littered her drawing desk and her lap, and frustration set in.

One of the seamstresses came to stand beside her desk. "Katya?"

"Yes?' While the woman talked, Katya sketched, eyes and mind on her project and not on the seamstress.

"You know how the date for delivery of the warrior costume pieces got posted incorrectly?"

"Um-hum," Katya mumbled. She really didn't want to revisit that whole thing.

"Well, I remember the date had been Thursday, the 25th. Did you change it to Friday?"

"No. I didn't change it."

"Well, I was just thinking that if I remember it had been Thursday, and it really was Thursday, then somebody might have changed it to get you in trouble."

The seamstress now had Katya's full attention. "Why are you telling me this now? That was all a month ago."

"I just couldn't get it off my mind. At first, I didn't think anything of it, then, it started to bother me."

"You think somebody would do that?"

"I don't know. I just wanted you to know that I think the date was changed."

"Look, let me think about it, okay? Thanks for telling me."

The seamstress was obviously relieved to make it somebody else's problem.

Katya watched her walk away. *Would Marty have done that?* He'd taken her and her mom to the Farmer's Market. He helped her get settled in the studio. He was her friend. Why would he hide her sketches and sabotage her delivery? It just didn't add up.

That question buzzed around her brain all afternoon while she sketched and cut and played with fabrics. Marty saw her struggling and showed her how to make chiffon petals of graduating sizes, then lay them spiral fashion. "Voila!" A flower, fun but still beautiful.

"I can't take credit for it. It was your idea." Katya told him, more puzzled than ever.

"You were on the right track. You would have gotten there eventually."

Even as Katya thanked him, she searched his eyes for a clue. *Did you betray me, Marty?* His eyes didn't answer. The flowers took up the rest of the afternoon. Sometime around four-thirty, Chubbs left for an errand.

Shortly after, Jerry rolled out of his office. "Come on, people, gather round. I have an announcement." Staff members set aside their work and clustered around Jerry. A low curious murmur bubbled through them.

Katya noticed that Marty held back, not his usual wise-cracking self. Did Jerry know something Katya didn't know? Was Jerry about to chew out the whole crew because he had discovered Marty was the culprit?

Jerry started to talk. "This is one of those good news, bad news things." He looked around to gauge the effect of what he said. "I'll start with the bad news, which is only bad news for the studio, but good news for one of our crew." *Strange way to make an accusation. It must be something else.* "Marty has accepted a job at Metronome, a much grander studio than our humble little Cheshire." Everyone applauded.

Jerry continued. "This afternoon we want to give him a sendoff. Marty, we hope you won't forget us when you move on. We wish you best of luck at this step up in your life. We hope to be hearing great things about you." More applause.

At that moment, Chubbs stepped out from the hallway rolling a serving cart with a cake and plates proudly perched on it.

Jerry started to sing. "For he's a jolly good fellow, for he's a jolly good fellow," and pulled out a bottle of champagne. He popped the cork amid the singing and cheering, everyone crowding round for a glass. What use were her speculations now? If Marty was a villain, he'd be a villain someplace else.

***

Back at Lisa's, Katya's doubts about Marty wouldn't rest. If he was the bad guy, he got rewarded with a better job. Must be Hollywood justice. She wanted to stop thinking about it altogether. Here she was alone in this big house with nothing to do but think. About Marty. About her mom. About Lisa.

In spite of its size, Lisa's house felt more and more claustrophobic. After Kim discovered Katya with the photograph, Katya stayed in the bedroom, afraid to cross little Hitler's path. She needed air. She needed to get away from worries at work and worries at home. Did she dare drive Lisa's convertible? Lisa had said she could. She'd never driven such a fancy car. What if she wrecked it?

***

Katya didn't wreck it, but found it a dream to drive. It turned so easily she overshot a corner; the brakes responded to the slightest tap of her foot; the motor purred, barely audible. Some bluesy jazz spilled out of the radio, and Katya pretended she owned the car. In her fantasy she wore a cocktail dress of cobalt brocade and the party to which she headed was somewhere up in the Hollywood Hills.

Cruising aimlessly around she found herself near Chubbs and Elijah's house. The idea of sitting in their warm company, so different from Kim's animosity, tempted her. She was unsure if she knew them well enough, but the impulse to "drop in" Iowa style was too strong, and she gave in.

Standing on their columned entryway, she pushed the bell. Full, lovely chimes sounded somewhere within. Katya took a deep breath and told herself not to be nervous.

The door pulled open and Jose motioned her inside, just as if he remembered her from the dinner with her mother.

"Who is it, Jose?" Chubbs called, her voice coming closer. She entered the room. "Katya, dear. Come in. What can I do for you?"

Chubbs motioned her into a small sitting room with a television and comfortable chairs. Framed photographs covered the walls, Chubbs and Elijah together. Chubbs with Lauren Bacall, Elijah with Dean Martin. She gestured to Katya to sit down. "Jose, bring us some coffee would you, please?" She turned back to Katya, "So nice of you to drop by. I'm just having a lazy evening. Elijah has been on the longest phone call in his office."

Katya wanted to explain why she came. "I'm house-sitting for Lisa Graham . . ."

"Uh huh." The two syllables issued both an invitation to continue and the slightest hint of curiosity.

Katya hated lying to Chubbs, but she thought Chubbs would forgive her. "Her big house and her scary housekeeper make me lonely. I kind of wish I hadn't agreed to it."

Chubbs smiled at her. "Maybe you should start looking for your own place. I know Cheshire doesn't pay you much, but I bet you could afford a studio apartment."

The idea of her own place cheered Katya. "I would love that."

Chubbs looked up as Jose brought in a tray. "But of course, if you're ever in a bind, our pool house is always available."

"That's so nice. Thank you."

Jose left and they sipped in silence, glancing at the television.

Hollywood's perky blonde gossip monger, Rona Barret, took the screen dressed in a bright pink dress that matched her pearly lipstick. "Good evening, Hollywood. It was said that a certain balding director and the singer whose current hit is topping the charts were lunching together at Chasen's. Could it be the fresh face of the singer will be lighting up the big screen sometime soon?"

Chubbs chuckled. "I know who that is."

Rona chirped on. "Across the pond, there's talk that a certain starring duo are being warmly welcomed by the Brits. The female lead in a spy spoof has been seen in London's exclusive Marquee Club with members of the royal family and their circle. Could it be Hollywood royalty meets the House of Windsor?

"And that's Lisa Graham for sure." Chubbs watched Katya as she spoke.

"So that's why I haven't heard from her. Royalty?" Then she realized she had given herself away, a house sitter wouldn't care what Lisa Graham did in London. And besides, she was tired of hiding her relationship with Lisa, Chubbs had probably already worked it out, anyway.

Katya knew her face was turning blotchy with emotion. The news frightened her. She couldn't compete with royalty, for Pete's sakes. Who could? Yet, it surprised her that Lisa would betray her. Katya felt she had misplaced her trust. That hurt like an open wound.

"It's Lisa isn't it, the actress you and your mom fought about?"

Katya nodded, fighting back tears.

"It doesn't have to mean anything. She's just having some fun."

Katya wasn't convinced. Down deep, down where you can't deny the truth, Katya knew she had been cast aside. She gave Chubbs a brave smile. "I hope you're right."

Just then Elijah stepped into the room, yawning and stretching. He spied Katya. "Well, hello there. How long have you been here?"

"She just dropped in and we were watching Rona." Chubbs patted the spot beside her on the couch. Elijah sat down.

Katya stood up. "Thanks for the coffee. I better get back."

Chubbs and Elijah walked her to the door, their arms around each other. Their easy, warm relationship made Katya feel even lonelier.

# CHAPTER FORTY-FIVE
## Katya

The week after Marty left Cheshire, all his work landed smack in Katya and Pam's laps. Katya welcomed the extra hours and missed lunches. At Lisa's, tension kept Katya and Kim in their rooms. Only dinner coaxed them out, Kim to fix it, Katya to eat it. It struck Katya as a silly way to live.

Lisa hadn't called her once from London in the two and half weeks since she left. Rona Barrett hadn't gossiped about her.

Like fireworks, a decision flashed through Katya's head. She'd leave Lisa's house. Now. The sooner the better. When she told Kim, the odd little woman's brow narrowed and it looked like she might cry.

"Don't I fix good dinners?"

"Of course, you do. You're a great cook. My leaving has nothing to do with your cooking."

"Don't leave, Miss Katya. Miss Lisa won't like it if she thinks I not take good care of you."

"Don't worry, Kim. I'll tell her you were good to me."

Katya gave up trying to convince Kim and went to pack. She had only begun when a soft knock sounded. Katya opened the door to find a humble Kim standing there.

"Come." Kim gestured for Katya to join her.

Katya nearly refused, but the plaintive note in the housekeeper's voice convinced her.

Kim led her down the servants' stairs, through the kitchen to her quarters at the back of the house.

The room surprised Katya. If she were going to imagine how Kim lived, she would have guessed plainly, just like her looks. Instead, this squat woman with the short straight hair and square face liked pink. So much pink. And ruffles. Ruffles everywhere, on the bed and on the curtains. Ruffled pillows. A distressing number of pink ruffles. China dolls dressed in ruffled dresses stared down from a shelf. Ruffles skirted the lampshades.

Pride shone in Kim's eyes. "You like my room?"

Katya gulped. "It's very pretty," *and blinding.*

Kim pointed to a pink, ruffled chair. "Sit."

Katya obeyed.

From her bedside table, Kim took out a beat-up cardboard box and handed it to Katya.

Katya gave Kim a questioning look, and Kim thrust the box at her again. "Look."

Katya rifled through the box. There were dozens of pictures and a soldier's medals. *What did this stuff mean to Kim?* "What is this about?"

Kim picked up the photo Katya had found in the book and pointed to the soldier. "He my husband."

"You were married to this soldier?" Katya stared.

"He Miss Lisa's brother. He die." Kim's chin quivered.

"Oh." Lisa had told Katya she had a brother, and he had died. She hadn't said he had been married to Kim.

"After he die, his parents kick me out. They hate me Korean. I can't get job. English no good. Cannot read or write much. Miss Lisa, she took me in. Her parents kick her out, too, because," Kim hesitated, "you know." Then she went on, "Lisa love her brother. She give me job here. Cook. Clean. If you leave, she think I don't take good care of you."

*How much to tell this sad woman?* Katya began, "Lisa hasn't called me. She has new friends. It feels funny staying here. I want my own place. I'll write her a note and leave it. Why did you act like you didn't like me?"

"I'm afraid Miss Lisa will not need me anymore if she finds someone else to take care of her."

Katya patted Kim's shoulder. "From what you told me, I think Lisa needs you as much as you need her."

"I hope so. I have no place else to go."

*That makes two of us.*

\*\*\*

Now that she'd decided to go, Katya couldn't get out of Lisa's house fast enough. The time she'd spent here felt twice as long. Weeks without a phone call. Weeks of feeling out of place.

After her visit to Kim's room, Katya packed. Within forty-five minutes she moved her few belongings from Lisa's color-coordinated padded hangers and perfumed closet shelves to three wobbly cardboard boxes and two brown paper bags.

The little girl in her wanted to go back to Weaver, back to her mother's house, back to before she learned what she was made of.

*No way she could do that.*

As the taxi pulled away from Lisa's place, Katya wondered what all she was leaving behind.

\*\*\*

Katya lay her head back against the taxi's dirty seat. She wondered if he could just drive her around and around forever, so she would never have to get her life organized. Maybe she was wrong to stay on at the studio after her internship ended. What if Chubbs and Elijah weren't home? What if someone was already staying in their pool house?

Katya hated herself for her mistakes, her inexperience, her youth. Most of all she hated herself for getting involved over her head. Right here. Right now. She was swearing off relationships for a long time.

\*\*\*

The taxi driver unloaded her and her belongings on the curb. Warm light shone from the upstairs windows. *Good Lord, were they going to bed?*

She had no choice but to go ahead with her impulsive plan. She couldn't spend the night on the curb. Summoning courage, she walked to the front door and rang the bell, expecting Jose to answer the door.

Instead, Chubbs answered, wearing her nightclothes. "Katya! Whatever is wrong? You look like you've shrunk."

"Is the offer of your pool house still open?" She turned and gestured to her belongings piled at the curb like trash waiting for pickup.

"Of course, dear. Come in. Jose, would you take Katya's things to the pool house, please?"

She followed Chubbs through the house, out on the patio, and to the pool house.

"Thanks, Chubbs. You're a lifesaver."

"Nonsense, girl." She showed Katya around the little bungalow, much smaller than Lisa's pool house, but just as pretty. "You can unpack later, but here's the bedroom. Jose, bring those things in here, please."

Katya sat down on the bed like she was dropping a too heavy load.

Chubbs sat beside her. "Wanna talk about it?"

"Just got fed up hanging out in that huge house, not even knowing what was going on with Lisa. Stranded like I was on an uninhabited island. I decided to swim away, I guess."

"Well, glad you came to us. We can talk about you finding your own place. Not that you're not welcome here."

"Yes, please. That's what I want. A place of my own. No relationships confusing the situation."

***

Chubbs left and Katya got ready for bed by the light of the bedside lamp. Its soft light lit up the welcoming room. Pale blue carpeting beneath her bare feet. Soft lime green sheets to snuggle between. And best of all, knowing she had made the break from Lisa.

# CHAPTER FORTY-SIX
Anna

The Sunday after Mrs. Edelman's visit to Anna's shop, she and Dave lounged around her living room surrounded by sections of the Sunday paper. Curled up in her favorite chair, chewing on a pencil, Anna held the "Home and Family" section folded so that only the crossword could be seen. Dave stretched his long form on the couch behind the funny papers. Anna heard him chuckle, and she knew he was reading Beetle Bailey.

He lowered the comics and asked, "You want to go down to the café for lunch? The after-church crowd would be gone by now."

"Not while I still have this." She fingered the white bandage on her forehead. "People are going to stare at us, anyway; I don't need a bandage announcing me as the Scarlet Woman." Anna laughed when she said that, but the possibility did worry her. Funny how when nobody knew about their affair, Anna really was the other woman. Now, Fran had set Dave free, but Shannon clearly felt a claim to him.

"You're not the other woman, anymore."

"Shannon thinks I am."

"Well, you're not. If she's gonna take things out on anyone, it should have been me, not you."

"She is a confused young woman, that's for sure. I feel sorry for her mother. Did I tell you she stopped by the shop on Friday?"

"You told me. Now let's stop talking about them. It's us I care about." He put Beetle Bailey aside, sat up, and patted the couch beside him. When Anna came to sit next to him, he put his arm around her and pulled her close. "Has anybody really said anything?"

"No. I'm just afraid they will."

He squeezed her tight. "I bet some French toast would make us feel better."

Anna nodded. "Who's cooking?"

"Me, of course. You stay put. Finish that crossword."

***

The sound of Dave singing *Chattanooga Choo Choo* filled the house, and Anna smelled the French toast sizzling in the pan. She knew Dave prided himself on knowing every one of the train's stops. His singing talents, the result of college training, excelled his cooking ones; but he had mastered breakfast menus.

Anna set aside the crossword to finish later, and Dave appeared carrying two plates of French toast covered in butter and syrup. He sat them down on the table and said, "Coffee coming up." He brought it in and sat beside her.

They ate in silence. Dave looked up. "This is nice."

"It's delicious." Anna forked another bite into her mouth.

He chuckled. "Not the food. Us. Together. On a lazy Sunday afternoon."

"I like it, too."

Another short silence. "Are you over Neal?"

Anna laughed out loud. "There is no 'getting over' because there never was anything between us." She paused. "Are you over Shannon?"

"Same answer." Dave set down his tray, took Anna's from her, and led her by the hand into the bedroom. "I kind of like the bandage."

Anna responded with a playful swat to his shoulder.

***

They did the dishes together singing along to whatever came on the local station, old songs like *Down in the Valley* and *Buffalo Girls*, even hymns, *The Old Rugged Cross* and *The Garden*. When Dave sang the hymns, Anna only listened. He was that good. "You should join the church choir."

"You think they'd let me in?"

\*\*\*

October began with a bright and sunny Monday morning, surely the sign of good things to come. Anna hummed *Chattanooga Choo Choo* and arranged the items she'd brought from the old store. She even took the bandage off her forehead. No more Scarlet Letter for her. And then, remembering Dave's comment about it, she smiled.

A woman came into the shop and interrupted Anna's happy thoughts. See, everything would be okay. People would come.

Then she saw the woman was Shannon.

Anna started to say, "Please le. . ." when before she could finish, before she could duck, before she could scream for help, her day exploded with a shotgun's soul-shattering blast that knocked her flat. An inky blackness sucked her in.

## CHAPTER FORTY-SEVEN
Dave

Nothing brought traffic to a halt in Weaver except the Homecoming and Fourth of July parades. So why couldn't Dave and Moe get to the hardware store? A policeman diverted traffic from Main Street to the right, into the residential district. A crowd of people stood off to the left. Others rushed to join them, crossing the street at a trot right in front of their car.

The red swirling light of an emergency vehicle rose above the crowd. "There's an ambulance over there, boss." Moe pointed down the side street.

Through the crowd Dave saw flashing lights and the cherry tops of all four of Weaver's police cars in front of Anna's temporary shop. Dave strained to see. "What the hell?" He didn't wait for an answer. He yanked on the handbrake and threw open the door. "Take over." He dashed from the car. Tension bit into his gut. *This can't be good.*

Between the onlookers, Dave saw a sheeted body on a gurney ready to be put in the ambulance. He pushed people aside to get closer. Was the face covered? Meaning . . . well, everyone knew what that meant. Close enough at last, he caught sight of a pale cheek. Anna's cheek.

A blood-soaked sheet covered the rest of her. Her eyes stared, vacant and unseeing. The blood scared the crap out of him. So much blood. "Anna."

"What happened?" he said to bystanders. Somebody said, "Gunshot." Somebody else said, "She's alive." He kept shoving until he was next to her.

"Stand aside, please. Stand aside, everyone." The uniformed policeman looked barely out of high school. The ludicrously young officer held out his arms as a barrier, nudging onlookers back from the ambulance ramp.

Dave wanted to push his way forward in spite of the policeman, but Moe caught up with him and grabbed his arm. "Boss, I heard people talking. Shannon Miner had a shotgun."

"Shannon?" Again, and louder. "Shannon?" Heat rose in his cheeks, and he loosened his tie. The siren, shrill and deafening, could have been the screaming of Dave's own heart.

Dave figured Moe had guessed about him and Anna long ago. Nothing escaped his old friend, but both men pretended there was nothing to know. "Easy, boss. Let's get back to the car. We can follow the ambulance."

Lead filled his legs, and Dave could only stumble. Moe pushed his arm in the direction of the car.

Behind the wheel, Moe stayed as close as he dared to the speeding ambulance.

Dave felt sweat pouring down his face, and he swiped at it with his handkerchief. The rest of him shivered.

\*\*\*

At the ER, the duty nurse said Anna had been taken up to Surgery on the 4th floor. "How long will surgery take?"

"Could be several hours."

Dave looked at Moe in dismay.

"You want me to wait with you?"

"Yes. No. You go on home." Then Dave remembered they had only one car. His own. "You want me to drive you?"

"Nah. I'll walk. It's not that far. Just pick me up for work in the morning." Moe gave Dave's arm a reassuring squeeze and left.

\*\*\*

Dave's dime clanked deep in the bowels of the waiting room coffee machine. Then a watery brown stream piddled into a paper cup. Dave expected it to taste bad, and he wasn't disappointed.

Across the room an anguished young couple sat shoulder to shoulder, their hands braided together, their eyes closed. He chose a seat looking away from them in a fake leather chair with a tear that leaked dirty white stuffing. He felt as ratty as the chair looked.

What if Anna died? What if she was paralyzed? Would this be the end of their long love affair? Would a quarrel over him end up killing her? To comfort himself he thought about when they had first come together.

*** 

Anna had moved out of the duplex shortly after Katya was born and bought her house on Martin Street. When the dress shop owner retired, Anna ran the shop until she could afford to buy it. In spite of her husband's defection, she and Katya had a modest but secure life.

Meanwhile, Dave engaged livelier bands with newer sounds than the previous Majestic owner, and the ballroom's rep improved. It wasn't the biggest or the fanciest ballroom, but it had the best music. He could count on good, steady crowds. That was good because the only thing he could count on about Fran was that she would drink. A lot.

The afternoon he and Anna met again, the skies were heavy with snow. "White sky" people called it. Her red dress caught his eye the moment he stepped inside the Main Street café, and he just knew. Well he didn't know what he knew, but some kind of feeling came alive in him. Something he hadn't felt in a long time.

Fran had become a weeping, stumbling ghost who prowled the house at night looking for Randy. He worried she would fall down or wander outside while he was at work. He spent his days sleep deprived and withdrawn. Then he saw Anna in her red dress looking like a million dollars with her clear brown eyes and shiny hair. Her pink cheeks made him want to touch them, light as a feather.

"Dave Frank, how nice to see you." She had smiled, and he was a goner.

He took a table close by so that they could continue talking. "How's Fran?"

And Dave said the best thing he could say. "She hasn't been well."

"I've never forgotten our friendship." And Dave read in her eyes what she didn't say, *And the way it ended.* "If there's anything I can do . . ." Her voice trailed off. They both knew there was nothing Anna could do.

After that first accidental meeting, he made a point of going to the café for lunch a couple times a week. Sometimes he saw Anna, sometimes not.

He hoped Anna might want to share more than a few friendly words between adjacent tables. One day when she *was* there, he said, "What about a drive in the country? We could bring some sandwiches."

Anna studied his eyes. He felt them burn into him searching for his real question. She must have liked what she saw there. "I'd like that. Tomorrow?"

And that's how it began. They parked like teenagers on a back road screened by trees. He pulled over behind the dense greenery, his hands trembling. He turned and caressed Anna's warm and lovely breasts. She came to him willingly, eagerly. They made love there on the front seat with the gear shift poking his thigh and the door handle hitting her head, frantic with desire as if they could bury all the years of loneliness in each other.

When their lovemaking was over and they straightened their clothes, embarrassment made them awkward. Neither of them had expected it to be quite like that, and they tried to turn back into the upstanding business people they usually were.

Dave saw the unopened brown bag on the back seat. "I think we forgot the sandwiches."

\*\*\*

When he had dropped her off at her car, they arranged for another meeting on another road on another day. And after that, lots of meetings. Sometimes they had just talked. They made each other laugh.

"Mrs. Beemer, you know her, the Baptist minister's wife, tried to get into a size twelve swimsuit. She nearly suffocated herself squeezing into it. Finally, she looked in the mirror, bulging out all over the place with the zipper only half way up, and said, 'Maybe I should go up a size.' I almost choked." Dave had laughed, too, and wondered just how long it had been since he'd done that.

On luckier and more rare occasions, meetings had been arranged in Des Moines or Omaha.

*\*\*\**

Dave recalled he was in the hospital waiting room when a doctor wearing a blood-spotted surgical suit came out to speak to the young couple. All the pain in their young faces melted away, and relief positively radiated from them. He wished them well.

When the couple followed the doctor and left, the wasteland of the waiting room grew even more depressing. Dave felt as rumpled and worn out as the magazines on the table, and as stale as the bad coffee he held in his hand.

After another half hour, another blood-stained doctor came into the waiting room and approached him. "Are you Mrs. Simms' family?"

"I'm her brother." Dave gave him his best unwavering gaze.

"The shot hit her left shoulder."

At the word "shoulder" Dave interrupted. "You said the shoulder, not the chest."

"No, not the chest."

Dave closed his eyes and exhaled, letting go of the worst of his fears. The surgeon's next words were lost to Dave. "I'm sorry." He shook his head. "I lost you for a moment."

The surgeon smiled. "Perfectly understandable. Why don't we sit down?"

Dave did sit, and the surgeon perched on the chair next to him. "I said she's lost a lot of blood, but we got out all the pellets. The shot missed the artery, so her prognosis is good. She's in recovery now, but she is on pain and sleeping pills. She won't wake up until morning. I suggest you go home and come back then. If you leave your number, we'll call you if there is any change."

Dave wanted more. He wanted to see her and with his own eyes, see she was okay. He wanted to plant a kiss on her cheek, stroke her hand, her hair, but he couldn't do any of those things, so he left.

Darkness greeted Dave as he stepped out of the hospital. The day seemed a thousand hours long, and he could scarcely remember earlier that afternoon when his biggest worry had been fixing the Majestic's wobbly seats.

***

The next morning Dave took the back way to the hospital through the north side of town next to the railroad tracks and the grain silos. The ambulance's sudden shrieking siren made him jump. He pulled over onto the gravel shoulder to let it pass, and realized he was at the very spot where he had stopped to help Shannon when she ran out of gas.

His heart went out to her parents, her little boy, and even to Shannon. He couldn't make himself blame her for her behavior, losing a beloved husband so young with their first child still a baby. He knew loss could do cruel things to people. Look at Fran.

If he blamed anyone, he blamed himself for starting the whole cursed chain of events that put Anna in the hospital. If only he could make everything all right again.

***

Lying in her hospital bed, without makeup, her hair soft on the pillow, Anna looked about twelve years old. He thought he might cry, but he didn't. She slept soundly. As her brother, he couldn't kiss her cheek or even caress it. He put his hand in his pocket as if he didn't trust it to touch her, anyway.

A nurse came in to check on her and told Dave she'd had a good night. *That was something, anyway.*

210

"I have to go to work, but I'll be back in a few hours." He forced himself to leave, to be practical. He remembered he had told Moe he would pick him up. Moe's car was still at the Majestic.

When Dave pulled into Moe's little house on the edge of town, an ambulance sat parked outside. Was it headed here when Dave had pulled over to let it pass earlier this morning?

Dave's stomach fell to his knees. *For Christ sake, what now?* He'd seen enough yesterday when they put Anna in one. He hoped this one had stopped at Moe's because it was out of gas. A flat tire maybe. He was kidding himself, and his heart pounded.

Nearby a neighbor stood, his hands in his pockets, concern in his eyes.

Dave pulled up to the man and rolled down his window. "What's going on?"

"It's the old guy who lives there. Heart attack they said. Called the ambulance himself, but it didn't get here soon enough, I guess."

"Are you sure?" He knew the answer. His chest tingled, and his stomach twisted. Another tragedy? Anna yesterday. Moe today. Were the people around him doomed? A dull weight descended on Dave's heart.

He parked and got out. Standing next to the medic, he said, "I'd like to say goodbye to my friend." The medic let him pass. With the same sadness he felt in the war when a buddy got killed, despair crept down to his toes.

He pulled the sheet back from Moe's face. "You were first rate, buddy." Then he stepped back. The medics climbed in, and the vehicle crunched over the gravel and down the road taking away a solid gold friend.

\*\*\*

A few days later, a man Dave didn't know showed up at the Majestic. "Are you Dave Frank?"

Dave nodded. "Yeah."

"I'm Chuck Morton, Moe Rasmussen's lawyer." The man handed him a card. "Is there someplace we can talk?"

Dave showed him into his office.

The man settled into his chair with his briefcase on his lap. He snapped open the clasps and removed some papers, which he put in front of Dave. "You are the heir of Moe Rasmussen's estate," he said.

"No. Moe had no estate." *Did he? Even if he did, Dave wouldn't be the one to inherit it. Would he?*

"Oh, yes. There's no doubt about it. These are the papers." And the man tapped the papers he had put on the desk. "Moe's wife left him a piece of family property fifteen years ago when she died, and now Moe has left it to you".

Dave pushed back his chair to distance himself from the papers. "I don't want it. I'm not worth it."

The lawyer nodded knowingly, as if he was used to that reaction. "Why don't you think about it? I'll leave copies of the papers and you can look them over. You have my number. It's on the card. You can call me after you think about it. Believe me, people often feel the way you do. They are the good people. The bad ones can't wait to get their hands on the money."

The lawyer shook his hand and left. Dave stared at the papers the man had left on his desk like they were a court summons.

## CHAPTER FORTY-EIGHT
Katya

In Chubbs' guest house, it was okay to mess up the towels and leave clothes on the bed, but Katya had mooched off others long enough: the studio's internship apartment, Lisa's place with its matching this and matching that, and now Chubbs' house.

Would she never get her own pad? Someplace where she could eat bologna sandwiches and watch *Bewitched*. Someplace to toss her flower power throw pillows. Someplace to blast pop music from her transistor and sing along.

There was no bologna at Lisa's or Chubb's, no cheap, tacky throw pillows. Built-in sound systems supplied music.

But that all might change. After work Chubbs was taking Katya apartment hunting. *Please let the day fly by. Please let there be no screw ups or rush jobs. Please no nasty surprises.* She and Chubbs pushed open the studio door and stepped inside.

Tension hung in the air like static.

Katya knew something was up. Before she could ask, Jerry wheeled out from his office, his eyes narrowed. "There's a phone call for you in here. Man by the name of Dave Frank says it's an emergency." Jerry's all-business voice gave nothing away.

Katya had never had a personal phone call at work. Curiosity filled the faces of her coworkers, but dread was what she felt. With her heartbeat on hold, she went straight to Jerry's office and stared at the phone receiver lying on the desk like a loaded weapon. *Dave Frank. She didn't know any Dave Frank, did she?* If she didn't pick it up, then her day could go as planned. Katya gave Jerry a look and he gave her a nod of encouragement. "Do you want us to stay?" Chubbs waited at the doorway.

"Yes, please." She picked up the receiver. "Hello." She heard a confidence she didn't feel in her own voice.

"Katya, this is Dave Frank, a friend of your mother's."

"Yes?"

"Your mother was shot a few days ago. I know you two are not getting along, so I didn't call before."

Katya's throat closed up. When she tried to speak, a squawk came out. She tried again. "Shot?" She turned her gaze to Jerry and sank into his chair. "Is she alive?"

"Yes."

"But who shot her?"

Jerry rolled his chair closer and kept his eyes on her face, a wrinkle between his eyebrows.

"An unhappy employee."

"But why?"

"A misunderstanding."

A phone call from Mars would have made more sense. "I don't understand any of this."

"There's more." He cleared his throat as if stalling.

*This is going to be bad.* Katya squeezed her eyes tight shut. She began to rock her head and neck, powerless to hold still. "Yes?" Her voice broke.

"She has a bad infection. You should come home."

"Is she going to die?"

"You should come home."

Katya's chin trembled, and her nose ran. She swiped at it with the back of her hand.

The man's voice again. "You should come back to Weaver as soon as you can. Here is a number where you can reach me. Let me know what plans you make, and I'll do what I can to help."

Katya's hand shook as she tried to write down the number. Her whole arm shook. Tears spilled out on the notepad on Jerry's desk.

Jerry took the phone from her. "This is Katya's employer. She's very upset. Can I help?"

Jerry was silent as he listened and wrote a number on the notepad.

"She'll be in touch. Thank you." Jerry put the phone down without a sound, and handed Katya his handkerchief.

Katya sobbed. Words poured out of her in a jumble. "I don't know how Mom knows this man. I know who he is, but I don't know what he has to do with Mom. And Mom is mad at me anyway. We had a big fight. You know, I told you about it, Chubbs. I didn't think she'd ever speak to me again, and now she's been shot. And he says I should come home." She looked from Jerry to Chubbs. "Is she going to die?"

For several weighty moments no one spoke. Katya sniffed, and blew her nose, and cried in a shuddering, hiccupping way like a child.

Chubbs came to stand beside her and rub her shoulder. "Honey, hospitals can work miracles. It will just help her—and you, too—if you are there."

Chubbs' words lit a flicker of hope inside her. Could this horrible thing bring the two of them back together?

"Let me take you back to our place and help you pack."

Katya nodded again, unable to think.

"Don't worry about things here. Just stay in touch." Jerry said.

"Thank you." She tried to rein in her galloping emotions. Clearing her throat, she tried again. "Thank you," and it sounded normal.

***

Chubbs took charge and Katya let her. She packed, made flight reservations, called Dave Frank, and paid for the flight. Katya made a half-hearted objection—she had no savings—but Chubbs shook her head, so Katya saved her energy.

***

Katya slept in fits and starts on the flight. Weird dreams played through her sleeping mind like bad drama. Lisa shooting her mom.

Her mom with blood on her face. Each time she nodded off, she woke with a twitch and remembered why she was on a plane.

When a rumpled unshaven man greeted her in Omaha, a man who had to be Dave Frank, Katya rushed to him. "How's my mom?"

He was straight with her. "The wound is infected. Her fever is very high."

"Is she conscious? Has she asked for me? Is she getting better?"

He said flatly. "You can see for yourself as soon as we get there."

While waiting at the conveyor for her luggage, Katya made strange low, humming sounds. Sounds she'd never made before. Sounds she couldn't stop making. She rocked back and forth on her heels. Dave told her to sit down. He'd get her bag.

*\*\**

Neither talked while they raced for the car and exited the airport. When the road finally sang beneath their wheels, Katya started again with questions. "Where is the shot? Not her face? Oh, please not her face."

"She was shot in the shoulder. The shot missed the artery."

"You think she'll be okay, don't you?" If she could get him to agree, then it would be true.

"I hope so." He didn't lie to her, and he didn't tell her anything more frightening than she needed to know.

Katya stole looks at the man at the wheel of the car. Whiskers sprouted on his chin, some brown, some gray. Redness rimmed his eyes. Exhaustion seeped out of him like sweat. *He must care very much for Mom, whoever he is.*

"I appreciate all you've done. How did you know where to reach me?"

The man didn't answer right away. "There was a letter from you at your mom's house."

Where had *he* been that he found the letter?

The man sniffed and rubbed his nose. "One other thing. I told the hospital that I'm your mom's brother. Otherwise I couldn't get any information."

Katya nodded. It wasn't a bad lie. "I understand. I'll call you Uncle from now on." The man said nothing, and Katya lapsed back into silence, too, and turned to gaze out the window.

Neon orange leaves trimmed trees and golden corn blanketed the fields of Southwest Iowa. The hills rolled down and up in a soothing way she had not appreciated when she lived here. Her heart beat steadily, no longer racing. The familiar landscape breathed courage into her lungs.

***

The sun hovered above the horizon, fierce and orange at eight in the morning. Katya, thankful she didn't have to figure out anything for herself, squinted as she and her "uncle" crossed the seemingly endless hospital parking lot.

They took the elevator that smelled of stale smoke to the fourth floor, sharing it with a patient on a gurney and a plump nurse whose uniform nearly burst over her generous chest. The fluorescent light made the patient greenish and Katya turned away from him, not wanting to associate the look with her mother.

As they got off the elevator, the sound of laughter and the smell of coffee greeted them from the nurses' station. Two nurses waved to Dave. He and Katya continued on to a room three doors down the corridor.

Sick dread filled Katya, but she had to see her mom with her own eyes. She had to know just how bad she was. Desire for her mom to stay alive coursed through her. She must live. She *had* to live. Katya would stay and make her live by the sheer force of her own love.

She made promises to God she knew she wouldn't keep. She'd start dating men. She'd even get married, if that's what it took. She'd do whatever her mother asked. *Just, please please please God, don't let her die.*

A nurse appeared with gowns and masks. Katya's hands shook as she dressed in the unfamiliar clothes, putting the gown on backwards first, then taking it off and putting it on again. The mask caught on her ear and sat crooked on her face until the nurse straightened it and turned her by the shoulders to tie the gown in back.

While standing in the doorway to her mom's room, Katya whispered, "Be still my heart." It helped. It was a prayer.

Her mother lay motionless on the pillow. For one terrible moment, Katya thought she *was* dead, but then she saw her chest rise and fall. Katya moved closer, bending to kiss her cheek.

The nurse put her hand on Katya's shoulder and shook her head. "The infection."

Katya nodded and pulled her hand away. "It's Katya, Mom. I'm here." She stared intently at her mom's face for some hint that she understood. None came.

The nurse motioned for Katya and Dave to step away from the bed. "Her fever is still high, but it hasn't gone up anymore. That's what the danger is. If it goes up, we will know that the infection has entered her bloodstream and . . ." The nurse didn't finish the thought. "But we are doing everything to prevent that."

Just then, her mother's whole body jerked, as if electricity shot through it.

Katya thought she had imagined the jerking, and started to speak when again, her mother jerked and the sheet covering her moved like a live thing.

Blood rushed to Katya's head. "What's wrong with her? Help her."

The nurse pushed a red wall button, and an alarm sounded. Within minutes, a rush of rubber-soled footsteps came from the corridor. Where moments before, the room had been silent and watchful, activity now burst into it. Strange wheeled equipment came speeding in, tubes flying, pulled by what seemed like a dozen white-masked, white-clothed, white-shod people all rushing to connect the strange equipment to her mother.

Horrified, Katya stood back, breathing open mouthed through her own mask. Would her mother die right before her eyes? She clung to Dave Frank's arm. His hand covered hers, sticky with sweat, and she could feel it tremble. The white-coated people blocked her mom's face.

Dave pressed gently on Katya's upper arm. "Sit down." She shook her head. He remained standing by her side. After an anguished half hour, the hubbub settled down.

One by one, the white people left the room murmuring to each other and making notes on clipboards. The one with straight blonde hair wearing the nametag "Nina" stayed behind. A stray blonde lock fell over her left eye, testament to the furious pace of treatment. She brushed it away. "Mrs. Simms had a seizure from her high fever. We got the fever down a few degrees, and it is dropping even more now."

Dave and Katya exchanged a look of relief. The experience had made them partners now. Hesitant ones, but partners all the same. Weary now, Katya's knees gave out and she wilted into the chair.

"Thank God." Dave, too, looked about for a place to sit. Not finding one, he leaned against the wall and closed his eyes, his head tilted back, his chin lifted to heaven.

Nina said, "She is very weak and needs sleep. You may as well get some rest yourselves. We'll call you if anything happens."

Dave nodded at Katya. "I think she's right. You look exhausted."

Katya nodded, too. They retraced their steps, only this time with weights in their shoes, shed their gowns and masks at the nurses' station and got on the elevator. Down they went. Through the lobby and out to the parking lot. The return journey to the car seemed even longer than when they had arrived. In spite of the sun high in the sky, an October chill sent a shiver through Katya. She remembered she hadn't brought a coat. Maybe an old sweater would be waiting at the house.

The house. An unexpected longing to see the house she grew up in surprised her.

\*\*\*

Dave dropped her off and waited while she went in the back door. The first kitchen floorboard creaked like it always had, and the yellow walls still made her think of butter. But why were dirty dishes in the sink and a half full cup of coffee on the table? Her mom never left the kitchen untidy.

\*\*\*

Katya climbed the stairs heavily, shivering from the chill in the house. The stale unused smell in her bedroom made her feel like a stranger. Swaddling herself in the bedspread, she flopped on the bed. Sleep took her as if it had been waiting.

When she woke, she was stiff with cold and confused about where she was. Out the window, dusk descended, and she knew she had slept all afternoon.

Stretching one arm out from beneath the bedspread's warmth, she clicked on her old lava lamp and waited for its red and orange lava to bubble up, smoosh out, and then drift back down to bubble up again. Her mom had brought the lamp from Omaha after Katya had pestered her about it for weeks. Handing it to her in a Brandeis bag, her mom had said, "It beats me why you want such an ugly thing," but she laughed when she said it.

After Katya watched the lamp cycle through a few times, she thumped across the room in her stockinged feet, still wrapped in the bedspread. The dresser drawer squeaked when she opened it. The sweaters were all jumbled together the way she had left them when she went to Chicago, but a familiar sleeve peeked out from the tangle. She pulled it loose, tossed the spread back on the bed, and pulled on an old blue cardigan.

Downstairs, she turned up the thermostat, and the furnace groaned, and the radiators clicked as they came to life, heat spreading up and out like lava in a lamp.

Now that she had rested, her thought turned to food. Three cheese burgers from the Main Street Café would just about satisfy her. Instead, she rummaged through the refrigerator and found bread and butter. The cupboard produced a can of chicken noodle soup and cocoa mix. Soup, buttered toast, and hot chocolate. A feast.

She sang along to the radio, just like she used to, her steps taking her back and forth across the kitchen. Soup on the stove. Bread in the toaster. Water in the hot chocolate mix.

Petula Clark sang about going where your worries couldn't find you. Where was that? Katya wondered. She smiled when the toast popped up browner on one side than the other, the way she remembered toast. It surprised her to learn later that it could be browned evenly on both sides.

She arranged her food on a yellow plastic plate. Nothing said home like Campbell's chicken and noodle. She dunked her buttery toast in it, remembering how her mom did that, too. Hot chocolate was better made with milk, but there wasn't any in the frig.

The hospital hadn't phoned, so that meant no change, which seemed like a good thing. She wasn't sure how hospitals worked. Now she was ready to go see her mom again.

After clearing the table, she washed the dishes—even the ones that had already been there. As she swished soap around the dried-on coffee in the cup, she wondered again who had used it. She stored the last plate in the cupboard, and then fished around in her purse for Dave's phone number.

Before she found it, the phone rang, and it was Dave. "You want to go to the hospital, don't you?"

"Yes."

"Pick you up in ten minutes."

Katya turned out all but the front door light and waited in its warm glow. Countless times she had waited in this spot for Charlie's dad to pick her up and take the two girls to a movie or a ball game. This visit, she had been too busy, too worried about her mom, to think about her high school friend. They had exchanged a few letters last year and then nothing.

Dave's Buick stopped beneath the street light and she hurried out.

"Did you get some rest?"

She climbed in. "I was out cold for four hours. You?"

"Same."

"You eat something? The hospital cafeteria isn't too bad if you're hungry."

"No thanks. I fixed some soup."

Nothing more was said until they reached the parking lot. Impulsively, before she could overthink it, Katya said, "How do you know my mom?"

Dave busied himself with setting the handbrake and checking the lights. "We were old neighbors."

Katya didn't remember him as a neighbor, but she let it go. She wanted to know about the shooting and she didn't know who else to ask. "Who shot Mom? Why did they do it? Do you know?"

Dave stopped his fiddling with the car's controls and pursed his lips. Then he closed his eyes and released a mighty sigh. "It's because of me."

Katya blinked. "What?" Surely, she had misheard.

"Me. It's because of me." Dave spoke louder, regret in his voice.

"I don't understand."

Now that he had turned off the motor, the car became chilly. In the dim light of the parking lot, he turned to her. "Katya, I don't know if it's my story to tell. I've been thinking a lot about it, and I just don't know. Maybe I should—"

"No." The word hung in the chill air of the car.

He stopped.

"I want to know. I have to know." She stiffened and hit her thigh with her fist.

He sighed again. "Okay. I'll tell you why your mother was shot if you tell me what you two fought about in California."

He had her cornered, and she knew it. It was a fair bargain, but she barely knew this man. She didn't want to face his disgust. "That's a trick, but I will do it. Just please don't be shocked."

"Deal." Clearly satisfied, Dave said, "What do you say we go see your mom first?"

## CHAPTER FORTY-EIGHT
Anna

Anna drifted up from shadows, but exhaustion kept her from fully waking. A prod on her shoulder—more than a tickle, less than a pinch. Z*zzzzzz*. A buzzing insect noise reached her from far away. She struggled to wake up and slap down that pesky insect; but her eyelids wouldn't open. When she tried, they fluttered and closed again. Light from the hallway penetrated the veil of her lashes. Sun dazzled her through the window. Her eyes refused to stay open and dreams of gunshots and ambulance sirens carried her away.

***

Voices replaced gunshots, and their pleasant murmur interested her. This time her eyelids opened when she told them to. Two blurry figures came into view. Her gaze shifted to the right where night had turned the window into a dark rectangle.

When she saw the figures again, their masked faces confused Anna. Her voice slurred, thick with sleep. "Who are you?"

The tall figure touched her hand. "Mom?" she said. "It's me, Katya."

"Katya." Anna summoned strength to clasp her daughter's hand. "You're here."

"I'm right here, Mom. I won't leave you."

Anna kept a grip on Katya's hand, afraid she would disappear. The warmth of her daughter's touch made Anna stronger. "So happy. You make me happy." Her mouth wouldn't smile like she wanted it to.

Anna rested her eyes. Time passed before she sensed another person near her bed. She might have heard the whisper of his breath, or caught a whiff of Old Spice, but Anna knew who it was.

She forced her eyes open again. "Dave, you're here, too." She released her hold on Katya and touched Dave's white gowned arm.

"I'm here, too." The sound of Dave's voice was as potent a medicine as Katya's touch.

A wrinkle formed between Katya's brows and a slight frown pulled her mouth down. Anna could see that her easy recognition of Dave worried Katya, and she gave her daughter as reassuring a smile as she could muster.

A nurse came in then and made them go away, but because the two people she loved most in the world returned her love and shared her pain, she didn't feel alone.

## CHAPTER FORTY-NINE
Dave

Dave and Katya left Anna's room reassured that she recognized them. As they entered the hospital elevator for the fourth time that day, Dave hoped Katya had forgotten about exchanging stories.

"Are we going to talk in the car?" Katya said.

Dave scrunched up his face. "Let's get a cup of coffee in the cafeteria."

At ten at night, the cafeteria's fluorescent lights glared down on empty booths and tables. Pans and silverware clinked from behind the counter where a lone employee tidied the cooking area, the only sound in a place usually abuzz with the voices of worried families.

They sipped coffee they'd picked up in the cafeteria line. Neither said a word. Dave stared into his cup trying to find the right words in there.

"Who first?"

Dave still didn't talk.

Katya sighed. "I'll go." Except she didn't. Instead she started to cry, not sobs, but sad weeping. Dave handed her a fistful of napkins. "It's too awful. I'm too ashamed. I tried to fight it, but I can't."

"Unless you've killed somebody or robbed a bank, nothing can be that bad." Dave knew his lame humor probably fell on deaf ears; but to his surprise, the corners of Katya's mouth turned upward for a moment.

"Here goes." She breathed in deeply, her chest expanding. When she exhaled, she closed her eyes. She began with her eyes closed. "There was a girl named Paulette in Chicago, but I was afraid to be found out and I treated her badly." She opened her eyes

226

and a torrent of words flowed out, tumbling, escaping into the air. "Then there was this actress in L.A. My mom met her. We went to her house with a bunch of friends." Little by little, Katya's face relaxed as if the telling set her soul free.

Dave just nodded and kept his face as blank as he could. He wanted to take her hand to comfort her, but he didn't.

Katya stopped to blow her nose and draw breath. She rubbed her eyes and kneaded her forehead as if her head ached. "My mom saw."

"What did your mom see?"

Katya gazed brazenly into Dave's eyes as if daring him to disapprove. "My mom saw her kiss me." With that confession, Katya's body shrank into itself as if waiting for a blow.

When Dave didn't speak, Katya flashed her eyes at him, sparks flying. "Say something."

Dave let out a sigh as weighted and weary as doom. "I knew you were different."

Katya's mouth opened into a perfect O. "Different? In what way? And how did you know?"

"I knew you weren't a small-town Weaver girl, crazy about boys, just waiting to get married. There was more to you than that. I thought you might be . . . well, the way you are."

"How could you have known? I didn't."

"I'd seen it before. With singers, musicians, in my green room. In the war. You weren't interested in boys. You lived in your own little world with your art books and your mother and that funny friend you had. What was her name?"

At that Katya smiled. "Charlie."

"Yes, Charlie, the one with the bad arm."

Katya heaved a sigh to match Dave's. "I'm so tired."

Dave nodded. "So that's what you fought about? Your mom can't accept it."

"She said she'd never speak to me again." The look on Katya's face was a mixture of sadness and anger.

"You know she didn't mean that."

"I think she did."

Katya wasn't done. "And then Lisa dumped me. That's the actress. She dumped me for somebody she met in London or for a fancier friend than a girl from Iowa. I don't really know. Now that I'm here, away from California, I don't really care like I thought I would. Now all I care about is my mom getting better and making up with her."

In spite of Dave's suspecting Katya was the way she was, that was not what he had speculated Anna's fight with her had been about. Maybe Katya finishing art school, maybe spending too much money, all the things that kids her age do that aggravate their parents.

"Now I kept my end of the bargain. I want to know who shot my mom. And don't tell me it was a misunderstanding."

"You're right. Just let me get my thoughts straight." Where to start? "Okay. Now, just let me tell it. Don't interrupt." Dave steepled his hands and focused his gaze on his fingers. "Your mom and I have been friends for a long time."

"You mean you used to live next door to each other?" Katya inclined her head.

"I thought I said not to interrupt." Dave heard the impatience in his voice and got it under control. He began again. "Yes, that's true, but it's not what I mean. I mean *friend* friends." He gave Katya a look, and understanding rose up in her face.

"You were having an affair?"

"Yes." God, the telling relieved him, even though his words hurt Katya.

"Even when I was still at home?"

"Yes." Now, she's mad. Now she'll let me have it. He watched as the information registered painfully on Katya's face.

"You mean all those years she was deceiving me? Hiding it from me? And you, too?"

"If you want to judge us, then yes." Couldn't she just let it go? He was too tired for a battle.

"But if that's true, she's not the mom I thought she was. Did you seduce her? Lead her astray. She never would have done something like that on her own."

Dave let that go. He shrugged. "She was lonely. I was lonely. My wife is an alcoholic."

"Why didn't you leave your wife and marry my mom?"

For the millionth time he replayed the reason he couldn't leave Fran. "Because my wife blamed herself for our son's death. Even though I stopped loving her, I didn't want her to be alone. In the end, she left me." He grimaced, aware of the bitter joke.

Katya shook her head and looked like she might cry again. "This is very confusing. What has all this got to do with Mom getting shot?" He watched the struggle in her face between her tears and her defiance.

"Your mom broke it off with me in the spring, before my wife left me. It was a few months before she went to California. She started to see somebody else, and I started seeing Shannon." He paused to let Katya take that in. "Shannon sometimes watched the shop for your mom, but I didn't know that or I never would have asked her out.

When the car smashed up your mom's shop, we accidentally saw each other, realized we still had feelings for each other, and got back together. Shannon was jealous and unstable and shot your mother out of revenge."

Katya's face wrinkled up in distaste. "I can't take this all in. My mom always seemed so perfect to me. She was my idol. I worshiped her. And now I find out she was running around with a married man and lying to me about it."

"You made me promise not to be shocked. Can't you do the same for me?" His voice rose in exasperation.

"She's a hypocrite. I don't see what right she has to judge me, to despise what I am when you're both cheats and liars." Katya's voice started to sound hysterical.

"We're human, Katya. Just like you, we tried to fight it, but couldn't." He kept it to himself that they hadn't tried very hard.

"Yeah, maybe." Katya grabbed her sweater and purse and stood up, towering over him.

He had to look away from her accusing glare.

"I just want to go home."

Exhaustion numbed Dave's brain. He wanted to go home, too.

Silently, they crossed the parking lot, Katya walking fast ahead of him. He quickened his step to keep up with her since he felt responsible for Anna's daughter while Anna was in the hospital. Now uncomfortable truths linked Katya with him. They knew each other's secrets. It would take Katya time to accept what she had learned.

Katya walked right past the car.

He realized she intended to walk home. "Katya, don't be silly. Just let me drive you home."

She kept walking, and Dave got in the car. He drove up to where she was and talked to her through the open window. He felt like he was in some third-rate television drama. "Come on. You don't have to talk to me."

She stopped. The look on her face total exasperation, but she walked around the car and got in.

At Anna's house Katya opened the car door without looking at Dave. Her back to him, she said, "I don't want to go see Mom tomorrow. I need to think. I need to take this all in."

Dave didn't fight her. He thought of something that might soften her, might win her over. "I'd like to show you something."

Now Katya looked at him. "What?"

"It's too late now. I'll show you tomorrow. Will you come with me?"

"Why should I?"

"Please. It won't take long."

She closed her eyes in contempt. "This better be good."

Dave waited for her to agree.

"What time?" Exaggerated patience filled her voice.

"Not too early. I'll call first."

As Katya crossed in front of the car, Dave rolled the window down again. When she was alongside it, he said, "Thank you." But Katya didn't respond.

*** 

Dave picked up Katya after ten the next morning.

"What's this all about?"

"Just be patient. I'll show you." Then he dug around in his pocket and handed her a set of car keys. "These are to your mom's car. Use it. It shouldn't just sit there. The battery will get low."

She frowned, but tucked the keys in her purse.

Dave drove slowly, ponderously. No matter how much time had passed, this was never an easy trip for him.

He arrived at their destination, turned off the ignition and set the parking brake.

The sneer on Katya's face had been replaced by softer eyes, eyes that held a question, although he suspected she already knew the answer.

The tidy lanes and rolling hills of the Weaver Cemetery lay before them. Only one grave existed for Dave. The rest were mere background. He started to walk past the Olsens' double stone, past the twisted and ancient oak that shaded the grave to which he headed.

He stopped. Katya stood beside him, all openness now.

"Randy Frank. 1951-1953." Katya read the inscription on the stone.

Dave nodded his head towards the grave. "This is my son." He gazed at the stone. "I want you to make up with your mom. Death is final. I don't have a chance. You do. If you won't do it for yourselves, do it for me. She'll never be happy with me until she settles things with you. You're first in her life. You always have been. I've always known that and accepted it."

Sympathetic now, Katya asked softly, "How did he die?"

Dave continued to stare at the grave stone, all curlicues and flowers with a naked cherub. He had wanted something plainer, but at the time, he did anything Fran wanted and this stone was her choice. "He ran into the street and was hit by a car."

Dave stole a sideways look at Katya. "Your mom and dad were there when it happened." He had no desire to tell her who had been driving. Now was not the time for another painful secret.

CHAPTER FIFTY
Katya

The familiar smell of French Fries and coffee burst upon Katya as she opened the door to the Main Street Cafe. Memories of countless post-game hamburgers, Saturday morning donuts and hot chocolate, and after-school Cokes rushed over her. For a moment the warmth of the memories almost made her cry. Instead, she smiled when she saw Charlie, her best friend growing up. They hugged and laughed and talked at the same time. Finally, they settled down and took a booth. Talk came easily, jumping from their studies to fashion to the Beatles.

Charlie shook her head in wonder. "You're in Hollywood. And here I am studying business at Weaver County Community College. I feel like a hick."

Katy face looked stern. "There's nothing wrong with that. It's a good field and lots of opportunity. I mean, what do you think movies are if they aren't a business?"

Charlie laughed. "Come on, Katya, there's a big difference."

Silently, Katya agreed, but she didn't say so. "Well, it doesn't matter to me. You will always be my best friend. Hey, why don't you come stay with me when I get a place of my own?"

"I would love that." Charlie stopped to take a bite of her burger and a slurp from her malt. With a full mouth she asked, "Are you dating anyone? Somebody famous?'

Katya nearly choked on her own mouthful. "No. No one special."

"Maybe you'll date Frankie Avalon."

"He's married." Katya laughed. Dating talk made her uneasy. She turned the attention on Charlie. "Are you going out with anybody?"

Charlie shook her head, "Naaaah. A couple of losers that think just because I have a bad arm, nobody will want me and I'm an easy mark."

"The jerks."

"Don't worry. I let them know otherwise."

Katya wanted her old friend to know about Lisa. She needed somebody to accept her, to tell her it was okay to be the way she was, but she didn't have the courage to risk rejection. Instead, she asked Charlie something that had been bugging her. "What have you heard about my mom getting shot?"

Charlie's pale blue eyes searched Katya's face.

Katya knew she was trying to decide how much to say. "Just tell me anything you've heard. Really, I want to know everything."

Charlie took a deep breath and began. She spoke with care. "I heard that Shannon Jackson shot your mother because of Dave Frank." She stopped, and Katya nodded for her to continue.

"Dave and your mother had been having an affair for years and Shannon thought your mom stole Dave back to start up again."

"Did you know any of this before the shooting?"

"No, and at first I didn't believe it, but then I heard it from people that don't usually gossip, and I knew it was true."

"Dave Frank is the one who called me in California to tell me Mom had been shot. Last night, when I asked him why, he told me." Katya watched the meaning of that sink in for Charlie.

She needed Charlie to understand. "She lied to me, Charlie." She saw nothing but treachery in her mother's past. "She lied to you, too. Oh, not in so many words, but we thought she was one way, and she wasn't like that at all. She's a liar and a cheat, yet she pretended to be such a great mom." She used the same words she had used with Dave and the same indignation rose up in her like lava in a lamp.

Charlie's face flushed. "She *was* a great mom. That was real."

"Don't you feel betrayed? I do."

"Your mom has always been great to me. I figure the rest isn't any of my business."

"Well, *you* can say that, but it's *my* business."

Only kindness shone from Charlie's eyes, and Katya didn't want to be kind. She wanted to stay mad because her mom had betrayed her and that hurt. It hurt deep down, like a shift in her foundation. Now her mom could suffer. But Katya couldn't sustain her anger and her shoulders fell. "It seems like the mom I knew wasn't the real one. That she only pretended. What should I do? I don't want to go visit her in the hospital. I don't know how to act." Katya's chin began to tremble and she put a fist to her mouth. She refused to cry. She had wasted enough tears.

"Look, Katya. I saw your mom with you. That wasn't pretending. She loved you. Would it help if I went with you to the hospital?"

Katya's confusion lessened. "Oh, Charlie, that *would* help. Thank you."

*** 

When Charlie and Katya walked into her mom's hospital room, her mom smiled.

"Charlie," she said in a voice that tried to be hearty, but was still weak. "So nice to see you." Katya's mother took Charlie's hand sideways in her good one. "Isn't this a mess I've gotten myself into? Do you think I'm awful?"

A stab of jealousy took Katya by surprise. Her mom was so comfortable with Charlie.

Charlie laughed. "I could never think you're awful, Mrs. Simms. I think getting shot is awful, though. I hope you get better soon."

Katya's mom patted Charlie's hand and let it go. She looked up at Katya. "How about you, honey? Do you think I'm awful?" There was no smile in her voice.

Dave must have told her he had confessed. She felt cheated out of her revenge. Katya had wanted to confront her, to surprise and hurt her. Charlie stepped into the gap left by the question. "Mrs. Simms, I have another friend to see on the second floor. I'll be back in half an hour."

Katya watched Charlie leave and turned back to her mother, whose injury gave her an unfair advantage. Katya's effort to control her feelings and her tongue made her heart hammer. "Well, yeah, Mom," She turned sullen. "I think you have a lot of getting well to do before we can talk about it. And I may have to go back to California." Katya invented the bit about California, but now that she had said it, she wanted to do it.

Her mother's face paled. "You hate me, don't you?"

"Yes, I do." It felt sensational to let it out, no matter the consequences. "You lied to me my whole childhood. You were my idol, and now I find out you're just a big fake!" Her breathing came hot and heavy.

Her mother's face flushed and her eyes filled with tears, and it made Katya glad. She couldn't stop herself now. "You said I was terrible for being with Lisa, but you're just as bad. Worse. I can't help the way I am. You didn't have to be a cheat and a liar and a fake, but you chose to do it, anyway, no matter how it would make me feel." Katya heard herself shouting.

A nurse appeared at the door. "What's going on in here?" She started for Katya, but just at that moment Charlie appeared, hurried around from behind and reached Katya first.

"Now stop it. Come on. I'll take you home."

Looking for someone who understood, Katya's eyes darted at Charlie, then the nurse, and then her mom. She found no sympathy. Her mom was sobbing now, and Katya didn't care. Let her cry her heart out. See what it feels like.

The nurse said to Charlie, "Take her out of here. She can't upset our patients like this. Go on."

Katya took flight, her shoes smacking the floor. She bypassed the elevator and ran down the stairs, Charlie in pursuit. When she got outside to the parking lot, she stopped and pounded her thighs and groaned with pain.

Charlie herded her into her car and Katya didn't fight her. When they were seated inside, Katya was surprised to see Charlie's eyes flashing indignation. "How could you do that? Your mother has been shot! Don't you get it? You probably set her back a thousand years."

Katya flung words at Charlie. "Not you, too. Isn't anybody on my side?"

Charlie looked at her in disgust and started the car. As she drove, the two friends sat in hot silence.

Katya decided since she had come this far with Charlie, her friend was going to know the rest whether she liked it or not. She shifted her whole body around so that she faced Charlie. "Will you just stop the car for a minute? I want to tell you something."

Charlie frowned and knit her brow, but she did as Katya asked and pulled over to park in the side parking at the Philips station. When they were stopped, Charlie turned to her. Her voice was hard and flat. "What is it?"

Katya stared boldly into Charlie's face, her heart whacking away at her ribcage. "When Mom came to see me in California, she saw a woman kiss me." There, she couldn't take it back now. The revelation lay between them as palpable as if it breathed.

"A woman?" Disbelief filled Charlie's voice and face.

Katya began to sweat, but she refused to back down. "You heard me."

"I don't understand." Charlie's voice came from a strange place. It fluttered in the air like a wounded bird.

"Now you know." Katya wasn't going to explain the facts of life to her. She could look them up in the encyclopedia if she was that naive. "My mother was shocked—just like you are—and she accused me of all sorts of things and said she never wanted to see me again. She judged me. That gives me the right to judge her, and that's exactly what I'm going to do. I don't expect you to understand." Katya let the chip on her shoulder slip an inch. Her chest sagged and her voice turned quiet. "I don't understand myself. I didn't choose it. I don't want people to despise me." Desperation made her beg. "I need you as my friend, Charlie. Can you still be my friend even if you don't understand?"

Warring emotions fought a battle on Charlie's face. She kept shaking her head as if to clear it. "I don't know. I need to think about it."

Katya shivered in the chill of Charlie's disloyalty. With as much humility as Katya could muster, she said, "Please, Charlie. I'm scared."

Katya put a hand on the car door, ready to get out when Charlie spoke. "You say your mom was one way and pretended to be another way. Well, it seems to me, you were doing the same thing. I don't know why you're mad at her."

Katya had fought this fight with herself. "I was a kid and she was an adult. And besides, I didn't know I was the way I am—a homosexual. That's the word." Maybe the hard truth would win Charlie over. "I thought I liked boys just like you, or I thought I would eventually. It just didn't happen for me and something else did. I don't expect you to understand."

"Just leave me out of it, okay." Charlie gripped the wheel and stared straight ahead.

"Will you still come see me in California?" One final pathetic plea for acceptance escaped Katya.

"I don't know," her friend said with studied indifference.

Charlie started the engine and it came to life, putting an end to the discussion and Katya's plea for understanding. They rode in silence to Katya's house where she left the car without saying goodbye. The car door closed with a final clunk, closing the door on the friendship, too.

Katya entered the house with a resolve she didn't know she had. She was leaving, now, as soon as possible. Well, morning. She mounted the stairs to her room, put the few clothes Chubbs had packed for her in her cheap flowered luggage. On impulse, she grabbed the lava lamp and buried it in the packed clothing, a weird reminder of what had happened the last few days.

Her mind concentrated on the future, on getting back to California and her career. The day had come when she was an outsider in her home. Weaver was the place she used to be from. Charlie was somebody she used to know. Her mother was the parent she used to love.

Her sleep was fitful. Each time she closed her eyes she heard the nurse demanding she leave her mom's room. When she didn't see the nurse, she heard Charlie's voice. "What do you mean? I don't understand." Now California meant safety. Circumstances had switched. The once strange place had become a refuge; her once familiar home had become a threat.

The last few hours before dawn, Katya slept hard, unrestful sleep. She woke with bitterness in her mouth, like bad-tasting medicine. After dressing, she decided to take a drive around town. Who knew when she'd be back? Orange and red leaves covered the trees and the ground around the school. She and Charlie had walked home together every day, watching the popular kids and wondering what made them tick.

Without planning to, she passed her mother's shop—nearing completion now—and pushed the worry from her mind about who would help her mother when she went back to work. Past the hospital and back down Main Street, out the other end of town and down the winding lanes of the Weaver Cemetery. She found herself at Randy Frank's tiny grave with the outsize cherub looming over it.

Katya stopped, pulled on the parking brake, and left the car. A connection with the dead child drew her to its grave. She hadn't felt it when she was here yesterday with Dave, but now—alone—some elusive alliance bound them. She had done exactly the opposite of what Dave had warned her against and widened the gulf between herself and her mother. Her new, older, more cynical self said she didn't care.

"What brings you here?" a voice asked from behind her. Katya turned to see Dave.

She was about to make a crack about asking him the same thing, and then realized the wrongness of that. "I'm not sure. I just felt the need to come here and think."

"About what?"

Keeping up her guard, acting defensively required work. She let all that go for a moment and replied honestly. "About going back to California. Weaver doesn't feel like home anymore."

"I wish you'd stay. You and your mother could work things out."

"I doubt it." Her defenses rose again. "Besides, I have a job to get back to."

"Well, if you insist on going, I'll take you to the airport."

"Thank you."

"Should I keep you up to date about your mom's condition?"

Katya considered his question. "No. If I want to know, I can contact you. I have your number."

"If that's the way you want it."

"That's the way I want it." Katya walked away and Dave walked closer to the grave, tidying it up, tossing aside small sticks and dried leaves.

It occurred to Katya that caring for the grave might replace having his son to take care of. His was a cruel story, and her own story didn't feel much happier.

# CHAPTER FIFTY-ONE
Anna

When Katya left town, Anna still called the hospital home. She lay in bed staring out the window, trying to imagine the years ahead without her daughter. No visits home. No shared stories of life in the world of clothing. No Christmas Eve dinner or exchange of presents. The pain in her heart was bigger than the pain in her injured shoulder.

One night she dreamt that a car came smashing into the temporary store and its driver had a rifle and took shots at the dresses which wriggled and jumped like specters. The driver yelled at Anna, "Your daughter's a pervert!" She woke sweating and thrashing. Her calls of "No. No," brought the night nurse running. Only after the nurse gave her a Valium could Anna calm her breathing and go back to sleep.

The next day, Anna shut out her feelings for her daughter with a door as unyielding as the one on a bank's vault. Her new life on this side. Her old life with Katya locked away. Fine. She'd have more heart to give to Dave. More energy to give to the store. More resources to restore her health.

\*\*\*

On the morning of November first, her morning nurse brought her breakfast. "We're kicking you out today." She fluffed Anna's pillows. "Have you lined up somebody to stay with you for a while? You'll need some help."

"Dave says he has found someone." Anna speculated that the nurses knew Dave really wasn't her brother, but had kept up the pretense. Small towns could get away with a few lies among friends.

When Dave arrived an hour later with Naomi, Anna's first impression was not positive. A tall, thin, tired-looking woman, Naomi stood behind Dave, still as a ghost. Mrs. Danvers.

"This is Naomi Harmon. She's going to be helping you while your arm gets better."

The woman nodded, more timid than threatening, as Anna first thought.

"Hi, Naomi."

Naomi stepped forward and gave Anna her arm to lean on as she stood up. The lady smelled of Ivory soap. Her arm was rough and warm, like a terry towel. Anna's feelings toward the woman softened. Maybe she would like the help of this silent woman.

\*\*\*

Anna's first glimpse of her house brought unexpected happy tears to her eyes. The sweet symmetry of the windows on either side of the door, the safe shelter of the peaked roof over the entry, the bushes round and fat all brought a grateful smile to her face. She had been more homesick than she knew.

Dave left for work, and Anna settled on her pretty teal couch. She remembered insisting that the furniture store cover the chair in matching fabric. "But it has perfectly good upholstery on it now." Anna had insisted, and the sales clerk sniffed. "It'll cost you." Anna never regretted the extra expense.

She let her little house enfold her in its orderly arms while Naomi went in the kitchen to fix coffee. Back in her beloved home at last, Anna put her head back and closed her eyes.

The comforting clink of Naomi finding her way around the kitchen came to Anna. Her new helper sang along to a song on the radio, the one by those four English boys with the funny hair and funny name. The one about love being easier yesterday. The plain, hardscrabble woman had a voice like an angel.

Naomi's sure footsteps sounded in the hall, and then the living room carpet silenced them. She appeared wearing one of Anna's old aprons. In her rough hands she held a delicate cup and saucer,

Anna's favorite china painted with Baltimore orioles and cornflowers. Although Anna had owned the dishes for years, they felt new and precious after the solid white chinaware in the hospital.

She sipped and breathed in the coffee's heady aroma. The strong coffee coursed through her veins, and she wondered how the hospital had dared call their weak brew by the same name.

On a small companion plate, Naomi had arranged crackers with butter and sugar on top. "Thought you might want a sweet to go with your coffee." Naomi set the crackers on the table next to the couch. "You need groceries."

Anna picked up the square, dimpled soda cracker, butter shining, sugar crystals winking in the light. She used to fix this simple treat for Katya when she was little.

"I haven't had these in ages." She crunched down on one, and its simple bright flavor took her back to Katya's tea parties on the front porch at her play table. Anna had gathered her knees beneath the undersize table, sipping weak Kool-Aid "punch" from cups the size of measuring spoons. Another life. Anna longed for it.

Coming back to the present in her living room with Naomi, Anna remembered her resolution to close her heart to Katya. She wiped crumbs from her cheek with her good hand. "Get a cup for yourself and join me."

After a moment's hesitation, Naomi went out to the kitchen and returned with another bird and flower-covered cup. She sat in the matching teal chair next to the shared end table and made quiet little slurping sounds when she drank, like a cat.

Anna had only planned to get to know the woman better. Where did she live? Did she have any kids? When instead, she said, "My daughter and I had a big fight." She astonished herself. *Where did that come from?*

"Yes?" *Slurp.*

And Anna's mouth kept talking, bypassing her brain. "I don't think she'll ever speak to me again."

Naomi nodded. "What did you fight about?"

Anna watched her pick a crumb from her dress. "She doesn't like men."

Anna could not read Naomi's expression. "My cousin was like that."

"Like Katya you mean, she . . .you know . . .didn't like men?" Anna couldn't bring herself to say it the other way.

"She killed herself." Naomi's face paled as she whispered the words.

That hit Anna with an impact as powerful as the shot to her shoulder. "God. That's terrible."

"I quit speaking to her. Everybody did. She was all alone."

Anna wouldn't think about that. If she did, her resolve would crumble and she'd crawl on her knees to reconcile with Katya. Anything to keep that from happening. Surely, Katya wouldn't harm herself, would she? Now she would never stop thinking about that.

"And you know, Katya found out about Dave and me." Anna put this information out there, cautiously, not knowing what made this woman tick.

"Uh huh." *Slurp.*

"Did you know?" Anna ventured this question even more guardedly.

Naomi didn't speak, she just pursed her lips. Anna read the expression. Naomi had known. "Did other people know?"

"Don't think so."

Anna's troubling thoughts found refuge in Naomi's unjudging attention. When Anna spoke, Naomi listened with her heart.

***

During the next two weeks, every time the phone rang, Anna's heart begged it to be Katya. Every pile of mail held the promise of a letter from her. But a phone call never came and a letter never arrived. Was she okay? Anna thought about Naomi's cousin, and her heart leaped in fear.

***

Rather than needing Naomi less as her shoulder healed, Anna needed her more.

One morning she asked her new friend, "What do you say we go down and look at the changes in my store?"

Apprehension ruled Anna's thoughts while Naomi drove the familiar streets to the store. What if she didn't like the rebuilt shop? She fidgeted in her seat, her stomach quivering.

"You okay?" Naomi said.

"Nervous. What if I hate it? What if the color scheme is all wrong? I chose it while I was in the hospital."

Naomi was practical. "If you don't like it, it can be changed."

"Right." Anna nodded her head and relaxed a little.

The minute she set foot inside the door, she grabbed Naomi's arm for support. Anna wanted to sing. "It's wonderful. It looks fresh and new. Even better than I expected." The tweed carpeting, freshly painted sky-blue walls, and gleaming silver and glass fixtures energized her. She moved slowly around the room, touching the cash register, her old friend, running her hand on the beautifully encased hanging rods. She stopped to look at herself in the antique free-standing mirror salvaged from her old shop.

Wilmer, the builder, watched her, hammer in hand. "Well, what do you think?"

"I think it is beautiful, Wilmer, you've done a great job."

"Let me show you the addition." He and his son had cleverly connected the main shop with the small space next door. A perfectly curved arch and a small step invited shoppers to explore the new area.

"Lots of finishing, but we're done with the big stuff." He paused. "Want to see your office?"

Her office made Anna clap her hands—or as close as she could come to clapping—in delight. Indirect lighting around the top gave the room a warm glow. Anna pictured herself closing out the day surrounded by that glow. The space was no longer the little cubbyhole where Katya had done her homework, but Anna wouldn't think about that. She would keep thoughts of her daughter locked away.

She went back out front where Naomi waited patiently. "Let's bring this place back to life, Naomi. I'm tired of sitting around home."

"You mean me, too, Mrs. Simms?" Naomi looked surprised.

"I mean you, too, Naomi. And from now on, I'm Anna. I'm not Mrs. Simms."

\*\*\*

Each morning Anna became a little more independent, needing Naomi less and less at home. But she had become more and more necessary at work. Anna expected some rush inventory orders to arrive. Under Anna's supervision, Naomi unpacked, pressed, tagged and hung a dozen dresses and twenty blouses.

The woman worked tirelessly, barely stopping for a cup of coffee or a sandwich. She hummed along to the radio, surprising Anna by knowing the words to most of the pop songs.

\*\*\*

Katya's old friend Charlie stopped by. "Oh, Mrs. Simms, you must be proud. Isn't it fun to come to work here every day? I would love to work in a place like this."

"Well, would you like to?"

Charlie wrinkled her brow, "Would I like to what?"

"Work here."

And within a few days, Charlie had overhauled Anna's accounting system and showed Anna some display techniques she learned in merchandising class.

With some of the money Charlie saved her, Anna stocked the Attic, that's what she named the new annex, the teen area.

Wilmer moved on to other work, but his son Lars stayed behind to assemble new racks, and hang light fixtures in the Attic. Charlie bossed him around like she owned the place. "A little higher, to the right, there."

What Charlie didn't notice, but the two older women did, was that Lars had a crush on Charlie, size extra-large. His face glowed with devotion. Not until Anna said, "You know, Charlie, I don't think you need to push Lars quite so hard."

"You think I'm being too bossy?" Charlie sounded surprised.

"I think the guy would cut off his right arm for you."

And the only word for the look on Charlie's face was amazement.

Anna chuckled and wondered how any woman could be so oblivious to a man in love with her. And then it came to her: Katya would never be in that position, and Anna's heart withered a little.

With Anna's guidance and the help of her unlikely duo, Anna's Style Shop and the Attic opened two weeks before Thanksgiving, just in time for holiday shoppers.

In what felt like atonement for less savory articles about Anna, Garson and *The Malcom County Tribune* gave her shop opening a front page, two-column spread with a storefront picture.

# CHAPTER FIFTY-TWO
Dave

Dave would make the Majestic shine like the royalty she was. He'd do it for Moe.

He'd wait until after the holidays, only weeks away now, and then he'd replace that damn air conditioner, their tormentor of the last year.

Then he'd do the fun stuff. New seats. Padded. Red maybe. Bathrooms with pink porcelain fixtures for the girls. He'd give the guys some privacy with stalls instead of those smelly urinals lined up like some army camp. He'd update the green room. Performers would look forward to a Majestic gig. And best of all, a real concessions counter with seats that swiveled like in a soda shop. He could see Moe nodding his head in approval.

When Dave came to work, the emptiness of the place taunted him. Every door he opened and closed echoed. The sound of his own footsteps annoyed him. He waited to hear Moe's tuneless whistle as he puttered; and a couple of times, Dave thought he heard it. But he had just wished it.

His long-time friend and handyman's death had left him off kilter. The routine of The Majestic ran itself while Dave found his balance again. Someday, maybe, he would find a replacement for Moe.

Maybe now that Wilmer was done with Anna's shop, he'd come talk about giving the Majestic a facelift.

\*\*\*

Dave marveled at Anna's recovery and how her remodeled shop kept her spirits high. At least for a little while. Naomi and Charlie had come at just the right time. But he knew thoughts of Katya haunted Anna, and didn't know how to help her. He was just there for her.

"What if she kills herself like Naomi's cousin?" Anna had only said it out loud that one time, but he had a feeling she thought about it a lot more times.

He didn't answer her. Just held her hand and let her cry.

When there was no word from Katya, anxiety built up and built up until she'd have a good cry and be okay for a while. Then the buildup started all over again.

Or she made nervous chatter about Naomi and Charlie. What a strange trio the three females made. "I think Charlie and Lars are getting serious. Aren't they funny? What a cute little couple. And Naomi sings while she works. Did I tell you that?" She had told him that at least three times. Dave hated her forced, phony talk. It made him want to yell, "Just shut up."

He'd always understood how Anna's love and concern for Katya came before her feelings for him. But these crying jags and nervous streaks went beyond simple concern.

As he went around the ballroom performing Moe's daily duties, he counted the ways the last months had worn him down—Anna's injury, Katya's visit, Moe's death—and now, Anna had become nervy and strange.

One obstacle after another had gotten in the way of his relationship with Anna. Maybe the universe was trying to tell them something.

***

For years Monday nights had been their night together. It was the only night the ballroom closed its doors. Monday afternoon, Dave called her from his office to ask her to dinner.

"I'm beat. Can we do it another time?"

His whole body slumped. Her answer disappointed him. It angered him, too. He picked up a pencil and threw it at the wall. When would Anna have time for him? He gritted his teeth.

Dave ate supper at the café. The Salisbury steak was tender and juicy, but he couldn't enjoy it. He cut off a bite and studied it.

The waitress passed his table, "Something wrong with the steak?" She startled Dave.

He turned to her in surprise, then collected himself. "No, it's fine. It's good."

She nodded and moved on.

When he finished, he drove by Anna's store and saw that the light was still on. It was eight o'clock. Was she still there? She couldn't go out with him, but she could work until eight? She wasn't too tired for that.

On an impulse, he stopped and went to the door. It was unlocked. He opened it and the bell sounded.

Anna came out of her office, the look on her face turning from curiosity to wariness when she saw him. "What are you doing here this time of night?"

"I could ask you the same question." Dave had an edge to his voice.

"Are you spying on me?"

Dave ignored that. "I thought you were too tired to go out, but I see you aren't too tired to work late." He shut the door behind him.

She turned her back to him and went back to her office, talking as she went. "You run your own business. You know you have to put in extra hours sometimes?" She sat down at her desk.

Standing in the doorway, his hat still on, Dave asked, "Is it absolutely necessary that you put in extra hours tonight on my only night off? Especially now you have two people to help you?"

Anna looked up at him and frowned. "I don't need to explain myself to you."

Dave's voice softened. "Look, Anna, I thought we were partners. I thought all we needed was the chance to be together, and everything would work out. But ever since Fran left me and it looked like the time had come, we have had nothing but one problem after another."

"You're blaming me for getting shot?" Anger filled her eyes.

Dave gave an exasperated sigh. "Don't be ridiculous."

"Then what are you saying?"

"I'm saying we either get married as soon as my divorce is final or we call it quits. I'm getting too old to figure out what you want anymore."

Anna's eyes turned big and round. She blinked several times.

"Well, what's your answer? I want to know now. No more messing around."

She sat down in her desk chair like she had gone weak. She stared at him, looking stunned, and whispered something.

"What did you say?"

Anna looked up at him, eyes shining. "I said yes. Yes. I said yes." Each time a little louder. She sat in her chair as if tied to it.

Dave pulled her to her feet and they kissed a kiss so joyous, so wonderfully sloppy and messy, it could probably be heard down at the Main Street café. Anna purred.

They came up for air, still laughing. "I should have gotten you a ring."

"You still can." Anna's eyes gently challenged him.

"We'll pick it out together right here on Main Street. Right now. That'll show 'em."

"The jewelry store is closed right now."

"Well, tomorrow then." Dave started to twirl her around and she grabbed for her shoulder. "Oh, sorry. For a moment I forgot all about it."

"Let's do that. Let's forget all about it."

"Well, do you still need to work late?"

Anna grabbed her coat from the nearby hanger, and switched off the light with a final definite click. "Let's get out of here."

CHAPTER FIFTY-TWO
Katya

Surprises awaited Katya when she returned to Cheshire's studio. A temporary illustrator had become permanent when worked picked up. And Pam had become head illustrator, changing her attitude and breaking through her shell. On Katya's first day she could barely conceal her surprise when Pam smiled and said, "Welcome back. How's your mom? We missed you." She hadn't spoken that many words to her the entire time they had worked together. Promotion agreed with her. Maybe ambition fueled her more than she let on.

Despite inside troubles regarding the *Lighting Man* costumes, the movie had been a hit with the press, who predicted it would become a "cult favorite." It had gained word-of-mouth momentum, and box office continued to be good. To Katya's immense surprise, repeat viewers showed up wearing imitations of her costumes. Guys wore red shirts with lightning strikes, the girls had fake jewels as big as walnuts stuck to their foreheads. Her designs had started a fad, and amused satisfaction rippled through her every time she thought about it.

\*\*\*

Katya still stayed in Chubbs and Elijah's pool house, the search for her own place on the back burner until after the holidays. As grateful as she was to them, she chafed every time apartment hunting got postponed.

On a November Saturday morning, Katya accompanied her hosts to the Farmers Market. While they went off in search of produce, Katya roamed through the fresh flowers looking for a bouquet to surprise them.

The mild November weather, the blue skies above, and the scent of the flowers in rainbow colors filled her with a quiet pleasure. While trying to decide between daisies and lilies, a voice from behind her said, "Hi, stranger."

She turned to see Marty, his basket overflowing with peppers and chorizo. "Marty." She didn't know what inflection to use, pleasant surprise or mild shock. She wanted to be pleased because he had always been nice to her, but she still wondered if he had sabotaged her work.

The best thing to do was ask him. If he took offense, at least she wouldn't be spoiling a work relationship. She would have lost a friend, but suspicion created a barrier between them, anyway.

"How is work at Metronome?" She picked up the lilies.

"Crazy. Some days I long for Cheshire and its small family."

*Yeah, families have feuds. Siblings have rivalries.*

They walked among the flowers. Marty took the lilies from her and replaced them with bachelor buttons.

She gave Marty an amused look. Nervy to exchange her flowers. Still, she kept quiet about them because she wanted to continue the conversation about work.

"Pam's head illustrator now. And Jerry hired a new guy while I was in Iowa." She decided she liked the bachelor buttons, their bright and friendly blue, their old-fashioned blossoms. A simple flower with no pretensions.

"You went home to visit?" He added some tiny white flowers whose name she didn't know. "That's better." He addressed his comment to the flowers.

Katya surrendered to his flower choices. "Family emergency. Long story." Fresh pain stabbed her. Distance didn't diminish the hurt from her mother's deceit and harsh judgement, and her long-time friend Charlie's rejection. Marty was about to add some snapdragons to the arrangement. "Hold on there, mister. Who's paying for this?"

He put the snapdragons back, and a pause in the conversation gave Katya the opening she had been looking for. "Marty, I have something to ask you, something hard."

"You mean, why didn't I like your flowers?" He picked up the snapdragons again and added them to the collection a second time.

"Well, yes, no. That, too." She laughed. "Flowers later. Something else first."

"Aren't you mysterious? What is it?" He put his hands in his pockets, evidently done with flower choices.

She stopped next to the tulip display. "Remember when I was working on that space movie?"

Marty picked up a bunch of red tulips, studied them, and put them back. "Yeah, there were a couple of wrinkles, but everything went smoothly in the end."

"That's just what I mean. Remember when I was late for the deadline with wardrobe?"

Marty looked thoughtful. "Sort of." Either the incident had honestly left little impression, or he was trying to downplay it.

"I know I wrote the right date on The Board. One of the seamstresses thinks somebody changed it, and I do, too. I think somebody changed it to make me look bad." Katya looked him in the eye.

"Why would somebody do that?" His eyes still roved the flowers.

"I don't know. Jealousy. Resentment. Could be anything."

"Yeah, so?"

"Wait, let me finish or I'll never get this said."

Marty nodded.

"And then I found my sketches in your drawer. You know, I was supposed to have them for my meeting with Jerry." She paused, drew breath. "Well, anyway. I dropped my eraser and it landed between your file cabinets. When I picked it up, that's when I saw my initials sticking out of some sketches in your filing cabinet, the sketches that had gone missing." Her mouth went dry.

She had finally said it all to Marty. He would either be insulted or sympathetic.

He stopped walking and turned thoughtful. Looking her directly in the eyes in a way a traitor would not, he said, "I found those, too, when I moved to Metronome, but the movie was already released so I never did anything about it. I don't know how they wound up in my files."

That's what she wanted to hear. "You mean it wasn't you who took them?"

"Of course not. Don't be ridiculous. Why would I take them?" Impatience crept into his voice.

"Well, twice somebody made me look bad. I don't want to believe it, but I had to ask if it was you." To cover her discomfort, she shifted the flowers to her other arm.

"Me? You must think I'm a jerk." His voice rose and a hurt look came into his eyes. He appeared taller than ever.

She wanted him to understand why she had to ask. "No, Marty. I think you're a friend. That's why I was shocked to find my sketches there. And of course, that made me suspect you might have changed the date. I really didn't want it to be you, but who would it be then?"

"Honest, Katya. It wasn't me. I liked working with you. You're one of the things I miss most about Cheshire." Marty's usual good humor returned.

"Now *I* feel like a jerk, but you see why I had to know. Who do *you* think did it?"

"I don't have a clue. There are some quirky people there, but nobody strikes me as mean and petty. Look, you've got your flowers. I've got my chorizo. Why don't we go out to lunch? We can catch up on happier subjects."

"That sounds heavenly." Katya laughed and sighed at the same time.

A voice from behind them said, "I did it."

Marty and Katya turned to see Pam, a sheepish look on her face.

"I was about to say hi, when I heard what you were talking about. I listened." She wore a rueful expression.

Katya frowned. "What do you mean, you did it?"

Pam shrugged. "Just what I said, I did it. It was stupid. I was mad because you got to do the futuristic stuff and I was stuck on that dumb Western. I figured if it looked like you weren't doing a good job, Jerry would take you off the project and give it to me." She shrugged again.

Katya gave Marty a "Help me" look. To Pam she raised her eyebrows. Her body tensed. "That was a pretty rotten thing to do."

Pam nodded and looked at the ground. "Yes, it was. I'm sorry. I wouldn't blame you if you told Jerry."

Katya gave Marty a second look that begged him to intervene, at least say something.

At last he did. "Look, let's go find a bench and sit down."

Katya frowned at him, rolling her eyes. *Was that the best he could do?*

***

The three sat on a park bench next to the flower section, Marty between Katya and Pam like a referee. The smell of tacos drifted over from the nearby food stand.

Pam spoke to the ground, her shoulders slumped in defeat. "What are you going to do?"

Katya stared at the flowers. Was she going to become somebody that went around bearing grudges against people: her mom, Lisa, Pam, Charlie? A huge sigh escaped her, releasing tension she hadn't noticed accumulating. "I won't tell Jerry."

Relief emanated from Pam. "Thank you." Awkward silence hovered over them.

*What happens now?*

Marty came to the rescue. "Look, I'll treat you both to lunch if you promise to play nice together from now on."

Providing exactly the distraction needed, Chubbs and Elijah arrived at that very moment. "Hey, look, the whole gang is here."

Marty explained about lunch and asked them to join him and the girls.

"Why don't you three go ahead? We were hoping to have a lazy afternoon."

Katya thrust the flowers at them. "Enjoy these at the same time."

Their faces lit up. They accepted them with a hug and a kiss. "Have fun."

***

"You're living with Chubbs now?" Marty sipped water at Paty's diner. They had lucked out and gotten the last turquoise padded booth.

"It was supposed to be temporary, but every time we say we'll go out apartment hunting, something gets in the way." Katya passed around the stacked menus.

Marty stared at the menu, but spoke to her. "Did you move there when you left the intern apartment?"

As she flipped the menu over to read the daily specials, Katya wondered if she should tell them the whole Lisa story. Since it was a day for confession, she decided to come clean on the house-sitting situation. They had all afternoon. "No, I house-sat for Lisa Graham for a while. It wasn't really house-sitting. We had a . . . personal connection."

Marty and Pam exchanged a look, which Katya noticed. "What?"

Before they could explain, a gum cracking waitress interrupted. "What can I get you three kiddos today?" Crack. Chomp. Crack.

"I'll have a tuna melt," said Pam. "And a Coke."

Marty and Katya chimed in together, "Same." And they all laughed at their timing.

When gum chomper left, Katya picked up where they had left off. "So, what did you guys mean by that look. I saw it. You know I did."

257

"We thought you and Lisa were involved. I mean, we weren't sure, but there aren't many secrets in this business."

Gum chomper returned with three Cokes on a tray. *Clunk, clunk, clunk*, she set them in front of the thirsty three.

"Does everybody know?" Katya asked, dumbfounded. She sipped her Coke thinking how careful she and Lisa had been.

Marty said, "Probably not the seamstresses. They stick to themselves."

"Does Jerry know?" Somehow Jerry knowing seemed almost like her mom knowing.

Gum chomper returned with the sandwiches. The three drew back to give her room. *Clunk, clunk, clunk*. They were served, and chomper descended on the booth next to them.

Pam took a bite, and with a full mouth said, "If he does, he doesn't care,"

This was more than Katya had expected. "You mean Jerry wouldn't be shocked."

"Shall we tell her?" Marty asked Pam, wiping a crumb from his cheek with a cheap diner napkin.

"Jerry has his own secrets to keep."

"What do you mean?" Katya frowned and put her sandwich back on the plate, waiting for an answer. *Was Jerry involved with the mob, with drugs? Was their classy boss not classy after all?*

Marty explained with a snicker, "He's too busy juggling other men's wives."

"Jerry?" Katya asked, flabbergasted. "But I thought . . ." she didn't finish the sentence. The words just slipped out, she wished she hadn't said them.

Marty grinned "Only his legs are paralyzed, honey." And he took a satisfyingly big bite of tuna.

Katya gulped, embarrassed, and they all laughed it off and went back to their food. Katya contemplated all she had learned today.

Just when she thought her brain couldn't take in any other revelations, a well-known older actor and a woman about his age came in, and Pam spotted them. "Oh, shit." She studied the tabletop.

Katya watched them look around for a vacant spot, and finding none, turned to go back outside to the umbrella tables.

To Pam, Marty said, "The coast is clear." She raised her head.

Without noticing him come back in, the man appeared alone beside their table. They all jumped in surprise. "Hello, Pam," staring at only her, as if the rest of them were part of the turquoise plastic covering the booth. "Can I speak to you alone for a minute?" Katya couldn't remember his name, but she had seen him in at least one spy movie.

"I have nothing to say to you. I'm with my friends." Pam's eyes flashed at him.

"Are you avoiding me, Pam?"

Katya watched Pam's face redden and tears moisten her eyes. She pulled herself up straight, shoulders back. "I am *not* avoiding you. We are not seeing each other at all anymore. I told you."

The man, sandy-haired and handsome, despite his sun-hardened face, said. "You know you don't mean it."

Katya tried to keep her face blank. She stole a look at Marty, but his eyes were downcast and his shoulders slumped, as if he was trying to disappear.

Katya involuntarily jumped again when Pam's voice came out in a hiss, "We are done talking about this. Your wife is waiting," special emphasis on the word wife.

The man didn't change expression, but Katya saw his cheek muscle twitch. "I'll call you." He turned

"I won't answer."

The man studied Pam for a few lengthy seconds, and then quietly left.

To his back, Pam said, "Go back to her like you always do."

When the older man was safely out of range, Marty came back to life, "Holy crap, Pam. Are you okay?"

Pam ate her French fries at a furious rate, as if they held salvation. Her face had turned even redder than before. Like a small, pretty dragon, her breath came loud and fast. "I just want him to leave me alone so I can get on with my life." Then she picked up her purse, slammed a few dollars down, and stood up. "Pay for me, will you? I'm getting out of here."

Gum chomper stared open-mouthed at Pam's back, and then turned to them. "Well, what ruffled her feathers?"

Neither Katya nor Marty answered.

"Will that be all?"

Marty nodded.

And she slammed down their ticket with an explosive crack of her gum. A few moments of astounded silence followed Pam's hurried exit. Katya blinked rapidly, and drew back when Marty looked at her.

"Well, now *all* the secrets are out," he shrugged and grinned.

Katya shook her head and laughed, not at Pam but at the sheer incredulity of all she had learned today. She raised her hands palms out protectively. "Well, please, if there are any more, just don't tell me. My surprise meter is about to explode."

\*\*\*

They cruised Toluca Lake streets lazily, enjoying the sun shine compliments of Marty's convertible. When they headed back toward Chubbs' house, Katya said, "Lots of drama goes on beneath the surface of people's lives. I had no idea Cheshire had so many stories."

"Just people trying to find a little happiness, to be a little less lonely."

Katya looked over at Marty. "What about you? What makes you tick?"

Marty grinned ruefully at the road ahead. "Let's save me for another day."

"How about you and your mom? Did you make up? I remember when she left Lisa's, she was pretty upset."

Katya looked down at her hands, shaking her head. "No, things got even worse in Iowa."

"Well, I'm sorry to hear that."

"Thanks." She realized they were close to Lisa's neighborhood. An impulse to stop surprised her. Would it be too bold to just park in front of Lisa's house, walk up to the front door, and ring the bell?

In the midst of Katya's trip to Weaver, her mom's injury, the hard feelings, and the abrupt departure, her anger at Lisa had been defused. Now she wanted to settle any hard feelings.

"How about we stop at Lisa Graham's house?'

"Any particular reason?" Marty looked puzzled.

"Just want to make things right with her." In her head, Katya was already inside the house.

"Look, why don't I drop you off. I'm getting low on gas. I'll go fill up and be back in thirty minutes, okay?"

*** 

The musical tones of the doorbell sounded deep within the expansive house. Standing there on the tiled entryway, Katya heard Kim's *tip tip tip* footsteps through the closed door. During her stay here, Katya had become attuned to them.

"Miss Katya." Kim looked surprised.

"Kim, how are you?"

Kim stepped back as Lisa came forward, her smile warm, her beauty still dazzling. "Katya, come in."

A moment's awkwardness – should they shake hands, embrace, kiss? Lisa gave her a quick hug.

"Kim, how about some coffee?"

"Yes, Miss Lisa."

They went to the Paris room, at least that's how Katya thought of it, as cozy as she remembered.

Kim brought coffee on a tray, and they waited for her to leave before talking.

"So, is my name mud with you?" Lisa looked sheepish.

Katya settled back in her chair, sipped the delicious coffee, and said. "Not now. But yes, for a while. Until other things came along."

"I heard you went back to Weaver."

"My mom had um. . ." Katya paused for the right phrase. "Problems in her life and wound up in the hospital."

"I hope she's okay."

"She's a lot better."

"You want to tell me about it?" Lisa asked, real concern in her voice.

"Maybe someday, but not today. It's long and complicated and Marty will be back soon. He went to gas up the car. I just thought we could talk a little and be friends. I saw on Rona Barret that you had some pretty famous acquaintance in London." Katya couldn't believe her own nerve in asking.

Lisa laughed, but there was bitterness to it. "British royalty has a history of using American film stars and then closing the royal circle back up with the Americans on the outside."

"Is that what happened to you?"

Lisa nodded. "One night I was the toast of the town. The next night I was soda without fizz." She shrugged, and Katya could see the memory still caused her pain.

A smug and satisfied breeze blew through Katya's head. *Ha ha for you.* She recognized her own pettiness at Lisa's pain, but didn't regret it. She wasn't that noble.

Lisa asked, "Can we still be friends?"

"Yes. That's really why I stopped."

"No hard feelings?" Lisa's eyes had laughter in them.

Katya blushed and shook her head. "No hard feelings."

"And what did you do to Kim?" Lisa relaxed and took a chatty tone. "When I mentioned you, she said that you moved out, but that you were nice. You liked her dinners."

"Kim and I found we had a few things in common." Katya looked at her nearly full coffee cup, and drank down the rest. "I really do have to go." She got up to go and Lisa followed her to the door.

Katya hovered on the front step a moment.

Lisa leaned against the door. "Really, let's stay in touch. What are you going to do now?"

"I'm going to live in Chubbs' pool house until I find a place of my own."

Lisa nodded. "Good."

Katya got in Marty's car.

She was glad she had come, and even more glad to leave.

## CHAPTER FIFTY-THREE
Katya

*Dave Frank called. 12:30.* The scrawled note hung crookedly from a piece of tape on the pool house door.

Fleetingly, Katya thought something had happened to her mom, but her instincts said otherwise. What did he want? How was she ever to put the messy Weaver visit behind her if he kept pestering her? Katya didn't want to know what he wanted. She'd left her home town mad, and she wanted to stay that way.

Besides, it could only be bad news. She didn't call.

***

The following week, Katya had nearly succeeded putting the call out of her mind when she got caught. While watching TV, the phone rang and she knew who it would be. With flat resignation she answered, "Hello."

"This is Dave. Remember me?"

She scoffed. How stupid did he think she was? Katya couldn't keep the exasperation out of her voice. With her free hand she wound and unwound the telephone cord as she talked. "Of course, I remember you." She didn't ask what he wanted. She wanted him to squirm.

"Did you get my call last week?"

"Yes." She wouldn't explain why she didn't return it, either. The cord caught and wouldn't unwind, she had to shake her hand to free it.

"Katya, please listen and don't hang up on me."

She steeled herself, ready to do exactly that. Clasping the receiver with both hands, she said, "What do you want?"

"I want you to come to Weaver for Christmas."

That was the last thing Katya had expected to hear. Cord winding started anew. "Why on earth would I do that?"

She could hear Dave take a deep sudden breath. "Oh, for Christ's sake. Will you drop the holier-than-thou thing? Look, you need to put things right with your mom. You don't have to accept everything, but don't you see how childish you are both being?"

"It is no business of yours!" And then, for good measure, added, "For Christ's sake." She hadn't sworn much since art school, but maybe she'd start again. It felt good.

"I'm making it my business."

Katya had a ridiculous urge to either laugh or throw the phone at the man. He was wearing her down. Would the man ever stop? "Look, have you talked to her about this?" She remembered the gum cracking waitress at Paty's, and wished she had some gum to chomp.

"Will you come? Please?"

"You *haven't* talked to her, have you?" She pursed her lips and got up to pace.

"As soon as my divorce becomes final, your mother and I are going to get married. She will never be happy with me until she is happy with you. You have always come first with her. I've known it and accepted it. I'm asking for myself."

"If I do come, and I'm not saying I will, I won't beg." She stopped mid pace for emphasis.

"No one's asking you to."

Katya's sigh came from the bottom of her soul. "I'll think about it." She didn't say good bye, but she put the receiver back in the cradle carefully.

Now the ball was in her court. Was that a good thing? She wished the whole mess clean away as she flopped on the bed. Despite her defenses, renewed hope came like a flicker and then a definite flame until she could no longer resist it. She pictured herself and her mother talking about fashion, laughing at *Dick Van Dyke*, and eating in the kitchen with the radio on.

Without over thinking, Katya dialed Dave's number. "Okay, I'll give it a shot. But you prepare her, you hear me."

## CHAPTER FIFTY-FOUR
Dave

A cold rain beat down. With his top coat collar turned up, and his hat pulled low over his eyes, Dave wrestled the Christmas tree off the top of his car. A wet, dripping tree that Anna would not appreciate.

Anna stood with the front door open. A path of newspaper and towels protected the carpet. "Honey, you're getting soaked." And then she sneezed.

Dave dragged and carried the sodden tree along the path, which tripped him up while the tree caught in the towels. "Where do you want it?" He wiped the rain from his face with a free hand.

"Ohhh, I don't know. This isn't how I planned it." She put her hand on top of her head, trying to think.

"Believe me, rain was not in my plan, either."

He had already put on the tree stand outside. With nowhere else to put it, he stood the cursed tree up right in front of the television. "It's going to need to dry out before we can put lights on it. Unless you want me to electrocute myself."

Anna sneezed again.

"Look honey, you feel lousy. Me and the tree are soaked. I think that's all we should do today. Let's finish tomorrow night." Monday night, their night.

He started to pull her into his arms to comfort her, but she pulled back because he got her wet.

"I need to get into some dry clothes. Is there anything you can do about my overcoat?" The wet wool smell got stronger by the minute.

*\*\**

As he showered, Dave cursed out loud. "Damnation." He had intended to talk to Anna about Katya and Christmas while they decorated the tree. Both talking and decorating plans got all shot to hell. He would have to screw up his courage again tomorrow night.

Dave dressed in Anna's bedroom, where he kept a few clothes, not sure he should bring all his stuff. They lived in an awkward limbo, one of the things getting married would put an end to. They'd be together. Clothes, Christmas trees, and houses.

***

Monday brought success with the tree. Dave plugged in the lights.

Anna said, "Oh, lovely. Katya always liked the bubble ones. Sort of like her lava lamp."

This was shaky ground. Anna was allowed to talk about Katya, but Dave wasn't. He sneaked a peak at her eyes to judge her mood. He was never sure how mention of Katya would affect her, but she looked calm.

Anna took the top off a box of red ornaments and handed them to Dave. "You do the red. I'll do the green." And they worked contentedly together for a few minutes. A green one here. A red one there. The piney scent of the tree surrounded them.

Dave took a deep breath and plunged in. "Honey, I talked to Katya."

Anna's mouth dropped open at the same time she dropped the ornament she was holding. It smashed into green smithereens. "Dammit."

Dave knew she wasn't swearing at the broken ornament.

When Anna kneeled to pick up the pieces, Dave kneeled to help her. He talked to the top of her head, bent over, intent to ignore him. "Please, listen."

Anna looked at him then, a look like a volcano about to erupt. Slow, smoldering, unstoppable. "No. You listen. You had no right to do that. It's my business. How did you even know how to reach her?" Her eyes blazed.

268

"It's a long story."

Anna's head of steam petered out. "Why would you even do that? You know it hurts me to talk about her."

"I did it for us." He took her hand, pulling them both to a standing position and led them to the couch. He had her attention. "I invited her here for Christmas. We can never be happy with this secret between us. We are partners. We share problems. Secrets."

"Christmas? You invited her for Christmas and didn't tell me?" Anna threatened to blow again. "Do you have any idea what we fought about?"

Dave nodded. They might be fighting but the truth was coming out.

"How? How do you know my most private thing?"

"Katya told me." He said it cautiously, knowing Anna wouldn't like it.

"Katya?" Her head shot forward and her eyes widened big enough Dave almost heard a pop.

"When? When have you been nosing around behind my back?"

Her tone made Dave cringe, like he had done something wrong, even though he didn't see it that way. "When you were in the hospital."

"You've been keeping secrets from me, too." Her tone was self-righteous.

Dave couldn't take anymore. He raised his voice. "See. This is what I mean. If you do not bring this out in the open, it will always be between us. Just like now."

Anna slumped. He knew she knew he was right. She started to talk and cry at the same time. "It's ugly, Dave. I'm ashamed. What did I do wrong?

Her sobbing was pitiful to him. He raised her face to his and looked into her eyes.

"Honey, you did nothing wrong. You are the best mother to her anyone could ever be. And she is a good daughter."

"But how can you say that? It's perverted. It's disgusting." Her shame turned her face red.

"I was never sure, but I suspected it." He used the quiet voice again, knowing what he said was hard to hear.

"Why would you think that about her? About me?"

"I've seen it before. The music business attracts people who don't feel accepted elsewhere. Maybe the film business too."

"You don't think it's sick?" Hurt and shame contorted Anna's beloved face.

"That's not for me to say." He paused, and said, "Or you."

"It would feel good for it to be like old times with her." Anna leaned back with a lost look in her eyes.

"Honey, you do know it can never be the same, don't you?"

Anna nodded. "I feel sick."

Dave knew Anna would need some time to adjust. He tried to put himself in her place. If Randy had lived and Dave discovered he was homosexual, how would he feel? All he knew was being homosexual was better than being dead. H. didn't say so, though. Anna could only take so much at a time.

"But you can at least try to have some kind of connection with her."

"What will people say? What will they think?" Anna's cold dull eyes stared at the ceiling. Defeat and weakness filled her voice.

"No one needs to know."

"But I'd know. You'd know."

Dave didn't have an answer for everything. He said, "Just talk to her. Just open up to each other."

"Is she coming?"

Dave nodded.

"She wants to make up?" Anna asked the ceiling.

"She only agreed to come. Beyond that, I can't predict." Dave slumped back, too. All this emotion wore him out.

"Neither can I."

She looked like a small animal, wounded and trapped. He'd never seen the look on her face before. What had he set in motion?

## CHAPTER FIFTY-FIVE
Katya

Not one bit of holiday joy lifted Katya's spirits. And it was Christmas Eve.

Apprehension made her shoulders tense and her face tight, as she sat on the passenger side of Dave's car huddled against the door like a cornered mouse. Fields of corn flew by full of dried stalks, flattened and forlorn. The gray white skies had smelled of snow when they left the Omaha airport, and she realized she hadn't seen snow since the night she had been cruel to Paulette on the street in front of the art school dorm.

By the time Dave pulled his car into the parking space in front of her mom's shop, Katya had emptied herself of all expectations. This would go the way it would go. She resolved she would not let her emotions get the best of her. No shouting. No smiling. No crying.

Like a prisoner facing his first day of incarceration, she dragged out of the car and up to the window of the shop. Through the glass, she saw her mother standing at the cash register. As if pulled by a magnet, her mom looked up, and they locked eyes. Katya's stomach cramped. She clenched her teeth and narrowed her eyes.

Dave propelled her gently by the elbow into the store, where she took in the changes: the carpeting, the twinkling new display racks, the arch between the main store and the new annex. The changes increased her sense of living outside her mother's life. From the hallway by the office, Charlie stared at her with fear in her eyes. Then, like an animal threatened, she ducked back inside. Is that what their friendship had come to? Her friend was afraid of her?

A woman Katya didn't know stood motionless and rail thin, her face without expression. Finally, Katya looked at her mother, hard, long, taking the measure of her. Who should speak first?

"Katya, Merry Christmas," her mother said cautiously, the words sounding like a question.

Katya didn't speak, whether from confusion or spite, she wasn't sure.

Her mother's eyes revealed nothing about what might be going on in her head. She excused herself with a shaking voice, went back to the office, and spoke to Charlie in low tones about closing up. She came our wearing her coat and handed the tall woman a gift and wished her a happy holiday.

Katya's heart pounded as she stared hard at the cash register. *Oh, hurry up, Mom. If we're going to get out of here, then let's get out of here. I feel like I'm on public display.* If she had to stand here like this any longer, she might scream.

Then her mom disappeared in the office again.

Katya looked at Dave and, in a whisper more like a growl, said, "I'm getting out of here."

Dave put a hand on her arm. "Just hang on a minute."

Katya shook it off, but stayed put.

At last, her mom came out. "We can go now."

Katya wished she had never come to Weaver, to her mother's shop. She should have made her mom come to her in California.

As they stepped outside, Dave said, "Why don't we drive around and look at decorations? It's starting to get dark. People will be turning on their lights."

Katya recognized fake cheerfulness in his voice, like an over eager salesman. Her insides twitched at the sound.

In the tense circumstances, driving around appealed to Katya. She dreaded being stuck in the house with the two of them. "Yes, let's do that." In Dave's car, she took the back seat where she could watch her mother in the front. Her every nerve stood alert and ready to pounce.

Getting the three of them inside the car and settled seemed to last a lifetime. Katya feared the whole holiday would be equally labored. Dave said, "Let's go up on Snob Hill," the overblown name for the town's handful of grand houses, owned mostly by professional people: the town doctor who had always seemed old to Katya, the pharmacist, the vet, a few more Katya didn't know.

Katya's mom nodded and made a gesture with her hand that said, "Just get going somewhere, anywhere."

\*\*\*

"Looks like old Doc Crank's wife went all out." Now Dave's voice had taken on an unfamiliar tour guide tone, which was more irritating than the artificial jollity. "And all blue lights there. What do you think of all blue lights, Anna?" The phony happiness returned.

His yammering set Katya's teeth on edge. She took deep breaths and unclenched her fists. She couldn't tell the effect on her mom, but the back of her neck looked rigid. He kept talking and talking. "And red and green lights, just like your tree, Anna."

Katya heard her mother's intake of breath. "Oh, shut up!" Katya's mom said it, but if she hadn't, Katya would have. In a calmer voice she continued. "I'm sorry, Dave. You didn't deserve that." She expelled breath noisily.

She turned to Katya, her face like stone. In an equally hard voice, she said, "Where should we start?"

Dave pulled onto a side street and stopped the car, but kept the motor running. The heater blew hot, dry air in their faces.

"I don't know This wasn't my idea." She looked out the window and not at her mom.

Dave broke in, the false voice gone. "Both of you need to stop acting like children. Get down off your high horses, unless you want to spend the rest of your lives hurting each other. Or estranged, as good as dead to each other. Is that what you want?"

Katya said, "I don't know what I want."

Dave said, "Cut it out."

She'd never heard him shout before.

Katya took a breath so deep she felt it in her toes. "I want to work things out, Mom." More softly. "I really do. I have missed you like crazy. Please, Mom." Her defenses fell like a leaning tower, and it felt good to let them go.

Her mom turned awkwardly from her spot in front and reached her hand out to Katya.

Katya took it, and her mother gripped it hard.

"Honey, I don't want this wall between us, either. But I am so confused and worried. I don't understand how you feel. I don't think I ever will." Katya looked into her mother's beautiful face, a face she thought she knew well.

"I'm not asking you to understand. God knows, I don't. Just accept it. Accept me." She was begging, the thing she said she wouldn't do.

Her mom's voice broke. 'I'm trying to."

Katya gripped her mom's hand mightily. Then she let it go and said without meanness, "Now I need to know how you could have lied to me all those years when you two were together. You hurt me, Mom. I felt left out. Betrayed." The words were coming now, saying things that needed to be said and freeing her locked in emotions.

Her mom sighed. She paused to blow her nose. "I did betray you. I knew it when I did it, but I loved Dave. I still do." The two shared a look that proved her mother's words. "He didn't want to leave Fran because she blamed herself for Randy's death and drank to forget. I understood that. I felt sorry for Fran, too."

Katya said, "But not enough to keep you from stealing her husband."

Dave spoke. "Katya, Fran wasn't interested in me anymore. She wasn't interested in anything but drinking." Then he looked over at Katya's mom, and held the look unwaveringly. He said, "She needs to know the whole story."

Katya's defenses shot up again. She looked first at one, then the other. "What whole story? You mean there's more?" Just when Katya felt peace might be possible. What else could there possibly be? Her head started to pound.

"Honey, it was your dad, my Joe, who ran into little Randy and killed him." Her mom looked at Dave and her features softened. "Randy got away from Fran, ran into the street, and at the moment the sun blinded Joe and he hit Randy." Sobs came from a deep injured place and her mother couldn't stop them. "It was terrible. I saw it happen. It still haunts me." She composed herself and went on. "Joe was shattered. He couldn't live with himself. He ran away because life was intolerable for him. He didn't run from me, especially not from you—I didn't even know I was pregnant when he left." Her voice broke again, but she got control of it. "Just a few years ago, he killed himself and left his money to me. It was your father's money that sent you to art school."

Katya shrank. Small. She felt small, small, small. She whispered, "Oh, Mom. That tears my heart right in two." The awfulness shattered her. She choked out, "I didn't even know him, but I feel bad for him. That's why I felt the connection to Randy in the cemetery. We're all connected." Salty, hot tears slid down her cheeks. Her mom passed her a handkerchief embroidered with violets.

Dave spoke quietly. "Let's go home." He put the car in gear, and the idling engine rumbled awake.

\*\*\*

As they drove the familiar streets, a small flame of hope ignited in Katya's heart. Relief made her limp. She lay her head back and closed her eyes, tired through and through.

Her mom's house—Katya's home—stood dark, looking abandoned on a street where every other house had made some effort at holiday lighting.

"Wait a minute," Dave said.

Katya could tell the happiness in his voice was unforced, not fake like in the car.

He left them standing on the front sidewalk and entered the house by the back door. In a moment, the outdoor lights sparked on and bathed Katya and her mother in a gentle glow. The Christmas tree lit up through the window like a bright greeting.

Katya watched as the bubble lights warmed, and their insides rippled up, just like her lava lamp, just like the hope bubbling up inside her. Earlier she had sensed the coming of snow. Now it arrived in puffy flakes, landing gently on her face, sweet as blessings.

## CHAPTER FIFTY-SIX
Anna

Inside Anna's house, the Christmas Eve ham perfumed the air. "Naomi, bless her heart, took off a few hours this afternoon to get this feast started. I asked her to join us, but she wanted to celebrate with the people at her rooming house." Anna hung her coat in the closet as she spoke.

In the kitchen she tied a poinsettia-printed apron around her waist and tossed two others to Dave and Katya.

The apron made Katya appear mature and responsible to Anna's eyes. Dave tied his high on his chest and preened like a runway model. Katya and Anna rolled their eyes at his antics, but he gave them an exaggerated nose-in-the-air response. The success of his reconciliation scheme had gone to his head. She wouldn't spoil his moment.

"Dave, would you mash the potatoes? I'll try to make gravy without lumps. Oh, and honey, . . ." Anna stopped, realizing the endearment might mean either Katya or Dave. She corrected herself, "Katya, would you put some Christmas music on the stereo? And set the table, please. The good stuff."

Katya put on Frank Sinatra's Christmas LP, and his words about being home for Christmas rang true in Anna's ears. Her daughter was home, and not just in her dreams. And Dave joined them openly.

As if Dave read her thoughts, he held the potato masher microphone style, and sang along.

Anna laughed and said to Katya, "He's out of control."

"No wine for him."

The three worked together, sharing familiar tasks like a family. Katya put cutlery at each place setting, and Anna combined flour and water to thicken the gravy, whisking it mightily in her battle against lumps.

In triumph, Anna placed a bowl of silky gravy next to the ham. "Success," she said. The three whipped off their aprons in unison, which made them smile, and took their places. The Yule log sported pine sprigs and ornaments, serving as a cheery centerpiece.

Anna clapped in appreciation. "Look what you've done with the Yule log." She smiled at Katya and again studied the place settings. "And you found the old place cards." She admired the juvenile crayon-printed *Mommy* and *Katya Ann* that Katya had made in elementary school. A new card set by Dave's place, one with more accomplished penmanship, the "D" on Dave round with a final flourish. Anna picked it up, smiled her appreciation at her daughter, and returned it to the table. "Everything looks pretty," she said. "I especially like the greenery and ornaments. Inspired."

"I raided the Christmas tree," Katya answered, faking a guilty expression.

"Always knew you were a bit of a thief," Dave said, as he poured small amounts of Mogen David wine in the Fostoria tumblers.

Dave didn't like Mogen David, said it tasted like syrup, but he humored Anna. He swirled it in his glass, inhaling it and raising his glass in a toast. "To this blessed Christmas."

The three glasses clinked. "To a blessed Christmas," they repeated. A mixed blessing for sure, thought Anna, but one she determined to live with.

As they ate, Katya mumbled, "I didn't bring presents." She shrugged and ducked her head in apology.

Her daughter had come under protest, and gifts might be considered peace offerings. Anna understood that. "You are our gift."

They finished the meal, at ease with one another. Dave pushed back his half-eaten piece of pumpkin pie. "I couldn't eat another bite."

Anna agreed, and added, "Let's leave the dishes until later. I *did* buy a few presents." She shrugged. The plan to reconcile might have gone awry, and presents would have made an awkward situation even worse; but Anna remained hopeful.

The stereo switched to Johnny Mathis, who sang about the marshmallow world in winter. Anna handed Dave a package with the telltale shape of a shoe box. To Katya, she passed a small but weighty present wrapped in snowmen paper.

Dave opened his first. "New slippers! My big toe thanks you." He gave Anna a kiss on the cheek.

Anna blushed and gave Dave a smile. She peeked at Katya to gauge her reaction to the kiss, but saw no disapproval. Dave's kiss revived the memory of the kiss Anna witnessed Katya receiving. She regretted her extreme reaction. "Katya, open *your* present now."

Katya removed the tape one piece at a time. She slipped off the paper and folded it.

Anna watched her daughter's face, hoping the gift would please her.

One by one, Katya removed four pottery coffee mugs in the shape of owls. One had a goofy smile, one had half-closed eyes, one's mouth formed an O, and the last had a single tear on its feathery cheek. Katya held up the sad one and said, "Aww," chucking it under its pottery owl chin. "Thanks, Mom. They are really clever."

The wisdom of owls would be welcome as they faced their unknown future.

"For when you get your own place."

"I love them," said Katya, but Anna heard *I love you* because she wanted to.

Dave gave Anna a new toaster. "Your toast will be done on both sides now."

Anna fingered the gold and silver locket he gave her the night before. "Just between us," he said when he fastened it on. "I'll give you something less personal tomorrow."

And to Katya he gave, at Anna's suggestion, a gift certificate to the record shop for a new album.

Only one gift remained. Anna pulled out a big square box wrapped in snowflake-covered paper. "We can all enjoy this one. You two open it together."

They exchanged a puzzled look, and Dave said, "She's the boss."

Katya shook it, and the contents rattled. "Ha! I know that sound."

"Well, don't tell. Go on, open it." Anna's two loves sat side by side, working together. *This is how it should be. If only . . .*

Her mind wanted a handsome young man sitting next to Katya with his arm around her. But such thoughts were a bitter waste, and Anna made them go away.

Dave pulled open the tape, and handed it back to Katya. She unwrapped the snowflake paper to reveal a jigsaw puzzle of a thousand pieces, a picture of the famous Hollywood sign on the hill above Los Angeles.

"Tomorrow can be a lazy day. We'll put the puzzle together in our PJs." Anna beamed at Dave. "Will you make us one of your special breakfasts?"

He nodded, "Love to."

***

The puzzle of their relationship lay ahead of them like the assembly of the Hollywood sign. It could take shape with little effort, amid laughter and fun. Or the enormity of the task might daunt them, the temptation to give up strong. In the end, with love and cooperation, they might create a satisfying and happy result that would please all of them. That was the wish in Anna's heart.

## EPILOGUE

Naomi showed Anna the pale pink suit as soon as she unpacked it from the Pendleton shipment. "Look at this beauty."

Delight took away Anna's breath. "Oh!" She left the cash register for a closer look, stroking the butter soft wool. The delicate color reminded her of the inside of a sea shell, not that Anna had seen that many sea shells.

In June, Anna and Dave walked down the aisle of the Weaver Lutheran Church. The pharmacist and his wife completed the wedding party. Dave's eyes lit up when he saw Anna so stunningly dressed. In the lapel of his dashing navy suit coat, a pink rosebud repeated the color.

As he uttered his vows, his voice cracked and his eyes misted over, causing Anna's heart to melt like chocolate held fast in a child's hand.

Anna mailed a framed wedding picture to Katya along with a letter. They planned to visit her on their California honeymoon.

The memory of their emotional Christmas together still filled Anna's thoughts. She struggled to accept Katya's double life and let go of shame and disappointment. At least Dave, Naomi, and Charlie, the people she saw most, knew the truth, sparing her the strain of deception.

Anna never mentioned it at the shop. The initial shock of Katya's sexuality hardened Charlie's heart against her daughter. Nothing would ever change that. The break between the two friends, who had once been close, wounded Anna daily.

Katya had written a letter in return, sharing her news. She had found her own place, a tiny house close to where her intern apartment had been. Anna was glad she made no reference to her fateful visit there last July.

Katya also wrote, *And Mom, you'll never guess who I ran into. Dottie from art school! She is going to work on some animated shorts for Hanna Barbera. And she married an instructor she had a crush on. He is a lot older—at least thirty—but they are happy together. I'm glad things are turning out well for her. We picked up right where we left off.*

*We shared a Milky Way just like old times and she filled me in on the other girls. Remember crabby old Mona? She married her engineer and is going to teach elementary school art. Don't think I'd want to be one of her students. And do you remember Paulette? She invited us to pizza that very first day when I moved into the dorm? Dottie said she will soon be coming to California, too, to work for Harvey Comics.*

Katya's written words pleased Anna almost as much as her presence. Her daughter would not be lonely in her new life. Anna herself longed for Katya every day. Maybe all mothers felt that way. *Our children are only ours for a little while.*

Anna folded the letter in half, kissed it as if it held Katya's spirit, put it back into its envelope, and pressed it to her heart.